TIME OF TRIAL

HESTER BURTON

TIME OF TRIAL

London
OXFORD UNIVERSITY PRESS
1973

Oxford University Press, Ely House, London W. 1

GLASGOW NEW YORK TORONTO MELBOURNE WELLINGTON
CAPE TOWN IBADAN NAIROBI DAR ES SALAAM LUSAKA ADDIS ABABA
DELHI BOMBAY CALCUTTA MADRAS KARACHI LAHORE DACCA
KUALA LUMPUR SINGAPORE HONG KONG TOKYO

ISBN 0 19 272042 2

© *Hester Burton 1963*
First published 1963
Reprinted 1965, 1972
First published in this edition 1973

To
R. W. B. B.
with love

Printed in Holland
Zuid-Nederlandsche Drukkerij N.V.
's-Hertogenbosch

CONTENTS

1 *The Pargeters*

On that unlucky Monday late in the summer of 1801, Margaret Pargeter awoke to the chimes of the City churches striking six. She had lived all her life in Holly Lane and knew exactly how the chimes crossed and knotted in a skein of peals—and then unravelled again. St. Alban's in Wood Street started first, and then St. Giles' Cripplegate, and St. Mary's and St. Alphage's and then, not quite together, St. Olave's in Old Jewry and St. Anne's in Aldersgate. Last came the lordly boom of St. Paul's almost overhead. With the first note of St. Paul's, she opened her eyes and lay watching the blobs of sunlight on the ceiling, waiting luxuriously content for the madrigal of the bells to unwind itself, and wondering with a smile what new thing the new day would bring.

A minute later she was frowning. She had forgotten that it was a Monday. The intricate unweaving of the chimes had resolved itself not in a silence but in a single, melancholy bell, which beat on and on. It was St. Sepulchre's bell, tolling the last hours on earth of the prisoners in Newgate who were condemned to die. There was nothing new in a Hanging Monday. It was always brutally the same: the tolling; the holiday crowds; the penitent prayers; the hanging; the cheers. Nor was it new that Margaret should push it all urgently to the back of her mind. She was young. She was just seventeen. And frankly —without shame—she preferred the happy things of life.

Under the relentless intoning of the bell, the City stirred itself to another week. The cheerful sounds of the living crept up into her room, timidly at first with the chip-chopping of chisel against brick, and then more boldly with footsteps, a greeting, and a laugh. And then with the sharp clatter of a horse's hooves and a shout and a volley of oaths.

She jumped out of bed. Few horsemen ever ventured through the narrow passage which joined Holly Lane with Paternoster Row.

It must be a drunkard or a runaway thief.

She ran to the window but was in time to see only the crouched figure of the rider and the flank and tail of his horse as he swerved sharply up Cheapside. But behind him stretched a trail of havoc. Immediately below her, outside her father's bookshop, sprawled a carpenter, swearing loudly as he picked himself up. The rider had knocked the poor man's tool bag off his shoulder and scattered his saw and hammer and plane about him on the cobbles. Farther up, a milkmaid cowered flat against the chemist's door, her milk pails still hanging safely from her yoke, but her dress splashed dark with mud and her face still white from the fright she had had. The builders and joiners had stopped shoring up the walls of the tenement on the corner and were standing in a knot, staring up Cheapside and shaking their fists.

Margaret laughed. The day had begun with a bang.

She wrapped up her nakedness in the large window curtain, leant on the sill, and waited for Robert Kerridge to come out of the house.

He was late. His first demonstration at St. Xavier's Hospital began at half past six.

The carpenter wiped himself down, picked up his tools, and shuffled off to join his companions in repairing the tenement; and the mikmaid left the shelter of the doorway, crossed the lane, and disappeared into the Pargeters' kitchen. Margaret wrinkled her nose in disgust. She hated the smell and look of scalded milk, and today they would be with her all day long, for Monday was her saloop day in the bookshop; she would have to serve saloop to every customer who bought a book and to every starved poet who came to her father for advice. Across the lane, Libby, the chemist's servant girl, came out into the sunshine and unhooked the shutters of his shop.

A door banged immediately below, and footsteps rang in the covered alley that led to the back of the house.

It was Robert.

In a moment the crown of his new felt hat appeared beneath

her window. She knew about the hat. He had bought it on Saturday with part of his next month's allowance, which had come up on the Yarmouth mail on Friday night. It was grey and tall, with a generous brim and a fine silk cord—a hat fit for a prince.

The medical student stood for a moment snuffing the cool morning air and adjusting the set of his neck cloth, and then crossed over the lane and looked at himself in the rounded glass panes of the chemist's window.

She watched him entranced.

He turned his head from one side to the other, clearly dissatisfied with the distorted image that the bottle glass threw back, and then, seeing that the chemist's door was glazed with modern panes, turned to this more accurate mirror to admire anew the nobility of his hat.

Margaret had never seen anything more surprisingly absurd. She had never thought to catch the clever, adult, handsome, and altogether splendid Robert Kerridge preening himself in the open lane. It was the sort of silly, childish thing that Margaret herself might do, but not Robert, the poised and wise. Not Robert, the best and most hard-working anatomist of his year.

When he tipped his new hat to the back of his head and squinted sideways to catch sight of his profile, she burst out laughing.

The medical student spun round on his heel.

'Meg,' he cried.

Meg. Meg. He knew how she hated this ugly shortening of her name. It was teasing and patronizing and vulgar of him to use it. She dropped the curtain and leant half out of the window.

'I'm *not* Meg.'

On her last birthday, she had extracted a promise from all her friends that she was now to be called Margaret. Suzannah and Eugenia and Jane had promised, and Mrs. Neech their housekeeper and Robert and her cousin George. Even her brother John had grudgingly admitted her right to the name with which she had been christened.

'I'm *not* Meg. I'm Margaret Washington Pargeter.'

Robert looked up at her, his eyes travelling quickly over her rumpled brown hair and her features still blurred with sleep, his wide mouth twitching with laughter.

She flushed with anger. When would he cease treating her as a child?

'Dear Mistress Pargeter,' he said, taking off his beautiful grey hat and making her an extravagant bow, 'forgive me for telling you that you are showing your shift to the whole of Holly Lane.'

She gasped with dismay.

Then she tugged the curtains fiercely across the window, shutting out the light and the lane and the mocking young man, and stood for a moment in the dimness, a blush sweeping up her neck and over her cheeks as she listened to his footsteps growing fainter in the lane. She was not so much embarrassed as mortified and angry—angry that through a moment of self-forgetfulness she had made herself seem ridiculous to him.

Then she remembered Robert's look as he squinted sideways to catch sight of his Roman profile in his new hat, and her brow unclouded and her eyes suddenly filled with delight, and she flung herself down on her bed and laughed and laughed.

The new day had shown Robert as ten times more absurd than herself.

Three hours later, Margaret's brother John stood in the middle of his father's bookshop and scowled. He was on the verge of revolt.

He was a broad-shouldered, burly, out-of-doors young man who looked as though he would have felt more at home in the hunting field or leading a cavalry charge against the French. The bookshelves caged him in, and the dusty shaft of light that fell between the chimney pots, down through the little panes of the shop window, to fall in a pool at his feet, only emphasized the darkness and the smallness of his prison. The shop was full of glooms and heavy with the strange, snuff-like smell of old leather and damp paper and ink. Everything about it was an affront to him.

'I hate it!' he exclaimed, his eye sweeping savagely along a row of Tillotson's and Calamy's sermons. 'I hate its mouldy smell. I hate the poverty of it all.'

'But, John, it's not poor,' protested Margaret indignantly.

He scanned again the worn calf bindings of the second-hand histories, the tattered volumes of seventeenth-century travels, agricultural tracts and botanies, and the outdated manuals of husbandry and medicine, and turned to his sister, more bitterly convinced than before.

'It's trash. I'd not give ten pounds for the lot.'

Margaret stared at him incredulously and then turned abruptly to the large oak table behind her.

'Look at these and these and these,' she said fiercely, pointing her feather mop at the new books that had come straight from the presses: *The Works of Hannah More, Travels in the Interior of Africa,* and twelve volumes of Dr. Henry's *History of Great Britain.* 'They're worth five pounds alone. And look at all those glorious poets over there and Dr. Blair's *Sermons* and this new book which came out last week: *The Young Midshipman's Instructor, with useful Hints to Parents of Sea Youth.* Why, with the war and everyone so proud of the Navy, we'll sell dozens of copies of this.'

'You're a fool. Selling hundreds of copies wouldn't get us out of this.'

'Out of selling books? Out of Holly Lane?'

Her brother had flung himself moodily into the tattered Moroccan leather chair which their father kept for his best customers—when he remembered not to sit in it himself.

'Who wants to get out of it?' she continued. 'Father's happy. I'm happy. We have enough money to buy food.'

'Well, *I'm* not happy,' retorted her brother. 'And if you weren't a child, you'd see that we're as poor as church mice.'

So it was out at last.

John, who had first broken his articles with Mr. Mudge, the

attorney, and next thrown up a clerkship in a merchant's house, was now tired of selling books with his father! She had known it, really, for many weeks. He had been so moody and difficult all the summer that she could not imagine his taking to the trade in earnest. Besides, he hated reading and had no head for accounts.

'So you want to be an officer and a gentleman,' she said.

She had guessed where his new ambition lay, for she had watched him several times studying with rapt attention the columns in the daily papers that advertised the selling of army commissions.

He looked up, startled, and then scowled.

'I don't see why I shouldn't be,' he muttered. 'I'm strong. I'm healthy. I'm willing to live rough and to fight and take knocks.'

He was all these things, and as he spoke in his own defence he suddenly appeared manly and dignified—a brother one could respect.

For the first time in her life, Margaret felt very sorry for him. She and John had always been so exasperated with each other that neither of them had ever been able to look at the other steadily, with unclouded vision. She had not recognized till this moment the kind of person that he really was—a man who was all fingers and thumbs with his brains, but whose physical courage and common sense would never desert him. Of course he was right. He would make a splendid junior officer. He would love the man's life, the danger, the glory, the display. His broad shoulders were built for a scarlet coat.

What a grief for him that his ambition could be nothing more than a dream!

'You know very well why you can never be an officer,' she said sadly. 'We both know. Father will never stomach the buying and selling of commissions.'

Her brother swung himself out of the chair in a gesture of sullen despair.

'Who'd have a meddlesome, reforming, Jacobin bookseller for a father!'

Margaret stared at her brother, aghast, feeling the anger mount higher and higher within her. A wall of rage seemed to stand between them.

'He's not meddlesome and he's not a Jacobin,' she exclaimed hotly. 'It's not his fault if the world's all wrong.'

John had never before said quite such a dreadful thing. He was callous, cruel, impossible.

They were back in their lifelong squabble again.

'But it needn't be *he* that's got to put it right,' he retorted, kicking a book along the floor.

This was so exactly what Margaret herself had often thought that the anger drained out of her as quickly as it had come, and she turned away feeling sick and disloyal, as though it were she who was blaming her father, not John.

Margaret could scarcely remember a time when England was not at war with France or when an Englishman with a new idea was not suspected of being a traitor to his country. A new idea paved the way to reform; reform might lead to revolution; and a revolution to people living in England in 1801 meant only three things: mob warfare, the guillotine, and the triumph of the French.

'What good can he do with his dreams and his talk?' cried John, giving the book another savage kick. 'He'll only get himself arrested for sedition.'

'No, John, not just for talking.'

'What about Mr. Spence?'

'*He* published books.'

'Yes, but father agrees with every word in his books. He says so again and again. He'd be selling copies of them here, if you didn't always hide them.'

This was true. Every night, Mr. Pargeter asked for the copies of Spence's *Pig's Meat* and his *Restorer of Society* and Tom Paine's *Rights of Man* to see how many copies had been sold, and every morning Margaret hid them away again among the sermons. She was just as bad as her brother. She was afraid for her father. Terribly afraid.

Two months ago, the Court of the King's Bench had sentenced Mr. Spence to twelve months' imprisonment in Shrewsbury Gaol for publishing a plan for the improvement of society. Land, he had urged, should belong to the parishes, not to large farmers who let their labourers starve. Margaret, like her father, thought that it was both just and sensible that the fields of England should belong to the Englishmen who tilled them: that the villages and hamlets throughout the realm should govern their own affairs. Yet the Attorney General had called the plan 'a seditious libel', and the newspapers had mocked its author as 'a poor insane' and 'a crack-brained, half-witted organist'. Even the wretches in Newgate, where he had awaited his trial, had abused him, kicking him while he slept.

No wonder she was afraid.

John turned gloomily to his sister.

'You haven't made the saloop, Meg. He'll be back from the auction by ten.'

The bell at St. Sepulchre's tolled on and on over the sunlit City. On hanging days it tolled for four long hours. She felt its slow throbbing as she stood by the open kitchen window, grinding the cake of dried orchid root and measuring the sugar and the milk and water for the saloop. It made her despondent and sad.

Her father would grieve for his latest defection of John's—not openly in anger or reproach, but hidden away behind his kindness and hopeful faith in the wisdom of men. He would feel puzzled and sad, not understanding how much more important rank and position and worldly regard were to others than they were to himself. She could even guess what new trades he would suggest for his son—joinery, cabinet-making, engineering—not realizing for a moment that John was sick for a hat like Robert's and the right to swing his cane and live as an equal among gentlemen.

John was so hungry for the trappings of life that she wondered whether he had exaggerated their poverty. Were they really poor? She thought of the stink and filth in the tenement at the end of Holly Lane and decided that they were not. The kitchen about her was sweet and clean. She thought of the mobs earlier in the year who had rioted for bread, of the thousands of labourers and their families throughout the country who lived on the edge of starvation, and then she looked back across the the kitchen at Mrs. Neech turning the joint on the spit. With cleanliness and food and books to read, what more could one want?

She sighed. She could think of many things. She would like a high-waisted, white muslin gown with a fichu, like her friend Suzannah, the chemist's daughter, and to share Eugenia's spinet lessons with Signor Minio and to go to Brighton races every year with Jane and her family. She loved her father; she loved the musty smell of his books; she understood why he dreamed his dreams. But like John, she loved the good things of this world too. She thought one could suffer too much for a principle.

She stirred the simmering milk and wrinkled up her face. It was so odd of Father to be both a philosopher and a fuss-pot. Everyone else she knew sweetened their milk with juniper twigs, but Father insisted that all milk in the house be boiled. He said that it rendered the dirt in the cow-keeper's shop less injurious to the health.

The awful tolling stopped at the very moment that Mr. Pargeter and his friends from the auction turned out of Cheapside into Holly Lane.

The bookseller was an old man. His white hair fell to his shoulders in a mane and stood back from his forehead to reveal a brow of formidable height and breadth. The words were tumbling out of him like water out of a pump. To enforce his meaning, he had raised his hands and was thumping downwards through the air in a gesture all his own. It was as though a clergyman-turned-gardener had decided to give the blessing by prodding it into men's hearts with his thumbs.

'I tell you, gentlemen,' he was saying, 'that with every month of the war the gulf grows wider between us.'

'How, sir?' asked the foppish young man at his side.

'We are becoming a nation of two peoples: those with property and hopes; and those with no property and no hopes.'

'Granted that this be so,' said a sober gentleman on his right, 'what would you have us do?'

'Let that which separates us be held in trust for the use of all.'

'Sequester property, sir?' exclaimed the fop.

'Let the parishes hold it in trust for the use of the people. Let them administer the land and the houses.'

'Houses, sir? Surely not houses.'

'Here in London?' expostulated another of his friends.

'Especially here. The houses and tenements should belong to the parishes, not to the landlords.'

'Oh come, come, Mr. Pargeter,' protested another.

'Let a man labour in the certain hope that his exertions will earn him enough to feed his wife and children. Let a poor man live in certain hope of a decent shelter at nights with cleanliness and sweet water.'

'Why, so he may,' said the fop.

They ware passing the tenement under repair, from which came a stink so noisome and foul that the party pressed their handkerchiefs to their noses.

'Call you that cleanly?' asked the bookseller roundly from the safe distance of the opposite side of the lane. 'Is it even a shelter?'

The four men stood with their backs against the warehouse over the way and looked up at the rambling, dilapidated building which the workmen were trying to repair. It leaned drunkenly on one side so that the top two floors were tilted at an angle of thirty degrees; the plaster had fallen from the upper storeys revealing the crumbling ruin of the walls beneath, and half the windows were boarded with planks or stuffed with rags.

'The landlord is doing what he can,' said the sober gentleman.

'Too late. Too late,' exclaimed the bookseller. 'He should pull it down and build again.'

Margaret had run out to the front of the shop to greet her father, but seeing the group stationed opposite the tenement and catching sight of the downward thumping of her father's hands, she stopped in her tracks.

'Dear Lord,' she prayed. 'Please stop him. Please stop him before he says something seditious.'

While they had been talking, a small, dark-haired boy had crept out of the tenement. Margaret watched him summon up enough courage to run across the lane and tug her father by his coat flaps.

The bookseller looked down at him absent-mindedly and then, suddenly seeing the child in focus, shook his head sadly.

'You are very dirty, Elijah,' he said. 'Have you forgotten to go to the pump this morning?'

The child nodded.

'Hungry?'

The child nodded again.

'Has your mother not given you bread?'

He shook his head.

'Ask her now. Where is she?'

'At the hanging, sir.'

'And she left you none?'

'You must go to the ravens, Elijah,' laughed the foppish young man.

'No, child,' said the bookseller gravely, taking the boy's hand. 'You must come home to my Meg.'

Seeing his daughter waiting for him at the far end of the lane, he raised his voice.

'Meg,' he called loudly. 'Here's Lord Binsey and Mr. Simkin and Mr. Jeeves for saloop, and Elijah for bread.'

That last evening before the disruption of their peace, Robert Kerridge raised his eyes from the anatomy manual he was studying and took a darting look at Margaret, reading a slim, drab-covered volume of poetry. He liked to catch her thus, her eyes bright, her cheeks flushed, and her lips very slightly apart, her whole mind and heart given to the matter before her. The candlelight shone richly in the deep browns and reds in her hair and softened and gentled the wide, strong brow which she had inherited from her father. Hers was a good face, he thought, not pretty—it was too individual for mere prettiness—but honest and intelligent and alive. The only childish thing about it was its nose. At night, as its owner tired, the nose grew wide and sleepy and pink, like a small child's. It amused and touched him, reminding him nightly that the daughter of his grandfather's old friend had still not reached womanhood—an assurance of which he stood in need. It was more comfortable for him to think of Margaret as a child.

'Father, you must write to him tonight,' she exclaimed suddenly, holding the volume of poetry tight against her chest. 'Write and ask him who he is.'

'Write to whom?' asked the bookseller vaguely, his mind still deep in the catalogue of Mr. Beckford's furniture which had been auctioned down in Wiltshire last week.

'To Mr. Cottle, of course. You said you would.'

'To Mr. Cottle? Yes, my dear. But I've forgotten what I'm to ask him.'

'Why, who this Mr. Wordsworth is. What is he like? Where does he live? And who is the friend who wrote the poems with him?'

'Ah, yes,' he murmured ruminatively. 'The *Lyrical Ballads*. Too plain and homely, Meg, for my taste, I fear.'

'More of your scribbling verse,' said her brother savagely, tossing aside the *Morning Post*. 'It's trash. It never sells.'

'It isn't scribbling verse,' retorted Margaret indignantly. 'And it isn't trash. How many times have I told you that it isn't earning money that makes poetry good? It's what it *is* that matters. And what it does to you inside.'

'Makes me sick,' jeered John.

'That's because you're ignorant and a boor,' rapped out his

sister. 'And you're not even right about the ballads not selling. Longmans published this second edition only last winter.'

Robert swallowed a smile. He enjoyed watching her when she was angry, for she revealed herself unawares when she lost her temper—much as she had revealed herself at the window that morning.

'Homer and Virgil and Shakespeare and Milton are manly spirits, my son,' said the bookseller gently. 'You are unjust to them and to yourself to condemn poetry because the versifiers of our modern age lack their wisdom and strength.'

'But, Father, Mr. Wordsworth's poems *have* wisdom,' protested Margaret.

'They show pity for the old and the sick and the poor, my dear. A pity expressed in a manly plainness of style. But they are not poetry, Meg. They are merely verse.'

Margaret bit her lip and returned to her reading. Despite her spirit, she seldom contradicted her father openly, though tonight the line of her mouth and the frown of concentration which had so quickly replaced her petulance showed plainly that she had rejected entirely Mr. Pargeter's opinion of her poet.

As the City bells chimed nine o'clock through the paling summer light, Robert's eyes wandered slowly round the little parlour, dwelling affectionately on the tattered brocade of Margaret's chair, the chipped delft jar in which Mr. Pargeter kept the spills for his cheroots, and then on the threadbare carpet at his feet. He wondered why he loved this shabby room—he who, like John, valued so much more dearly the bright varnish of worldly success. He was puzzled by himself. He hated failure. He wanted to be rich and successful, like his own father.

His gaze wandered up to the thoughtful old face of the bookseller, reading on through the list of Mr. Beckford's goods. It was a startling face for one who had lived most of his life in London and who had marked with sorrow the lives and misfortunes of his fellow men, for it was full of the simple strength of country things and reflected a brave, untroubled mind. Mr.

Pargeter's whole bearing made Robert think of the rugged stance of an oak-tree, standing calm and indomitable in the middle of a storm. There were seventy years to the growth of this oak-tree, and there was not an unsound limb or rotten branch that a storm could tear away.

Seventy years.

It was a long time in the history of a man. A long time in the history of two families such as the Pargeters and his own.

And Robert fell to wondering yet once again at the strange family connexion that had persuaded his parents to send him to lodge with this dreaming, unworldly man, so different from themselves in fortune and in personal beliefs.

His grandfather and the bookseller had been boyhood friends, fishing and poaching and swimming together along the upper reaches of the River Exe, and when his grandfather had married he had begged his friend to stand godfather to his first son.

It was all so long ago. So very long ago. And now, that god-son was his own father—self-confident, ambitious, successful, hard—as different from the family friend who had renounced 'the vain pomp and glory of the world' on his behalf at his baptism as it was possible for two men to be.

Robert, with his eyes still wandering idly round the little parlour, wondered whether the years would play such odd tricks with his own life and with Margaret's and John's. Would their children and their children's children come to peer at each other through such a briar hedge of tangled hopes?

Then the boom of St. Paul's joined the music of the bells.

2 *Disaster*

The disaster began with a yawning and wrenching of timbers, a strange shrieking yell of rending wood which brought the four in the parlour to their feet. Then came human cries, more yawning, and then, suddenly, an appalling, rumbling roar which went on and on. It rattled the parlour widows and then, with a final, dreadful subterranean tremor, seemed to shake the foundations of the bookseller's house.

They ran through the shuttered shop, flung back the door bolts, and ran into the lane.

Acrid billows of something choking and thick were sweeping down on them from the Cheapside end.

'There's a fire,' shouted John.

'No, it's dust,' choked Robert.

'It's the tenement,' cried Mr. Pargeter. 'It's collapsed.'

'Father!' gasped Margaret. 'The people inside!'

They struggled towards the tenement, nearly blinded by flying particles of plaster and rubble, choking and coughing in the thick air. The billows had blotted out the chemist's shop opposite; they seemed to wrap round each of them individually, like a hateful, smothering cloak.

'I can't see,' yelled John, who was ahead of the rest.

His voice came back to them thickly and far off, like the plaintive cries from a ship lost in the fog.

They stumbled on through the white dust till they stood in horrified silence before the huge heap of mangled masonry that had once been the tenement. Window frames, door jambs, rubble, blocks of brickwork, tiles, roof beams, and the stark, unpealed trunks of the pine trees in the walls were all jumbled and tumbled together in chaos. And over all, over the rising dust and the broken house, lay a silence so unspeakably dreadful that Margaret buried her face in her father's coat and wept.

'What can we do?' cried John, turning to the others, white-faced and helpless.

What could any of them do?

Five families had lived in the house at the corner of Holly Lane, and not a man, woman, or child, buried in that monstrous pile of rubble, stirred where he lay or called for help.

Slowly, little sounds came to them through the surrounding white fog of dust. Distant cries could be heard in Cheapside, and footsteps were hurrying towards them from east and west. Voices were approaching from the lane behind them, and Mr. Fisher and his apprentice coughed and spluttered through the dust to stand beside them.

'My God! My God!' muttered the chemist.

'Listen,' shouted Robert.

A roof beam groaned as it slipped down a slanting angle of floorboards and window-frames, and a new spurt of white dust billowed into the evening air.

'It was only the beam,' said John.

'No. Listen.'

The six of them stood transfixed in front of the ruin of the building, straining their ears for a human sound.

Very faintly, from the bottom of the highest mound of rubble, came a short, thin wail.

'There! Did you hear?'

It came again in a strange, buried, animal whimper.

'It's a puppy!' exclaimed Peter, the chemist's apprentice.

The creature mewed again.

'It's a cat!' said the chemist.

'No, it's not,' cried Margaret. 'It's a child.'

John and Robert stripped off their coats. Peter, the apprentice, was about to follow suit when Mr. Fisher grabbed him roughly by his coat and held him firmly by the neck.

'It's not our duty to go clambering to our death in that,' he said, pointing to the tenement. 'It's for us to tend the poor wretches who are brought out alive.'

He gave the boy a shake to enforce his meaning.

'Take the key of the shop,' he said, putting his hand in his coat pocket. 'Run home and fetch me the *aqua-vitae*.'

Mr. Pargeter was struggling out of his heavy coat to follow the two young men, but Robert, turning and seeing him, whispered urgently to Margaret:

'Keep him with you, Meg. Hold on to him. It's a task for John and me.'

Margaret ran to her father and took him by the arm.

'No, Father. Don't go.'

He shook her off, but she clutched him more fiercely.

'You have other work, Father,' she said. 'You must stay and fight this wrong.'

She wondered afterwards how she had ever come to utter such fateful words. Yet they must have echoed what was deep in her heart, for she urged him again.

'You must fight the landlords, Father, so that this wicked neglect never happens again.'

'Oh, Meg,' he said. 'You agree at last.'

Her brother and the medical student clambered up over the ruins of the house till they came to a dark space between the twisted floor beams of the second storey. They stopped for a moment to peer down the wrecked shaft of the stairway, strewn with planks and heaps of rubble, and then, first one and then the other, sat down on a jutting lump of brickwork and slipped heels first into the hole.

Margaret watched them with a sinking heart. The huge pile of masonry was still sighing and creaking every now and then as the heavy beams settled lower in the debris.

Weeks later, when Margaret needed to be consoled about her brother John, Robert described to her that horrible ten minutes before they reached the child.

In the dim light of the shattered stairs, they had groped their way downwards over the planks and heaps of plaster, now stooping, now crawling on all fours, and now lying flat on their faces and working their way onward with their forearms, like moles. The stench from the vault at the foot of the shaft grew stronger and more loathsome the lower they got; it sickened and

17

nearly stifled Robert; he had never smelt anything so foul. But John had clenched his teeth and plunged downwards without a word. Half-way down, the inside walls of the passage had collapsed, and over their ruins they saw the complete destruction of the first-floor rooms. Roof timbers and tiles and the mangled bodies and furniture from the upper rooms had been hurled through the gaping ceilings on the homes beneath. Death must have come instantaneously, for the families had been asleep in their cots. They passed four bodies lying in a single bed, their limbs so composed and their faces, in the faint glimmer, so wrapt in peace that they could have had no hint of the terror of their end. Lower down, on the level of the street, death had not come in so kindly a fashion. A woman had dragged herself out of her room, only to be buried in the passage by the collapsing wall. Her bloodstained fingers showed how hard she had fought to free herself from her tomb.

The weak bleat of the injured child sounded nearer then, and they had hurried along the dark ground-floor corridor towards it, dodging the cascades of falling plaster which were still gushing downwards from the rents in the drooping ceiling and eyeing with sickening dread the bulging wall beside them. As they went, they heard a distant rumble above and ahead, and the air was suddenly filled with tumbling bricks.

'Duck your head,' John had shouted.

They had stood together, burying their heads in each other's arms, choking and spluttering till the bricks ceased falling and the danger was past. When the dust cleared, they saw that a formidable obstacle now blocked the way. A great jumble of bricks and boards had filled up the gap in the passage.

'Start taking the bricks from the top of the heap,' said John. 'I'm going to look for a post to wedge that beam.'

In those few minutes in the darkness he had taken command.

When he returned with the post, they both worked frantically, longing to save the child quickly and be quit of that terrible, shifting ruin as soon as they could. They had torn at the fallen brickwork, cutting their hands and arms, their breath coming in choking rasps.

When they had made a gap wide enough to take the width of their shoulders, John had pushed him aside.

'I go first,' he had said. 'There may be something more to fall from the floor above.'

Before Robert had had time to protest, he had found himself looking at the soles of John's shoes disappearing into the hole in the rubble.

Thirty seconds later, Robert himself was through.

And the child cried quite close to them in the darkness.

They brought three people out of the ruin alive: a man, a woman, and the crying child.

The woman died on Mr. Pargeter's old coat, laid out on the hard cobbles of Holly Lane, her head resting on the bookseller's knee. The man was carried to St. Xavier's on a shutter by Robert and John, with one of his legs crushed and both his wrists broken by a falling beam.

Margaret picked the child up in her arms and carried him home. Though his hair was matted with blood and his forehead swollen and bruised, she had recognized the wizened little features beneath the thick coating of white dust.

They belonged to Elijah, the boy she had fed in the kitchen not twelve hours before.

Elijah tossed and whimpered all night in his sleep and clutched at Margaret as though to seek shelter under her body, just as he had found it under his mother's in the terrible moment that the house collapsed.

'How strange are the workings of the human heart!' her father had murmured when John and Robert had described how they had found the boy. 'She was a bad mother to him; she neglected and starved him. Yet when death faced them both, she must have clutched him to her and shielded him with her own body. The most loving of mothers could not have done more.'

Margaret had taken off the boy's filthy clothes and washed him in the hot water that Mrs. Neech, the housekeeper, had provided. And when Robert returned from the hospital he had gone to the chemist for a lotion to put in Elijah's dust-inflamed eyes and an opiate to dull his wretchedness. The boy had been too dazed to ask them what they were doing to him, and when they laid him in Margaret's bed he had fallen almost immediately into this drugged, unhappy sleep.

As she watched Elijah in the grey light of the summer night, struggling in his dreams against the violent wreck of his life, Margaret felt no happier than he. She was torn with grief. The disaster at the end of Holly Lane filled her with horror. She had never seen death so close before or properly understood the brutal suddenness with which it strikes. Those bodies lying crushed in the debris were people that she had seen alive, walking in the lane, only three hours before. All her life she had heard the children from the tenement crying desolately in their childish woes or laughing at their games in the street; she had lain awake at nights listening to the drunken shouts of their parents returning home from the gin shops and heard in the dawn their weary footsteps plodding off to work. Poverty had made their lives ugly and hopeless; but nothing in them had been so ugly or monstrous as their deaths.

The dust was settling on the rooftops and ledges and cobbles outside, and a faint glimmer of moonlight struggled through the last haze in the air to fall diffusely on the bed.

She stared at Elijah. He was not a pretty child. His hair was dull and coarse, his features pointed and drawn, and his joints were so sharp that she wondered that his elbows had not already cut two holes in the sleeves of John's shirt. He was so wizened that he did not look like a child at all, but more like one of those elderly elves she had read about in fairy-tales. She noted every line and crease in his bruised and sleeping face, and then frowned at her own thoughts. Elijah looked neither intelligent nor kind; the sharp savagery in front of her belonged to a vicious little animal rather than to a boy. She frowned again, angry with herself, and puzzled at the thought of the days ahead. How long would it take them to tame this wild creature, she wondered. And what onslaughts of silent disapproval would they have to withstand from Mrs. Neech?

Yet it was not so much the problem of Elijah that made her toss and turn so restlessly beside him through that anxious August night. It was something far closer to her. Something far more threatening to their future.

'You must fight the landlords, Father.'

What rage and horror could have driven such a protest out of her? It was so unlike her—so illogical. It ran counter to all her cautious, lying little acts in hiding away *Pig's Meat* and the *Restorer of Society* and Tom Paine's *Rights of Man* behind the sermons, and rendered useless all the anxious care that she had taken to save her father from arrest.

'You must stay and fight this wrong.'

What a dangerous, stupid, undaughterly thing for her to have said!

They had been standing together in front of that hateful ruin, the beams and the roof timbers still groaning as they settled more heavily on the trapped bodies beneath. No one should take any notice of what people said at such times. It was not fair. They should forget it.

Yet she knew that her father had not forgotten it, for directly he had seen Elijah dropping off to sleep, he had shut himself up in his snuggery behind the bookshop and bolted the door. When she had brought him coffee, he had shouted fiercely at her from inside, saying that he was writing *The New Jerusalem* and was not to be disturbed.

She was afraid.

She was not a fool. She was not cloistered from life. She lived in the heart of the City. She read the newspapers and heard the news discussed in her father's shop. When she went marketing with Mrs. Neech, she stopped to read the bills posted on the public buildings protesting against the high price of bread, against the low wages, against monopolies and government hirelings and Press Gangs—the cries of despair of a people goaded by need.

Yet England was at war. She was fighting for her life against France. Misery must be borne. Protests were treasonable.

Only last November, she had seen the Volunteer Corps marching off to Kennington Common to join the Life Guards in preventing artisans and journeymen from meeting to petition the King and Parliament for higher wages. She remembered Mr. Spence. Only two months ago, the Attorney-General had decided that his ideas smacked too much of the French Revolution and had thrown him into gaol.

What could the future hold for the author of *The New Jerusalem,* so passionately writing out his plea in the snuggery below?

Margaret shuddered with despair.

3 *'The New Jerusalem'*

On Tuesdays, Robert Kerridge's lectures at the hospital did not begin till after seven, and Margaret had time to dress herself and slip down the stairs to catch him at breakfast in the parlour.

'The boy's been tossing all night. Will you come to him before you leave?'

'Is he awake?'

'No. He's sleeping still.'

'It's the best balm,' he sighed wearily. 'But I'll come if you want me to.'

Startled by the weariness of the sigh, she studied him with more attention. Robert looked battered and spent, and the extreme neatness of his fresh shirt and well-brushed coat—his every effort to hide his hurt—brought a lump to her throat. Below the crisp wrist bands his hands stuck out swollen and cut. She could not bear to watch him buttering his bread. His fingernails were torn. She swallowed quickly and turned away, shocked and, in some odd and unbecoming way, made angry by the fact that the night's work had damaged his hands.

He looked up, sensing what her eyes were avoiding, and pulled his knuckles quickly out of sight under the hanging folds of the tablecloth.

'Take your father some breakfast,' he said, almost roughly. 'He must be famished.'

'He's not still up?'

'The light's shining under his door.'

'He's still writing?'

Robert nodded his head.

'And still very angry,' he said, beginning to smile.

'How do you know? Did he shout at you?'

'No, but his quill's tearing over the paper like a rusty nail on a slate. I've never heard anyone write in such a rage.'

His returning cheerfulness gave her the courage to look towards his hands again, but he kept them hid and returned her look with a wry, comical expression on his face.

'I might complain, Meg, that you haven't bothered to brush the dust out of your hair.'

Margaret blushed scarlet with shame.

'You shouldn't go poking about in people's thoughts like that,' she said angrily. 'They're private.'

'No, they're not. They're written all over your face.'

She went off quickly to the kitchen to fetch her father's tray and, walking back with it past the open parlour door and into the shop, she knocked loudly on the door of his den.

'If that's breakfast, Meg,' she heard him shout, 'leave it outside and I'll come for it when I've done.'

Robert was at her shoulder, smiling to make it up.

'And now for the child,' he said, leading the way upstairs.

He examined the boy lying askew on the bed and put his hand on his forehead and felt his pulse and then gave a darting look at his thick, dull hair.

'I'll write you a note for the chemist,' he said. 'Take Elijah across the road directly you've given him something to eat.'

'Is he ill?'

'No. Only suffering from neglect.'

It was a jangling, miserable sort of morning, with the tragedy of the night weighing heavily on everyone in the lane.

The boy roused himself soon after Robert left, and Margaret stood him up in the bed and asked him if he would like bacon and eggs and milk. The child stared back at her so dully as he nodded his head that she wondered whether he had remembered what had happened to him or whether he was still numbed by the drug.

'We'll go down to the kitchen and see what we can get.'

John's shirt tails lay in folds at his feet, and he had lost his arms in the sleeves. He looked like an old, unhappy little druid who had woken up two thousand years too late.

'I'll tie a ribbon round your middle first and hitch it up,' she smiled.

But the child stared back at her so mournfully that a wave of sadness suddenly swept over her. How could anyone ever make amends to him for the unlovingness of his childhood and what had happened to him last night?

'Come along,' she said quickly. 'It's not cold, and there are no nails in the floorboards, so you won't hurt your feet.'

Mrs. Neech awaited them in the kitchen with resignation stamped grimly on her face.

'He'll need some new clothes, Miss Margaret,' she said. 'I've just burnt his others in the yard.'

Margaret looked puzzled, not knowing where they were to come from.

'Your father can't hand him over to the Parish Overseer without a stitch to his back.'

'But he won't do that,' she retorted hotly. 'Not let the Parish take him. He couldn't!'

Mrs. Neech shrugged her shoulders.

'I don't know what Mr. Pargeter'll decide. But I'm not having a naked heathen in my kitchen, so out you go, Miss, and buy him some breeches and a shirt. It's not likely that you'll be sewing him a stitch yourself.'

This was unfair of Mrs. Neech. Margaret could not sew. Mrs. Neech had not taken it upon herself to teach her, and Margaret had been too indolent to bother to learn the art from anyone else. Suzannah Fisher did any odd sewing for her that she was compelled to have done. It was an equitable arrangement, for Margaret composed her a love letter in exchange for a hem. She filled her love letters with fine sentiments and quotations from the poets, and these delighted Suzannah's swains so much that the young men were always coming knocking at the chemist's door.

This morning, however, Margaret could not beg for the sewing of a shirt because Suzannah and Eugenia were away on a country visit at Shepherd's Bush.

Margaret sought the money box on the parlour shelf.

'There's that second-hand slop shop in Giltspur Street,' Mrs.

Neech shouted after her. 'They'll have what's needful. Something serviceable and clean.'

Mrs. Neech was a cross to them all, and they were a cross to her. She had come up from Oxfordshire with Margaret's mother and, when her young mistress had married the middle-aged bookseller of Holly Lane, she had remained to cook for them both, sniffing contemptuously at their narrow quarters and sighing continuously at Mr. Pargeter's lack of worldly good sense. Her young mistress had died at her daughter's birth, but Mrs. Neech had stayed on, faithfully and dutifully—sniffing and sighing ever since. They were tied to each other—the Pargeters and their housekeeper—by that most cruel and wearing of human bonds—a mutual faithfulness to the wishes of the dead. Young Mrs. Pargeter had begged her maid to succour her husband and her motherless children and had implored her husband not to send Mrs. Neech back to the country without money or prospects of a home of her own. They were bound to each other by a Gordian knot.

Margaret grumbled at the housekeeper as she strode up Giltspur Street, forgetting that she had cooked for them and washed for them for twenty years and remembering only that she did what she did sternly and, seemingly, without love. Elijah's arrival would add one more thorn to her crown of martyrdom, a thorn to be endured with disapproving resignation.

However, when Margaret, bearing the shirt and breeches over her arm, re-entered the kitchen, she found that the latest thorn had pierced Mrs. Neech into a most unresigned and unsaintlike rage.

'He's got lice,' she shouted, crimson in the face. 'The child is crawling with them. They're all in his hair.'

Elijah was sitting under the table gnawing a crust, like an animal.

'Take him to Mr. Fisher. Ask him what he can do.'

Margaret remembered Robert's frowning look at the boy's hair and the note that he had written for the chemist. So *that* was what he had meant! She could not imagine the exquisite

Robert knowing anything about lice, and it gave her a shock.

Mr. Fisher ordered Elijah to stand in the lane outside his shop and shouted for his apprentice to bring the camphor oil.

It was all over with brutal and surprising speed. Mr. Fisher held the boy firmly in the crook of his arm, and Peter poured the camphor oil over his head. The oil must have stung in the cuts and scratches, for he screamed and struggled in the chemist's grip.

'More. More,' said Mr. Fisher.

Peter soused the child's head with another pint and then started rubbing his hair roughly with a coarse rag.

'Oh, don't hurt him,' cried Margaret, for Elijah's screams were growing shriller and shriller.

Then the patient suddenly ducked his head and bit the chemist in the fat of his thigh. Mr. Fisher dropped him with a yell, and Elijah ran down the lane as fast as he could.

'Don't run away,' cried Margaret, running after him.

The child ran towards his home and then suddenly came to a halt, staring in front of him in horror. A group of onlookers was standing in a semicircle round the ruins of the tenement, gazing at it as silently as the child.

Elijah turned on his heel and with a howl of despair ran back up the lane and threw himself into Margaret's outstretched arms.

She did not know what to do with such grief. Father was still writing in the snuggery. Mrs. Neech was sullen at the sink, and John merely shrugged his shoulders; he was busy opening up the shop. So she heated some water, ran upstairs and stole Robert's lavendered soap, and scrubbed the hateful camphor out of Elijah's hair and eyes. Then she dressed him in the new clothes and poured him out a bowl of hot milk from the skillet on the stove. After the milk, Elijah's tears subsided into hiccups and sighs.

Margaret found a place for him in the shop, hidden away behind the stack of books that had arrived from the auction last night, and then went in search of the only book she could think of that might make him smile. It was a little book especially made for a child, containing poems surrounded by narrow borders of illustrations, drawn and engraved by the poet himself. She had loved it when she was younger, and she loved and honoured Mr. Blake, the strange acquaintance of her father's who had written it.

'Look,' she said, kneeling down beside him and opening the book at *The Little Black Boy*. 'He's a poet who loves children. Listen to this.'

And she read aloud:

> '*My mother bore me in the southern wild,*
> *And I am black, but O! my soul is white;*
> *White as an angel is the English child,*
> *But I am black, as if bereav'd of light.*'

Elijah could make very little of this poem; nor could he decipher the words printed on the other pages, because he could not read; but she left him contentedly tracing his finger along the extraordinary squiggles and twirls round the margins of the poems and gazing in wonder at the solid football of a sun behind the little black boy and his mother. It was so low in the sky that the black boy could have turned from his mother and kicked the sun half across the world.

Ten minutes later, Mr. Pargeter emerged from the snuggery, tired but exultant.

'It's done, John. It's done, Meg,' he cried. 'I can set it up in type today, and we can print it off tomorrow.'

John, who was adding the titles of the new purchases to the shop's catalogue, looked up and scowled.

'You'll help me with the inking and the screwing, won't you, my son? And, Meg, I'll need you for the stitching. I reckon that it'll run to a foolscap octavo.'

The old bookseller was so absorbed in an author's contentment that he failed to notice his children's embarrassed silence.

'We'll sell the pamphlet for a halfpenny a time,' he continued, striding up and down his bookshop with his arms linked fast behind his back. 'We'll have it out on the front trays and we'll get Elijah to hawk it round the streets. That's justice for you! The orphan of civic disaster distributing the *Plan for the New Jerusalem*.'

'No, it won't do,' protested Margaret. 'It won't do at all, Father.'

'Won't do, Meg?' exclaimed Mr. Pargeter. 'Why won't it do?'

'I don't know what you've written, Father, but it's probably a libel.'

'My dear child, a libel? Your father utter a libel?'

'Margaret's right,' burst out John. 'You're unjust to the landlord. He was doing his best. He was trying to repair the house.'

'Doing his best!' exploded Mr. Pargeter, suddenly scarlet with anger.

'Doing his best, John, when Mr. Fisher and I told him over five years ago that the house was unsafe? Doing his best, when the tenants went to him in a body last Christmas and told him that the building was in hourly danger of collapse? It's murder that Mr. Galliver's committed. Murder, John!'

'Then surely he'll be brought to justice?' replied Margaret.

'Can the judges bring those poor wretches back to life? It's too late, Meg. It's always too late. A disaster like this happens twice a year in London. Yet nothing is done. Nothing is done to stop it. The landlords continue to extort rents from their death traps.'

He looked first at his surly, despondent son and then back at his daughter, nervously fraying a piece of string between her finger and thumb.

'Come, Meg,' he said more gently. 'Sit quietly in the snuggery and read what I have written. If there's anything untrue or unjust, score it out. It is not Mr. Galliver I have attacked, but the system that allows such things. Nay, it is not even an attack. It is a plan. A plan to govern our lives better in this great City of ours. To bring light and health and hope to those who dwell in darkness. Come, my dear, leave that unhappy piece of string and read *The New Jerusalem*. And John, ask Mrs. Neech to bring me fresh coffee and rolls.'

Margaret settled herself in the snuggery and read the following introduction written in her father's vigorous and pointed hand:

THE NEW JERUSALEM

I adjure our rulers to view more closely the squalor and danger in which a large part of the poorer people in this and other of our English cities dwell. Let them reflect how quickly disease and death come to the children of the poor—how bereft they are of light and warmth and sweet air. Honesty and plainness go together. How comes it, sirs, that in this glorious nineteenth century, a rich man's horses be better stabled than a third part of our English commonalty? That not only do the poor suffer the degradation of filth but also the mortal danger of their miserable lodgings falling upon their heads? Fie upon a Government that rests satisfied in so much wrong when the remedy for the evil lies close at hand. Lords and Commoners, free the subjects whom you represent from so intolerable a misuse. Give the houses of our cities to the parishes of our cities that the parishes may order things rightly for the people who live within their bounds. A poor man's home should not suffer the wicked neglect of a private landlord, who squanders his rents elsewhere, careless from whence his wealth comes and indifferent to his tenants' plight. 'Tis said that an Englishman's home be his castle. Let it no longer remain the poor man's dungeon and his tomb.'

Margaret would have read further but at this point the shop bell rang, and ten seconds later her father called her.

'Meg, here's Mr. Simkin and Mr. Jeeves come to see how we are.'

The two gentlemen were wiping the white dust from the plaster of the tenement off their Hessian boots with her feather mop and John's bookshop duster.

'The devil of a mess you're in down the lane,' said Mr. Simkin gravely.

'Who would have thought such a total collapse possible,' sighed Mr. Jeeves, flicking the last of the dust off his heel.

'I have expected it these last five years,' replied the bookseller sadly. 'And I reproach myself. I reproach myself bitterly.'

'Why, what could you have done to avert the disaster?' asked Mr. Jeeves, his thin eyebrows arching in surprise.

'I could have written and published my plan before now. I am indolent. Very indolent. It should not take the death of innocent neighbours to drive one to one's duty. I should have published my plan years ago.'

'Your plan?' asked Mr. Simkin.

'Not the fantastical notions you diverted us with yesterday morning?' exclaimed Mr. Jeeves. 'Surely not those?'

'My plan for the New Jerusalem,' replied Mr. Pargeter with dignity. 'Margaret has the draft here in her hand.'

He took the bundle of sheets from his daughter and handed them to Mr. Simkin.

'Read it not as a mocker but as a Christian, and then give me your opinion,' he said quietly.

He turned back towards his two children.

'John, fetch the gentlemen chairs, and Meg, bring us some saloop.'

Margaret was in and out of the bookshop for the next hour attending to her father's clients, for first Lord Binsey and then Mr. Naylor and Mr. Benjamin Little joined the party, and then a young poet called Francis Love and a crabbed, choleric bookdealer called Mr. Stone. The little bookshop had long enjoyed a reputation as 'a lounging bookshop'—not so splendid nor as fashionable as Hatchards in Piccadilly, where wits and satirists mingled with dukes and duchesses and the greatest statesmen of the day—but yet a humble rendezvous where one could hear good talk and where the honesty of the bookseller's face and the youthful freshness of his daughter compensated for the dim light and the cramped closeness of Holly Lane.

Margaret spent much of the time in the kitchen grinding fresh powder from the cake of dried orchid root and mixing the water and milk and sugar; and by the time she returned to the shop the conversation had taken a new turn.

'And what do you think of this, gentlemen?' exclaimed Mr. Simkin, his finger on a new paragraph in her father's plan. 'The children of the poor are not to be put to work till they reach fourteen years!'

'Fourteen years!' laughed Mr. Naylor. 'Oh come, sir. It is not possible, not even in a Utopia!'

'Why not?' asked her father mildly.

'Why, sir, who is to support them in their indolence?'

'You would starve them still more than they are starved to-day,' protested Mr. Benjamin Little, 'for how would their parents then find the bread to feed them?'

'Besides, it is cruelty to the children themselves to keep them so long from employment,' objected Mr. Stone.

'How so?'

'Why, when they grow up, they will have to endure grievous heavy labours, and unless they be inured to toil in their tender years, they will sink beneath their burden, unfitted by the softness of their childhood for their duties as men.'

'Do we so inure our own children?'

'No, but we set them to learn their letters and their tables and put them under masters to make them tolerable scholars in literature and mathematics. They are not idle; we train them for their lives as men. We set our daughters betimes to their needles and teach them Italian and the use of the globe.'

'Why, so would I have the children of the poor occupy their childhood,' cried the bookseller, banging his fist down hard on Johnson's Dictionary.

Margaret left the shop to the roars of laughter that greeted her father's angry plea. She flushed and bit her lip, her eyes smarting with tears. Her heart ached for his dreams.

'The children from that tenement learning the uses of the globe!' she heard Lord Binsey crowing in his high, foolish voice.

Her father's clients were still quizzing *The New Jerusalem* when the parish overseer knocked at the kitchen door ten minutes later.

'I've come for the little orphan,' he told Mrs. Neech lugubriously, his tiny pig eyes disappearing into the fat of his cheeks in the effort to suit his expression to the solemnity of his task.

'And quite time too!' rapped out Mrs. Neech.

'Oh no,' cried Margaret, running up behind her. 'You can't take him. You really can't. He belongs here in Holly Lane.'

'No, he don't, Miss,' said the overseer not unkindly. 'With both his parents dead, he belongs to the parish.'

He shook his head solemnly, letting his dewlaps ripple and swing like the heavy ropes of two tolling bells.

'It's the parish, more's the pity, that's got to find him his clothes and apprentice him out to work.'

'But we've brought him a shirt and breeches already, haven't we, Mrs. Neech? And I know that my father will want to keep him.'

The overseer was a loyal servant of the ratepayers and was sharp enough to sniff a bargain.

'Perhaps I may speak with your father,' he suggested, permitting himself a ghost of a smile.

Margaret ran back into the bookshop.

'Father,' she said. 'They've come for Elijah.'

'Who have come, my dear? Be more precise,' asked Mr. Pargeter, still warm from the defence of his ideas.

'The parish overseer.'

'Well, show him up.'

There was no need for Margaret to show him up, for Mrs. Neech and the overseer had followed immediately in Margaret's steps.

'Good morning, Mr. Pargeter,' said the parish officer ingratiatingly. 'Good morning, gentlemen. I've come, sir, about this orphan boy from the disaster down the lane.'

He fumbled in his pocket and drew out a paper and read from it:

'Son of Josiah Dyett and Hannah Dyett deceased. Name of Elijah. Eight years old.'

'Eight!' exclaimed Margaret. 'I thought he was five.'

Mr. Pargeter turned swiftly towards his two children, catching their eye.

'Well, John? Well, Margaret? We want him to stay with us, don't we?'

'Adopt him?' asked Margaret, a puzzled look on her face.

'No, sir. Not adopt him,' expostulated John. 'We couldn't.'

'Why not?'

'We don't know anything about him.'

'We know he's a child in need of care.'

'But he may prove a thief or a rogue. He may bring us disgrace.'

'I could take him as an apprentice,' smiled Mr. Pargeter. 'How would you say to that?'

'A child of eight!' exclaimed John. 'What good would he be to us?'

'He can't read, Father,' Margaret confessed miserably.

'He'd be useless to us for years.'

'All apprentices are useless for years,' retorted the bookseller sharply. 'I know *I* was when I was bound to Mr. Fitch the printer. It takes time and pains to teach a child his trade.'

The overseer cleared his throat with noisy self-importance.

'Parish lads, sir, are apprenticed till they're twenty-four. You'd get your time and money back on Elijah Dyett by the time he was a journeyman.'

Mr. Pargeter frowned.

'We'll speak of this later,' he told the overseer. 'Return to-night and we can draw up the indentures then.'

When Mrs. Neech had led the parish officer away, Margaret, heedless of the fine company, flung her arms round her father's neck.

'Oh, Father, I'm so glad you've saved him.'

'Saved him from what?' asked Lord Binsey, a hint of amusement in his voice.

'From the workhouse, of course,' cried Margaret, turning a ferocious scowl on the ignorant young aristocrat. 'From being apprenticed to a waterman and taught how to smuggle and rob. From being apprenticed to a chimney-sweep and being smothered with soot.'

'Oh! Ho!' laughed Mr. Jeeves. 'So you think the parish is no very good foster mother to its orphans?'

'No. Of course it isn't. Hundreds and hundreds of parish children die, don't they, Father? And hundreds of others just disappear, and no one ever asks what's happened to them. You know it's so.'

Mr. Stone suddenly snarled so fiercely that everyone looked at him in amazement.

'Yet it is to this careless, inhuman parish that your father wishes us to consign our houses. "Give the houses to the parish," says he.'

'You mistake my meaning,' retorted the old bookseller hotly. 'In my New Jerusalem, *all* houses would belong to the parish. Can you believe that the rich would tolerate that inefficiency in their landlords which the poor and their children daily suffer at the hands of the parish? No, sir, they would not. By fighting for their own rights they would fight also for those of the poor. If *all* houses—rich and poor—and *all* orphans—rich and poor— were under the guardianship of the parish we should soon have a system of justice and enlightenment. We should live in a heaven upon earth.'

'Bravo,' laughed Lord Binsey, clapping his hands.

But the other clients looked grave and despondent.

'You mean well, sir,' said Mr. Simkin, picking up his hat. 'But I fear for the publication of your Plan.'

'Be advised by us,' urged Mr. Naylor, taking Mr. Pargeter affectionately by the arm. 'Don't print the thing.'

'Forget it,' said Mr. Jeeves.

'Throw it in the fire,' growled Mr. Stone.

'It won't do any good, sir,' sighed the poet. 'The ranks of the mighty stand over against us.'

When the clients had all gone, Mr. Pargeter turned to his daughter with a gentle cheerfulness that told her that he had set their darkest warnings at nought.

'And where, my dear, have you hidden my new apprentice?'

'Oh, Father,' she stammered, laughing, 'I'd ... forgotten.'

Indeed, in planning Elijah's future, they had all forgotten the boy himself.

'He's looking at Blake's *Songs of Innocence* behind that stack of books.'

Mr. Pargeter and Margaret and John stared down on the child, fallen in a heap on the floor, his legs curled up, his mouth half open, and his belly beneath his new breeches as tight as a drum. He was fast asleep.

'He looks like a puppy that's had too much milk,' murmured the bookseller.

'That's just what he is,' said Margaret.

'Then he's sure to be sick,' groaned John.

4 *The Bequest*

Events now took their relentless course.

Margaret could see straight to the bottom of the steep hill down which her father's hobby-horse was taking him; yet she could do nothing to call him back. John had failed. She had failed. His friends' warnings might never have been spoken. Mr. Pargeter was busy in the cellar sitting before his type cases with his printer's stick in his hand, putting together the words of his pamphlet. Nothing would stop him. He had been working below stairs all afternoon, humming gently to himself as his fingers sought out the appropriate letters in the case box and wedged them firmly in their place.

Yet Margaret made one more effort. She could not sit idly by.

'Robert,' she said. 'Speak to Father. He might listen to you.'

They were sitting alone in the parlour.

'Sometimes a man listens to a voice from another world,' she said.

Robert looked up from his studies and considered the matter. Then he smiled at her and shook his head.

'I know nothing of politics, Margaret. It would be an impertinence for me to talk to your father on such a subject.'

'Even when the impertinence might save him from prison?'

Robert was adamant.

'Your father is an old man and he knows the times. He understands what he is doing.'

'No he doesn't,' she retorted. 'He's so lost in his dreams and so sure that everyone is as good and kind as himself that he has no idea how cruel men are.'

'And what could I tell him?'

'That he's wrong to publish his dreams.'

'But he may be right!'

'He can't be right if all his friends think it will lead to his arrest.'

Robert did not answer immediately. He seemed to be fighting something out in his mind—something belonging only to himself.

'Margaret,' he said at last. 'I'm only twenty-one. How can I tell a man of your father's age that the thoughts of a lifetime are wrong? I know nothing of the ordering of society. I'm a medical student. My duty is to study the structure and diseases of the human body.'

He turned to her with a grave simplicity that she had never seen before.

'Look,' he said, lifting his anatomy manual. 'This is what I could teach your father. There's nothing else that I know which he doesn't.'

'Please, Robert,' she pleaded, almost in tears. 'You needn't speak for yourself, but please tell him how worried John and I are for his safety.'

He smiled suddenly—a half sad, half amused smile that took in not only Margaret's anxious face but also the shabby parlour with its chipped delft jar and took in, too, the face of the old man humming to himself in the cellar below.

'I'll do what I can,' he said.

As she listened to the rumble of the two men's voices below her, she felt her body relax. She had shifted her responsibility to someone else and, for the moment, she ceased from fret. She closed her eyes, felt a cool, fresh current of air from the open window brushing against her cheek, and wondered sleepily about Robert.

She had known him for two years—ever since he had come up from Herringsby to study at St. Xavier's. Yet she had never seen him so thoughtful and grave before; never seen him anything but sure of himself—a carefree monarch of all he surveyed. It was disturbing, this change in him. It made her ache inside; but she felt too tired to make up her mind what kind of an ache it was.

Too tired. Too tired.

She woke up to find him standing over her.

'It's no good, Margaret,' he said, smiling ruefully.

'What did he say?'

'He said that Jerusalem had to go on having its prophets even if its citizens persisted in stoning them.'

'What else did he say?'

Though it was scarcely a gay moment, Robert laughed.

'He said that if ever the pamphlet ran to a second edition he wanted to add two paragraphs suggesting that all doctors should be paid by the state and that all hospitals and operations and drugs should be free.'

Margaret lowered her eyes.

'Do you think he's a little mad?' she whispered.

'No, Meg. Only a prophet.'

Robert stood for a long time in silence by the open window, gazing out into the little garden with its tubs of dahlias and phlox.

'But I think,' he said slowly, 'that he hasn't thought at all what's to happen to the prophet's daughter—and his son, and his business, and his new apprentice.'

Robert was wrong.

Mr. Pargeter had planned very carefully what was to happen to Margaret and John and his business, should he be arrested for publishing his pamphlet. Elijah had arrived so unexpectedly on the scene that he had not yet had time to fit him into the plan. But he was a hopeful man and he saw no reason to fear for the future of his young apprentice.

Next morning he called Margaret down into the cellar. He had completed setting the pamphlet up in type and he had hammered the wedges into the two chases containing the pages of print. They were leaning up against the wall, ready to be laid on the press and inked.

'Margaret,' he said, putting his arm round her shoulders and drawing her towards him. 'You are anxious about my safety.

You would scarce be the good daughter to me that you are, were it not so.'

'Oh, Father,' she interrupted.

He pressed his finger gently over her lips.

'And I would scarce be a good father to you, had I not made provision for you in the event of my arrest.'

He led her to the back of the cellar, in the shadows behind the printing press.

'I want you to help me remove these loose bricks in the wall.'

She looked in astonishment first at her father and then at the irregularity in the brickwork.

'Why? What's behind them?'

'You'll see in a minute.'

Between them, they levered out the eight unmortared bricks. Then the bookseller put his hand into the dusty hole at the back and pulled out a little iron money chest about two feet long and fifteen inches high.

'Inside this,' he explained, 'I have kept your mother's jointure which she brought me when she married me. And when she died, I put her jewels away here, too.'

He carried the little chest from the wall and put it on top of the printing press. Then he fumbled in his pocket and pulled out his bunch of keys.

'Your mother was not a rich woman. We were neither of us ever rich. She brought me two hundred pounds as a dowry. And that is the sum that you will find here.'

He fitted the key in the lock and turned the spring. On top of the notes and the gold sovereigns lay a little soft leather bag. Mr. Pargeter picked it up and unwound its string.

'An amethyst necklace,' he said. 'And a ruby ring.'

The jewellery lay in the palm of his right hand, winking at them in the dim light. Margaret glanced up and caught a look of pain sweeping over her father's face, like a pucker of wind on a quiet lake. Then he smiled at her again, sadly but without hurt.

'They are not very valuable, my dear. But they are yours.

You were too young for me to give them to you when she died.'

Margaret's eyes filled with tears. She had been three days old when her mother died, and she suddenly realized the heart-break of that death and the loneliness of the grief that had prompted her father to hide her jewels for seventeen years in the cellar.

'Put them on,' he said.

He pushed the ring on her finger and fastened the clasp of the necklace at the back of her neck. Then he turned her round and held her at arm's length, his eyes travelling slowly over her rich brown hair and her strong, serious, young face, down over her straight, broad shoulders to her slender waist.

'There,' he said. 'Now you are a woman. A woman, like your mother.'

Then he returned to the heap of notes and gold coin.

'Before I start printing *The New Jerusalem*, we will go to Mr. Baltimore on Ludgate Hill and hand over this money for him to keep for you in his bank. It is for you to spend, if you need it.'

'But John?' asked Margaret. 'Should it not belong to John, too?'

'John has the shop, Meg. I want you to keep this. It is little enough that your mother and I can do for you. You must keep it for yourself.'

As they walked through the narrow passage at the top end of Holly Lane and then out into Paternoster Row, Margaret became more and more uncomfortable about the money, for she knew that with a hundred pounds John could buy himself into the Army. Should she tell her father how unhappy John was in the bookshop? She glanced secretly at his face. He was looking serene and happy, smiling at the pigeons circling round the dome of St. Paul's.

'Father,' she said. 'John could buy himself an ensigncy for a hundred pounds.'

'An ensigncy!' he exclaimed. 'What does the boy want with an ensigncy?'

'He's unhappy in the bookshop.'

'He's certainly remarkably inefficient,' sighed Mr. Pargeter. 'But an ensigncy! What an idea!'

They walked on in silence for a minute.

'Meg, I forbid my son to buy a commission. Let him earn one by merit.'

'But, Father, that's the way things are. You can't get a commission without paying for it.'

'Then he'd better stay a bookseller, my dear. I shall need someone to look after the shop if I go to prison.'

Margaret bit her lip. It seemed a cruel moment to quarrel with her father, yet she was sure that he was wrong about John. She took a deep breath, clenched her hands, and then burst out with her protest before she had time to feel afraid and stop.

'I don't think you're being fair, Father,' she said. 'You shouldn't force your principles on other people and, perhaps, ruin their lives.'

She gasped as she listened to herself. She had said more than she meant.

Mr. Pargeter stood still in the middle of the road.

'*I* ruin the life of *my* son! Is that what you mean?'

He was flushed with anger.

'First I articled him to Mr. Mudge,' expostulated the bookseller. 'And then when the law wouldn't do, I got him a clerkship with a merchant. What more could I do, Meg? What more could I do?'

'You've tried to make him like yourself,' she attempted to explain. 'And he isn't. You know he isn't. He's not bookish or clever or good at accounts. But he's brave and he's strong. He'd make a splendid officer.'

'Then he'll have to enlist as a private soldier and earn his promotion,' rapped out her father, stamping his foot down hard on the cobbles as he continued on his way to Ludgate Hill.

They walked on in silence, the bookseller swaying his head very slightly from side to side like a caged lion Margaret had once seen at St. Bartholomew's Fair. She had seldom known him so angry. And had she not been his daughter, she would never have dared to pursue the matter further.

'I can look after the shop,' she said. 'I know how you run your business.'

Mr. Pargeter shook his white mane.

'That's not the point, Meg,' he roared. 'And you know it.'

He made such a noise that three pigeons flew up from the gutter in fright.

'How can I publish my *New Jerusalem*,' he cried. 'When my own son soils his hands with the giving of Babylonish bribes?'

It was another hot, cloudless day, and as father and daughter walked on in unhappy silence towards Mr. Baltimore's bank, each hurt and made anxious by the other's pain, the heat and the hum and the sudden shouts and clatter of the great City gradually forced their way through to their attention. Country wagons were lumbering up Ludgate Hill with cheeses and vegetables and fruit; a dray rattled past with barrels of salted fish. And now that they were nearer the great river, the cries of gulls and the shrieks of winches unloading cargoes from the hoys and brigantines joined with the street cries of the women selling ribbons and laces and the old men shouting: 'Dust O! Bring out your dust.'

Margaret loved this bustle of life. Her father loved it, too. London was everything to them. They had always enjoyed the laughter and the calls and the curses of the street, the clop-chopping of horses' hooves and the grinding of iron-shod wheels and the hallooing of the watermen and seamen borne clear and distinct across the Thames into the heart of the City. They loved the sheer vitality of it all.

In such a buzz, two such hopeful people could not long be sad.

They stole a sly smile at each other.

Seeing this flag of truce, Margaret's smile grew wider and wider. It was good to be happy again. She had hardly smiled for a whole day and a half—not since they had first heard that terrible rending of the tenement beams.

She hated misery.

'He'll find his feet, Meg,' her father smiled. 'It's early days yet. He's only nineteen. A boy takes longer to come to himself than a girl.'

Of course he did, Margaret thought cynically. A boy could be a hundred things—a lawyer, a sailor, a merchant, a doctor. He was often confused and dazzled by the number of people he could become. A girl had no choice. She had to make up her mind from the start to settle down and be a woman.

'If John really dislikes the bookshop, perhaps I'll send him to your Uncle Allen at Burford. He can make a farmer out of him.'

The thought of John as a yeoman farmer was clearly pleasing to Mr. Pargeter. He wondered why he had never thought of it before.

'It's certainly a better career for a boy at this moment than the army.'

'Better than fighting for your country?'

'If the rumours in the City are right, Meg, there's not going to be much more fighting.'

'Why not?' she asked in astonishment.

'They say Lord Addington's ministry is negotiating with the French for peace.'

'For peace! But that's disgraceful! We're winning, Father. We can't give up the war *now*. Not now—when Nelson's destroyed the Danish fleet and we've almost driven the French out of Egypt.'

'Hundreds of thousands of Englishmen are on the verge of starvation, Meg. With peace, we could bring in food from the continent to feed them.'

'But it'll mean that the French will have won.'

'No, it won't. If peace comes, it will come as a result of treaty, not defeat. With corn to feed the people, we can live to fight another day.'

Margaret gave an angry shake of her shoulders.

'I wish Napoleon had never been born!' she exclaimed

savagely.

'So do we all,' smiled her father.

When they had finished their business at Mr. Baltimore's, they walked slowly homeward down the shady side of the hill, silent but content, each aware that though their difference of opinion about John had not been resolved, it was no longer dangerously explosive. Mr. Pargeter was more than fifty years older than his daughter, yet an extraordinarily quick and lively understanding existed between them. They read each other's thoughts in the twitch of a muscle, the turn of a shoulder, the fleeting gleam in an eye. Though unacknowledged and seldom exploited, it was a distressful understanding in a family of three, for it was as if two of them spoke a language unknown to the third. Through no wish of their own, it excluded John.

Walking alone together down the hill, however, they could keep silence or speak out with an equal sense of ease. And now, with the noisy normality of the world shouting and rattling about them, both felt some of the fears of the last two days slipping quietly away. John would find happiness somehow, somewhere. Elijah would forget his anguished past and grow back into a human child. Robert would regain his fearless grace. And perhaps even for the author of *The New Jerusalem* the future was not so black.

'I have a great belief, Meg, in the common sense of English justice,' said her father. 'They cannot imprison a man merely for suggesting a way for people to live in greater happiness.'

'What about Mr. Spence?'

'Poor Thomas. Poor Thomas. He was indeed unfortunate. In his case, both the Attorney-General and the jury forgot our English heritage—forgot the true reason that we are fighting against the French.'

'What's that?'

'Why, Meg, to preserve the ancient liberty of Englishmen to speak and write what we will.'

'May another jury not also forget?'

'I think not, Meg. I think not. One lapse of memory shows gross inattention to our historic past; a second would reveal a stark insensibility that I cannot believe of my countrymen.'

5 *Elijah*

Looking back months later on the quiet fortnight that followed, Margaret saw that it was only a lull in the storm that had already gathered about them— a lull in which clouds were massing below the horizon and winds mounting in the regions of the sky unknown to Holly Lane. Yet, at the time, the days seemed golden days. The arid heat of August mellowed into the glow of early September, and the morning mists and evening dews laid the dust in the City and for a few brief hours shrouded the hideous memorial of grief at the end of the Lane. They were selling blackberries in the streets and apples and small, sweet pears. And Suzannah and Eugenia came back from Shepherd's Bush chattering of picnics in the stubble fields and a harvest home in Squire Bamford's barn.

Suzannah was prepared to make a great fuss of Elijah on her first morning home and promised Margaret to measure him for a shirt, but when Margaret fetched him from the kitchen and she saw that he neither smiled at her nor thanked her for her promise, she dismissed him as an ugly, ungrateful little boy and wondered that Mr. Pargeter had been unwise enough to take such a wretched child into his house.

'He'll be stealing from you, Meg,' she said.

'He's not a thief and I'm not Meg,' snapped Margaret, stung to anger. 'And if you can't see that the child's still shocked and dumb with fright you're a greater fool than I thought you were.'

Suzannah was used to Margaret's bluntness when she lost her temper, but this was too much of a smack in the face even for Suzannah, and she walked straight out of the Pargeters' parlour, through the bookshop, her cheeks crimson and her head held high, and then out through the door and across the Lane without one backward glance at her companion.

Such an end to their long friendship would have grieved Margaret had she realized at the time that this was indeed its end. She would have run after Suzannah and begged her forgiveness. But they had quarrelled and made friends again so often in the past that it never occurred to her that they would not run into each other's arms in a few days and, laughing at themselves, make it up. So she walked from the parlour back into the kitchen, feeling the warmth in her cheeks and defiantly humming *All in the Downs the fleet was moor'd* half under her breath, and spent the rest of the morning eagerly pushing thoughts of Suzannah to the back of her mind and being gentler and more biddable with Mrs. Neech than she had been for years.

Mrs. Neech did not expect the impossible from Elijah. Margaret noticed with thankfulness that now that he was clean and clothed and had learned to sit on a chair at a table and use a spoon to eat his meals, the housekeeper left him in peace, content that at other times he should crouch on the floor and watch her as she moved about the kitchen, ironing the clothes or rolling out the pastry or stirring the pots on the stove. The child seemed lost in wonder and astonishment at the simplest household task. It was as though he had never seen clothes laundered or food prepared before or had ever dreamed that floors were made for scrubbing or that one polished brass and silver to make them shine.

It was Margaret's saloop day again and Mrs. Neech's morning for baking the week's pastry and cakes. With the scarcity and the poor quality of the diluted flour this was a task requiring ingenuity and care and, to help her, Margaret offered to go to the shop to buy the apples and plums. When these were carried home, she suggested snipping the seeds out of the raisins for the cake, but Mrs. Neech declined her offer, telling her that she had enough to do to mind her father's customers.

As she ground the orchid root, she watched Elijah staring at the apple peel slowly unwinding from the apple in Mrs. Neech's hand. It coiled along the table edge like a bright snake and finally broke free to fall on the floor at his feet. He covered it quickly with his hand and when Mrs. Neech had turned her back to attend to the stove, put the end of it hurriedly in his mouth.

'There's no call to take it sly-like,' said Mrs. Neech quietly, seemingly having eyes in the back of her head. 'No one's going to bite you, child.'

But with permission given him to eat the peel, Elijah lost interest in chewing it and pulled it out of his mouth and arranged it instead in a pattern in front of him on the floor. He was a strange child. He sat all that morning, Margaret remembered, languidly destroying one pattern and making another, long after the bright glow of the apple skin had dulled and its edges had begun to wither and go brown. Yet, though the apparent aimlessness of his game puzzled and irritated her, she felt that something so extraordinary was going on in the quiet kitchen that she did not dare to reprove him. It was there each time she brought back the empty saloop cups—an indefinable calm and naturalness, a feeling of rightness and peace such as she had never felt before in Mrs. Neech's presence.

It was as though the stern, middle-aged woman and the unwanted child were exploring each other, watchfully, wordlessly, and were learning a strange comfort in what they were finding.

It was like waiting for the spring to come. At the end of March, when the flower girls came to the City with their bunches of primroses, Margaret knew that the spring had already come to the country, and she walked down Giltspur Street to look at the plane trees in the quadrangle of St. Xavier's Hospital. They were obstinately dead, those plane-trees; they held the winter long after the country hedges had burst into tiny leaf, and she would go again and again to look at the silent, mournful branches, longing for April's joy to come to the City. And then one day, when she had almost given up hope, she found that the miracle had happened. Every twig in that sombre square was sprouting the golden yellow leaves of early spring.

So it was with Elijah during that quiet, brooding fortnight.

Margaret looked at him again and again, almost despairing of the child that lay imprisoned under so many years of fear and neglect. Would the thaw never come? Would he never break out and flower? Yet, imperceptibly the smudges were fading under his dark eyes; his hair was losing some of its unhealthy lankness; his body was putting on flesh. His mind began to stir.

A week after the destruction of his home and the death of his parents, he smiled.

Next day, Margaret came into the kitchen to find him standing on his head in the middle of the kitchen floor.

'Elijah,' she laughed in delight. 'What *are* you doing?'

But Mrs. Neech silenced her with a look.

'It's something he likes doing, Miss Margaret,' she said without a smile. 'You must let him be.'

Meanwhile, Mr. Pargeter printed off two hundred copies of *The New Jerusalem,* and Margaret, who could at least thread a needle and pierce it through a sheet of paper, sewed the sheets laboriously together and then ironed out the creases she had made with Mrs. Neech's flat iron.

John refused to have anything to do with the preparation of the pamphlet. During business hours he applied himself to listing the books on the shelves for the catalogue which his father was going to print at the end of the month; and in the evenings he went off to a coffee house opposite the Bank, frequented by young City clerks as restless and critical of their families as himself. He called the coffee house his 'club'; and at breakfast and dinner he threw its pronouncements defiantly into the family conversation.

'The Club says your story of a treaty is false,' he told his father. 'It must be. We're preparing to invade France. We've got hundreds of invasion barges ready waiting in Dover harbour. A friend of mine's seen them.'

The Club, it appeared, was die-hard Tory, and John, with the confidence of its opinions behind him, took to ridiculing his father's radical beliefs in front of him.

'You're a fool to pity the poor, Father,' he once announced. 'Try to help them and they'll bite your hand.'

Mr. Pargeter grieved at his son's boorishness, for he did not believe that a child of his could really lack pity for human misery. John was not himself. He was saying these things not because he believed them but because he wished to hurt his father.

Margaret, seeing her father's distress, grew daily more angry with her brother. Only Robert seemed capable of treating him to the mockery which he deserved.

'John,' he laughed, after John had delivered himself of an especially extravagant opinion. 'Those aren't even Tory beliefs. They're nonsense.'

Margaret looked at him in wonder. 'But Robert,' she said. 'I thought you knew nothing about politics?'

'Why, nor I do, Meg. But neither does John,' he laughed.

When the pamphlet was ready for publication, Mr. Pargeter laid a dozen copies of it out in the open trays in front of the shop. Then he began his afternoon walks round the City, putting *The New Jerusalem* into the hands of the passers-by.

On his safe return two hours later, Margaret could not restrain her relief and joy. She flung her arms round her father's neck.

'What happened? Was anyone angry with you? Was anyone rude?'

'My dear, my dear,' he replied, laughing. 'You should ask rather whether anyone was pleased with my pamphlet.'

'Were they?'

'We must wait and see. Wait and see,' he smiled almost gaily. 'Rome was not built in a day, Meg. Nor yet will the new Jerusalem.'

His cheerful hopefulness helped to calm her fears.

Every evening Robert hurried home from the hospital and swinging into the bookshop, looked Margaret full in the face.

'Is your father well,' he would ask. 'Is he at home?'

'He is well, Robert,' she would reply happily. 'He is in the parlour reading *The Times*' or 'He is in the yard picking the earwigs out of the dahlias.'

Mr. Pargeter was immensely proud of his dahlias, for they were some of the first plants of their kind to be grown in England.

And then Robert and Margaret would smile at each other and go to the old man.

Elijah continued to uncurl and put forth green leaves.

One morning he sat at the top of the stairs outside the attic room into which they had moved him to sleep, and yelled the street cries which he had heard all his life in the City about him.

'*Mackerel O! Four for a Shilling. Mackerel O!*' he cried in a shrill woman's voice. Then:

'*Sweep! Sweep! Sweep!*'
in a thin child's wail.

Margaret, hearing the shouts of the street coming from the very centre of the house, ran up the stairs to find him opening his mouth wide for yet another yell.

'*Dust O! Dust O! Any Dust today?*'
he bellowed somewhere deep in his throat.

'Elijah, what a terrible noise!' she laughed.

She had made a mistake, for the shy smile of pleasure died out of his face. It was clearly one of the things he was proud of doing.

'Do another,' she said quickly. 'I like it.'

'Do you?' he asked, the smile creeping slowly back.

She sat on the stair beside him, and he went through his entire repertoire, turning to her after each number for her smile of approval. His mimicry was uncannily true. Not only did he catch the particular lilt and timbre of each cry but he also settled his features in the expression of the hawker who cried them. Jaunty water-cress girls, sickly milkmaids, bustling country women selling eels, and the horrible, leering old man who hawked old clothes and rabbit skins along Newgate Street—

52

all passed before her at the top of the attic stairs. The doleful Elijah was a born actor.

Suddenly, the little colour that he had in his face drained away and he looked agonizingly strained and sad as he whispered hoarsely over and over again:

'*Thank you. Thank you. Thank you.*'

Margaret caught her breath, going as white as the child.

'Stop it, Elijah,' she cried.

It was the mad woman who haunted St. Paul's Churchyard at dusk and who stopped passers-by with this strange, heart-breaking sigh.

They sat for a moment, Margaret and the boy from the slum, clasping each other by the hand, swept together by a great wave of fear and incomprehension, baffled and frightened by the mystery of madness. The poor, harmless, crazed creature had haunted Margaret's dreams as a child; she must have haunted Elijah's, too, for his pale lips were trembling on the edge of tears. And yet there was nothing frightening in the woman herself; she was not violent or deformed or obscene in her language. It was just the incongruity of her thanking the world for her rags, and her matted hair and her poor, wild, puzzled eyes which shook them both so profoundly. Elijah had no idea why he was so moved, but for Margaret, the mad woman's whispered 'thank you' twitched aside a curtain and revealed a nightmare horror to life that she could not bear to contemplate. She wanted to know only the normal, laughing, happy things in the world.

'Never do it again,' she whispered. 'Please, Elijah, don't.'

The sun shone on and on in that brief, lovely autumn. The bees from the dahlias found their way into the kitchen and buzzed about the copper while Mrs. Neech boiled the plum jam, and a Red Admiral fluttered down from nowhere and basked on a pear that Margaret had put on the window-sill to ripen in the sun. She had never seen a butterfly so brilliantly gay and beautiful.

Every evening, Robert hurried home and asked the same question, looking into Margaret's eyes.

'Is your father well, Margaret? Is he at home?'

And now, almost laughingly, as though a danger that had been feared were now past, she replied:

'He is well, Robert. He is storing apples in the loft' or 'He is reading fairy-stories to Elijah in the yard.'

Yet, even in these halcyon days, two domestic events caused a rippling in the calm: John had one of his not infrequent explosions of family pride while selling a dictionary to a stranger; and Elijah, with a confidence made strong by the good food inside him, decided to show them all his gratitude.

John had always been over-conscious that his grandfather had received his education at Eton and King's College, Cambridge, and had for many years been the respected incumbent of a large parish in Devon and the close friend of Sir Lionel Peake. His father, in consequence, had been born a gentleman and so, by the nature of things, had John.

Margaret, who was arranging the books on the open trays, first saw the stranger picking his way fastidiously past the rubble at the end of the Lane.

He was dressed in the height of fashion. As he approached nearer, he gave her a heartlessly appraising look that was insulting enough to make her blush. He passed by her, eyeing the ribbons in her bodice and, once inside the dark shop, barked out his demands.

'A dictionary, my man,' he shouted into the shadows. 'The best French dictionary that you have.'

She heard John slam down a volume on the table.

'A guinea,' he said.

'I'll give you fifteen and six,' said the stranger.

'We're not hucksters,' shouted John. 'If you wish to haggle and bargain, go to the Jew with the barrow in Amen Court.'

The stranger shouted and John shouted; and then she heard

John stamp back through the shop and slam the parlour door behind him.

Margaret ran up the two steps into the bookshop and faced the customer.

'It is improper for a respectable bookseller to sell an author's books for less than the market price,' she explained coldly. 'Were you a frequent buyer and reader of books you would have known this.'

She took the dictionary down from the shelf again and put it in front of him. And, without a word, the stranger laid down his guinea, picked up the volume, and walked out of the shop.

As she watched him go, she found her father standing beside her.

'You are right, my dear,' he said, smiling sadly. 'The bookshop is no place for my poor John. He must go to your Uncle Allen. His sheep and cows and horses are too well bred to insult a gentleman.'

Elijah was now bold enough to adventure into the front of the house. He wandered about the bookshop, peering into the dark corners, and opened the long, thin drawers where Mr. Pargeter kept his engravings. He sat for hours staring at views of the English countryside and ruined arches and crusader tombs and moated castles and cathedral spires, astonished to learn what mighty things there were in the world beyond the confines of Holly Lane. He ran, too, between the customers' legs, smelling the blacking on their high boots and timidly pinching their buckskin breeches because he liked their feel.

He was occupied thus on the last morning that Margaret served saloop in her father's shop.

There were few customers now. Lord Binsey and Mr. Simkin and Mr. Jeeves had not been in the shop since the day that they had read the draft of *The New Jerusalem*. Indeed, though the Pargeters were too preoccupied to notice it, there had been a slow dropping off of all their friends. The Fishers had not once come across the Lane to pass the time of day, and Margaret wondered that Suzannah and Eugenia had given up sitting in their parlour window and calling down to her with news of dresses and visits to the tea gardens with Suzannah's young men.

That last morning, however, Margaret was busy with the saloop cups, for Mr. Stone had come to discuss the next auction with her father, and Mr. Love the poet was looking through the sheets of ballads. There was a young painter, too, sitting in the window, studying Albinus's great work on anatomy. He coud not afford to buy the book, so he was looking through the plates, pencil in hand and sketch-book beside him, every now and then copying the course of a muscle.

Late in the morning, while Margaret was washing up the cups in the kitchen, she saw Elijah coming through from the bookshop, looking flushed and happy. He ran to the open window, where her father had a pot of sweet-scented geraniums, and buried something in the earth by their stem. Then he ran to the housekeeper's rocking-chair and hid something else away behind her cushion. Last, he approached Margaret, pleasure and excitement sparkling in his once dull eyes, and presented her with a valentine.

It was a splendid valentine, drawn with the greatest delicacy of taste and art. A cupid was winging earthwards accompanied by a flight of swallows set against a primrose sky. His arrow was pointing towards a mossy bank where the flowers were painted with such distinctness that one could pick out violets and wood anemones and wild strawberries. Yet, exquisite though it was, Margaret saw at once that the artist had not completed his task. A space had been left on the flowered bank for the drawing of a reclining figure.

'Elijah, where did you get such a lovely thing?' she gasped.

The boy was delighted with her surprise, and his smile grew wider and wider, but he said nothing.

'Elijah!' she exclaimed, the truth suddenly dawning upon her. 'You haven't stolen it?'

'Stolen what?' asked Mrs. Neech sharply, coming in from

56

the larder.

Her eye fell on the valentine.

'And there's something in your chair,' said Margaret unhappily. 'And something else under the geranium plant.'

They found a fine cambric handkerchief under the cushion and a silver penknife in Mr. Pargeter's flowerpot; and they laid the things out on the kitchen table and stared at them miserably. It was clear what Elijah had done. He had stolen presents for them all from the customers' pockets.

'What shall we do?' cried Margaret, aghast at the thought of his thefts being discovered.

'He must put them back where he took them from,' replied Mrs. Neech firmly.

But Elijah, terribly disappointed and crestfallen at the sudden disapproval in the air, shook his head so that the tears shot out of his eyes.

'They're for you,' he sobbed, looking at them both. 'They're for you and Mr. Pargeter.'

'We don't take things from other people in this house,' said Mrs. Neech quietly. 'We're rich and we don't need to. And, besides, we think it's very wrong. You must take the things back.'

'But how can he?' asked Margaret, almost in tears herself. 'They'll catch him.'

'Not if he's clever, they won't.'

So one by one the presents went back into the three pockets. Margaret stood in the bookshop watching, her heart thumping with fear as Elijah glided up to the poet and slipped his hand along the skirt of his coat and then stood by the studious painter, pretending to look at his drawing.

Now, only one present remained to be returned. Old Mr. Stone was sitting at a table beside her father in a corner of the room that was difficult to approach. But Elijah was not to be defeated. He crawled under the table and pushed the bright valentine into the bookseller's huge coat pocket.

Mr. Stone with a valentine! Elijah had got it all wrong. He

had forgotten what he had stolen from whom. Poor, bachelorish, old Mr. Stone with a half-finished valentine!

The thought was so absurd that Margaret was overcome with joy. She ran up to her bedroom, gulping and choking, trying to stifle her laughter. And she was laughing, three minutes later, when she heard the shop bell ring and Mr. Stone's footsteps in the Lane below her window as he walked off towards his gloomy lodgings in the Strand with the valentine in his pocket.

It was as well that something in the course of that unhappy day made her laugh, for when Robert hurried home that evening and asked his question, Margaret leant her head on his shoulder and burst into tears.

'They arrested Father this afternoon,' she cried. 'They've taken him to the Poultry Compter.'

6 *Poultry Compter*

The Poultry Compter was indeed a matter for tears. Of all the prisons to which the City magistrates might have committed Mr. Pargeter while he awaited his trial, the Poultry Compter was quite the most horrible. It was an old brick building in Wood Street in a ruinous state of repair and notorious for its cramped and ill-ventilated cells. Gaol fever was almost as deadly here as it was in Newgate. It should have been pulled down years ago and one of Mr. Howard's new, airy, and well-regulated prisons built in its stead. It was terrible for Margaret to think of her father arrested like a criminal and confined in such a pestilential hole.

'He doesn't deserve it,' she sobbed on Robert's shoulder. 'He's a good man.'

Robert fumbled in his pocket for his lawn handkerchief and clumsily tried to mop up her tears. He did not know how to comfort her.

'Where's John?' he asked at last. 'Did he go with your father to the prison?'

She shook her head.

John was in the snuggery pacing up and down, up and down.

'He shouldn't have done it,' he shouted bitterly to Robert. 'He shouldn't have written that blasted pamphlet. He had no right to question the way things are.'

'No right?' exclaimed Robert. 'Then how can anyone reform the country's ills?'

'Ills?'

'There's so much that's wrong.'

'I don't see what's wrong. The country seems all right to me.'

Robert looked at John wearily. Margaret knew that he thought him a fool.

'You should have been at the hospital this morning,' he said quietly. 'A man and a child were carried in off the streets.

They both died this afternoon.'

John shrugged his shoulders.

'Fever, I suppose? Or gin?'

'Neither. Lack of food.'

'How dreadful!' exclaimed Margaret.

'No government can be expected to legislate against poverty,' her brother retorted grimly.

'Why not?'

John looked up startled, and then flushed.

'You're as bad as my father,' he shouted angrily.

'As bad? You mean as good. Only even there you'd be wrong. I haven't his courage.'

'Good. Bad. Good. Bad,' came Mrs. Neech's tart voice.

She was standing in the open doorway with a small rush skep in her hand and the old sharp look of disapproving resignation back in her face.

'I don't know whether your father's a saint or a fool, Master John. But I *do* know that he'll be a cold, unhappy, hungry old man tonight in that filthy prison they've taken him to, unless you go to him with a blanket and this basket of food.'

'I'll go,' said Margaret, grasping the handle of the basket.

She could not bear the shouting and anger about her. She wanted to go away quietly somewhere and put her mind in order. She wanted to be able to show her father quickly—at once—that she was ready and calm and steadfast. And yet, with John cursing their father for his folly and Robert angrily protesting his courage, she felt none of these things. She was distraught with grief and shame. John was his son. His only son. Whatever he had thought of his father, he should have been loyal to him at such a time.

Elijah had crept beside her and was tugging at her arm.

'Can I go with you?' he whispered.

Mrs. Neech guessed his request.

'You bide with me, boy,' she said. 'There'll be time enough for you to visit your master another day. And many a day, too. It's months they keep them before a state trial.'

60

The three of them walked in silence to the prison along streets that were soon to become all too familiar to them. John dreaded the journey's end. The degradation and humiliation that this whole family was suffering filled him with angry shame, and he avoided the eyes of the passers-by, as though staring at the cobbles straight in front of him in some way made him invisible and, therefore, not concerned with the ignominy that lay ahead. It was not he that was going to the Poultry Compter but a stranger who had never heard of the name of Pargeter. In the heavy silence of that walk, John was mentally contracting himself out of his family.

Margaret and Robert's thoughts, on the other hand, were drawing them closer and closer to Mr. Pargeter. Mrs. Neech's dour word had shocked them both into realizing the stark misery of prison life. Someone they loved and revered was going to suffer hunger and cold and loneliness; and, though they could bring him a little food and a blanket and visit him when they were allowed, nothing could make amends to him for the long and lonely night vigils, when he was locked up in a sordid and crowded cell with thieves and pimps and murderers. Nothing could save him from the anguish of being shut up away from his family and his friends and his home.

As they waited at the prison gate, a pot-boy came up and stood beside them, also waiting for admission. Over his arm hung a large open basket filled with broken victuals. Margaret saw a wedge of pork pie with a large mouthful bitten out of the middle of it and two mutton chops that had been over-singed on the grill and broken bits of bread rolls and half-eaten apples and the remains of a fly-blown hock of gammon.

'What's all that?' she asked curiously.

'Broken meats for the prisoners,' came the cheerful reply. 'Master always remembers them. Sends a basket round twice a week with the bits that's left on the customers' plates.'

'Customers?' asked Robert with a frown of incomprehension.

'Yes. sir. Them that eat at *The Shaven Crown* in Pump Lane.

My master's the landlord.'

John turned away, sickened with disgust and shame.

'It looks horrible,' whispered Margaret faintly.

'Them in there are pleased enough with it,' grinned the pot-boy, jerking his head towards the prison gate.

Margaret glanced down between the folds of the white linen napkin in the little rush skep she was carrying and saw the five neat, breadcrumbed lamb cutlets and the cheesecakes and the red-cheeked Norfolk apples that they had brought with them. And, not for the first time in the last two weeks, she felt a wave of tenderness for Mrs. Neech sweep over her.

At last, the prison porter opened the first gate of the Compter, and the four of them passed along a narrow flagged lane flanked by the debtors' rooms. There were more than a dozen of these, and each seemed more crowded and squalid than the last. The sudden, bottled-up noise of shouting and laughing came to them from the grated doors. Then they stood before yet another gate and, John having muttered the name of his father, they were taken through to the central courtyard of the prison, which was well-paved with large flagstones and had a cock of water which spouted up into the air and then flowed away along a narrow channel that ran across the yard. Were it not for the ugly clamour from the lane behind them and from the women's ward and the Jews' ward on either side of them, this might have been a pleasant spot, for the sky shone blue overhead and the spout of water caught the light of the sun.

'It's Mr. Stephen Pargeter you wish to see?' asked the turnkey again.

'Yes,' replied Margaret impatiently. 'He was brought here this afternoon.'

'Aye, I know about that,' grinned the turnkey. 'And I know about him. He's up on the leads.'

'On the leads!' exclaimed Robert.

'Do you mean on the roof?' asked Margaret.

The turnkey laughed as he nodded his head.

'What are you doing to him up there?' rapped out John,

swinging round sharply on the man.

'Doing to him?' asked the startled turnkey. 'Why, nothing. He's playing draughts with Mr. Nesbit.'

'But why on the roof?' asked Margaret, almost smiling with surprise and relief.

'Why, miss, the air's sweet up there and you catch the last of the evening sun. Mr. Pargeter's a real treat for Mr. Nesbit, Miss. It's not often we have a gentleman here. Not a gentleman who's quiet and friendly-like and good for a game of draughts.'

He led the way across another smaller courtyard, where the horrible, fetid, prison smell met them like a wall of fog. Here a huge nail-studded door led to the felons' rooms. And then up some brick steps they went, past the upper sleeping rooms where the air was heavy with sweat, and then up again by a winding stair to the roof.

Mr. Pargeter was sitting on a flat piece of roof with his back to a chimney stack, the westering sun suffusing his face and white hair and the brickwork behind him with the warm, golden glow of evening.

'Margaret!' he exclaimed joyfully. 'John! Robert!'

Margaret ran to him and, stooping, clasped him in her arms.

Then she turned to the man who had risen from the opposite side of the draughts board.

'I'm sorry, sir,' she said. 'We disturb your game.'

He was a stern, forbidding sort of official, dressed in a snuff-coloured coat that suited ill with his iron grey hair and coarse black eyebrows.

'This is my daughter, Mr. Nesbit,' said her father.

'At your service,' bowed Mr. Nesbit with stiff gallantry.

'Margaret, this is Mr. Nesbit, the Master of the Compter, who has paid me the signal honour of playing draughts with me this evening. Mr. Nesbit, this is my son John and our young friend Mr. Kerridge, of St. Xavier's Hospital.'

Mr. Nesbit again bowed his stiff bow. It seemed to creak like a key grating in a lock that had not been used for years.

The Master turned to John and Robert, while Margaret whispered in her father's ear.

'Father, we've brought you a blanket and some food. Mrs. Neech was quite sure that you'd be cold and hungry here.'

'That's very kind of her,' smiled the old bookseller, his face still lit by the sun; then his eyes puckered mischievously like a boy's. 'What's she put in the skep, Meg?'

Between them they poked the folds of the napkin away and looked down on the beautifully cooked cutlets and cheese-cakes and at the glowing Norfolk apples.

'Bless her,' whispered Mr. Pargeter, still smiling. 'She's a good woman, Meg.'

'Father, what else can I bring you?'

But Mr. Pargeter was gazing thoughtfully along the tops of the gables and over the wide, sunlit landscape of chimney pots and pigeons. He had not yet done with Mrs. Neech.

'We should have loved her more, Meg. Much more.'

Meanwhile Mr. Nesbit was in earnest conversation with Robert. He had mistaken him in the course of Mr. Pargeter's introduction for his son John.

'The magistrates should have committed him to Newgate, not here,' he was explaining. 'In Newgate they have special rooms set aside for state prisoners. Here, we'll have to lock him in with the felons.'

'With the felons!' exclaimed John.

'There's no help for it. There's nowhere else.'

'A little money would soon mend that, I suppose,' said John scornfully, ill concealing his loathing of the prison and his contempt for its Master. He was galled, moreover, that Mr. Nesbit should have mistaken Robert for his father's son.

'Money'll buy him a better berth,' he continued to bluster. 'How much?'

'John!' exclaimed Robert sharply. John had clearly failed to notice the kindness and concern in Mr. Nesbit's attitude to his new guest. 'I'm sure Mr. Nesbit is doing all he can to make things easier for your father.'

'So you're the son!' exclaimed the Master, turning his keen eye on the young man.

'How much?' repeated John insolently.

'Mr. Pargeter has already paid his prison dues,' replied Mr. Nesbit with frigid self-control. 'And as I told you but now, we have no separate rooms for such as your father.'

'Could he not be lodged with the debtors, sir?' asked Robert.

The Master shook his head.

'That would be against the regulations, Mr. Kerridge, and I doubt if Mr. Pargeter would fare much better. Their rooms are very overcrowded.'

'But my father to be bedfellow with highwaymen and drunken rogues!' cried John bitterly.

'My guests are rough and often diseased, Mr. Pargeter, but they are at least not drunk. We have no tap in the Compter. You must leave his welfare to us. For his sake, not yours, young man, I shall do my best to see that he comes to no harm here.'

And Mr. Nesbit, with a curt nod at them all, moved over to the far edge of the leads and turned his gaze towards the dome of St. Paul's.

'Yes,' Mr. Pargeter was saying to his daughter. 'Yes, bring me Milton's *Areopagitica* and, of course, pens and ink and a knife to mend the pens and several sheets of folio, Meg. I'll write them such a defence of my action that every juryman will acquit me on the instant.'

'Are you not feeing a counsel, sir?' asked Robert in surprise.

'Why, no, Robert. Who can defend a man better than himself? There will be no witnesses to cross-examine. No finer points of law. It is a very simple affair. It is *The New Jerusalem* that is on trial, not myself, and who can best defend a pamphlet but its author?'

'Are you calling no gentlemen—no friends to speak for you?'

'An honest man should not need the declaration of his friends to prove his honesty,' said the old bookseller simply.

For a week they visited him twice a day, bringing food and books and more paper. Sometimes John came by himself; sometimes Mrs. Neech chaperoned Margaret; and on one occasion Margaret brought Elijah. The boy was so delighted by the roof-top world in which Mr. Pargeter spent his daylight hours that he could scarcely pay attention to his master, but went peering over the parapets and looking down the chimney-pots in a fever of wonder and curiosity.

'He's mending, Meg,' said her father, smiling gently. 'Elijah is almost a child again.'

He looked tired and ill as he lay against the chimney stack.

'But you look pale, Father. Is it the nights?' she asked.

'Say no more, Meg. It's daylight now, and the sun is shining.'

Margaret sat down beside her father and picked up his hand and played with his fingers as she had done when she was a small child. And then she lay quite silent for a minute, looking up into the huge vault of blue, dazed anew by the amount of pain one could suffer in so beautiful a world.

'Meg,' said the bookseller quietly, 'John will have to leave us.'

'Leave us?' she exclaimed.

'He cannot endure my shame. It is too much for him, Meg. It is eating into his heart. We must help him.'

'But he must help *you,* Father.'

'I'm past a son's help, my dear. This is my trouble and only I should bear it.'

'No. No,' she protested vehemently.

'We must help him by sending him away.'

'Away? Where will he go?'

'To your Uncle Allen. I have written your Uncle a letter. And Meg, my dear, I have taken your words to heart. He goes with a draft for a hundred pounds. I have bent him to my will long enough.'

'No. It's not true.'

'John must be free to make what he can of life. If he wishes to buy himself an ensigncy, then he may do so.'

John left three days later, an unhappy, surly look in his eyes and a small new box for his clothes perched on his shoulder. And he walked down Holly Lane towards the coach station in Lombard Street without once looking back.

Nothing that Robert could say that evening would comfort Margaret or make her forgive her brother.

'He has run away,' she sobbed. 'Just when Father needed him most.'

7 *The Worst That Could Happen*

Mr. Pargeter's trial took place a week later.

Margaret sat on the public bench between Mrs. Neech and Elijah, frozen in her heart by the stark officialdom of the courtroom and by the cold intelligence in the eyes of the Crown lawyers who were lounging in the seats about the empty dock. What chance had her father, she thought, against minds such as these? They would not understand, let alone value, his large humanity; all their talents had been trained to assess matters of smaller concern—the niceties of the law; legal quibbles and distinctions; their whole purpose was to trip him up. She prayed hard that the judge and the jury would prove to be men with kinder and wiser faces—men capable of taking her father for the honest dreamer that he was.

It was, indeed, as Mr. Pargeter had predicted, a very simple affair.

When the judge and the jury and the bookseller had taken their places and the jury had been sworn, the Attorney-General rose with a great deal of rustling of paper to open the case for the Crown. The defendant was charged, he said, with having written and published a seditious libel entitled *The New Jerusalem,* and he called Mr. Nathaniel Twist, a hatter's assistant of Luke Street, Bethnal Green, as witness to the fact that the defendant had put a copy of the said pamphlet into the witness's hand at ten minutes before noon on the morning of August 31st as the witness was crossing London Bridge on his master's business.

'Do you deny giving Mr. Twist a copy of your *New Jerusalem*?' the Attorney-General asked Mr. Pargeter.

'Indeed, no, my Lord,' he smiled. 'I cannot remember Mr. Twist's face but I would not dream of questioning his truthfulness.'

'You cannot remember Mr. Twist?' interrupted the judge.

'No, my Lord. But then I gave what I had written into the

hands of so many people that I should be surprised if I remembered them all.'

The Attorney-General then addressed himself to proving that the pamphlet was both libellous and seditious. Taking a copy of *The New Jerusalem* in his hand, he slowly turned its pages, reading a sentence here and a paragraph there, and, by the skilful omission of the argument that lay between, represented her father's ideas as a scurrilous attack on the owners of property. By its inflammatory nature, argued the prosecution, this pamphlet was designed to stir up resentment among the poorer people against the Government.

Margaret flushed with indignation. She had read the pamphlet in its entirety and she knew that the Attorney-General's selections offered a cruel travesty of its purpose. Her father had not spared the feelings of neglectful landlords but he had certainly not encouraged their tenants to rise in revolt against the Government. He had suggested an ideal state of society. Nothing less nor more.

The reading of the passages had caused a commotion in the court. At her father's criticism of 'the wicked neglect of private landlords who squander their wealth elsewhere, careless of their tenants' plight' the members of the jury had muttered angrily among themselves; and at his suggestion that no child in England should be put to work until he were fourteen years of age there had been such a burst of laughter that the judge had threatened to clear the court.

Her father rose to make his defence amid the subsiding titters and whispers of amusement. These Margaret found harder to bear than the scowling looks. Nowhere, she despaired, among the man called to sit in judgement on her father was there a man wisely humble enough to give him an unprejudiced hearing. He had already lost his case. He had forfeited the sympathy of the jury, for the twelve jurymen were themselves all men of property. And the judge, once he had quelled the laughter, had relapsed into a comfortable daydream. The room was hot. She wondered whether he was about to fall asleep. The Crown lawyers smiled at each other languidly, clearly a little bored that they had won their case with such ease.

Her father must have sensed the atmosphere in the court as keenly as herself, for he gave her a quick, sharp look of understanding—a look that seemed to say: 'It is no worse than I thought. Do not fear.'

And then, putting aside his prepared defence, he turned to the judge and jury and addressed them in a quiet, untroubled voice:

'My Lord and Gentlemen of the Jury,' he said, 'I stand charged by the Attorney-General with having written a seditious libel. Your Lordship understands well the meaning of the charge, but I know not whether you, Gentlemen of the Jury, are similarly acquainted with its terms. A libel, gentlemen, is a written defamation injuring a man's reputation. Sedition is conduct which incites others to rebellion against the State. Before you find me guilty of what I am accused, you must convince yourselves, first, that what I have written against the landlords is untrue and, next, that the purpose of my pamphlet was a mischievous one: namely, to incite the poorer part of the English commonalty to rise in revolt against their Government.

'The Attorney-General has read you certain passages from my *New Jerusalem* which, by the omission of the matter from which they are culled, have given you a false and unjust impression of the whole. It is for this reason that I beg leave to read you the pamphlet in its entirety. It demands from you an attentive hearing of some five minutes' duration—a small request, sirs, when a man's honour and liberty are at stake.'

Half-way through her father's reading of *The New Jerusalem* there was a slight movement and shuffling along the public bench, and Margaret, looking round puzzled, found Robert beside her, lifting Elijah on to his lap. He was panting hard, for he had run headlong all the way down Giltspur Street at the close of his morning's lecture in order to be with her in time for the verdict. He turned to her eagerly now, asking a question with his eyes that he was too breathless to form with his lips.

For answer, Margaret swept a look round the courtroom.

'They're not listening,' she whispered. 'They've shut up their minds.'

Mr. Pargeter was reading gently and familiarly—as he had read to Margaret when she was a child—but the judge was not to be beguiled from his private dream, and the jury moved restlessly, resentful at having to attend. As for the Crown lawyers, they were leaning back in their seats with their eyes closed, comfortably resigned to waiting for the bookseller to have done.

Mr. Pargeter came to the end of *The New Jerusalem* and, looking up into the listless faces of the men sitting in judgement on him, was suddenly fired with rage.

'My Lord and Gentlemen of the Jury,' he boomed, his voice ringing with startling strength through the drowsy court. 'Consider what nation it is whereof ye are, and whereof ye are judges: "a nation not slow and dull, but of a quick, ingenious and piercing spirit, acute to invent, subtle and sinewy to discourse, not beneath the reach of any point, the highest that human capacity can soar to". So spake our poet Milton in defence of the freedom of our Press. So, gentlemen, speak I. If you condemn me for speaking the truth—for truth it *is* that I have written of the landlords, and you know it—then you condemn the liberty and the brave spirit of this great nation of ours. You curb its freedom.'

His fine, angry plea had brought everyone in the court to attention. All eyes were fixed on the old man with the eager face and the blazing eyes.

'Are we never to expect a happier state of things than the present? Is there never to be justice and equality and brotherhood between the rich and the poor? Are we not all God's Englishmen? And should not all such be fed and taught and housed in the dignity of such a chosen race?

'How comes it then, that I, who have suggested a remedy for our present ills, should be charged with sedition—for raising up strife among a people that I love? My action cannot bear such an interpretation. Lord Loughborough has said that: "Every man may publish at his discretion his opinion concerning the Forms and Systems of Government. If they be wise and enlightening, the World will gain by them. If they be weak and absurd, they will be laughed at and forgotten; and if they be made in good faith, they cannot be criminal, however erroneous."

'My Lord and Gentlemen of the Jury, you sit in judgement today not only on me, a poor bookseller, but also on the ancient liberties of your country and on the bold, inventive spirits that come after us who, in their patriotism, may seek—as I have sought—to find a way to remedy our social ills.

'For their sakes as well as mine, I pray that you consider well your verdict, pondering in sober truth how great a burden rests upon your shoulders this day.'

The twelve members of the jury were not men to waste much time in weighing their responsibilities to an abstract and timeless truth. They were men trained to grapple with the practical problems of the present hour. And these problems called them to make haste. Their counting houses, their banks, and their colleagues on 'Change awaited their speedy return.

After five minutes' absence, they came back into court with their verdict.

Guilty!

Her father was guilty!

Margaret looked across the crowded room at her father standing with bowed head—a frail, hurt, astonished old man —and her heart ached with an intolerable ache. He had really believed that he would win his case!

Robert had grasped her arm at the wrist. But as her eyes filled with tears and the image of her father standing alone in the sitting court doubled and blurred and fell, she could not bear to look round for his comfort. What comfort could Robert give? What comfort was there for anyone to give?

The judge was remanding her father in custody for another week. Sentence would be passed on him, he said, in the same court at the same hour on Friday next.

As the court rose, Margaret tried to struggle towards her father, but Robert held her firmly by the wrist.

'Not now, Margaret,' he said. 'Look, they're taking him away.'

'You go to him later, Miss Margaret,' said Mrs. Neech. 'You go to him tonight when you've put yourself to rights.'

To rights?

She brushed the tears angrily off her cheeks with her free hand and turned almost fiercely on Robert.

'We must go home, then,' she said.

What would they do to her father? Where would they send him? How long would they imprison him?

The questions hammered and banged in her brain till, as they passed the corner of Warwick Lane, they suddenly burst out into words.

'Robert, what will they do to Father?' she asked wretchedly.

'I don't know, Margaret,' he said simply.

His bleak truthfulness spoke to the honesty that lay deep in her nature and, for the moment, calmed her. Someone who understood her less well might have tried to comfort her with vain hopes. But not Robert. Robert would never cheat her.

'They must see that he's nothing but a poor, foolish old man,' said Mrs. Neech.

Her words were rough, but she spoke them with such compassion that Margaret turned to her with a new wave of affection and, seeing the gentleness in the stern housekeeper's eyes, her resolution fled. She suddenly burst into quiet, uncontrollable weeping.

'He's such a good man,' she sobbed. 'He'd never hurt anyone if he could help it.'

It was dreadful to be weeping in the open street. Dreadful. Elijah's hot, sticky fingers were clasping her hand in a tight, sticky grasp. For his sake, if not for her Father's and Robert's and Mrs. Neech's, she must somehow master her grief.

Mr. Stone was waiting for them outside the locked and shuttered shop.

'It's a bad business. A bad business, indeed,' he said.

They took him through to the parlour while Mrs. Neech went to prepare tea.

'Margaret,' began the old book-dealer, 'your brother was making a catalogue of the books in the shop. Did he ever finish it?'

'Yes, I think so.'

'Can you find it?'

'Yes, it's in the snuggery.'

'I'll take it away with me to study, if I may.'

'Of course, Mr. Stone, but why?'

The book-dealer sighed gloomily.

'I don't know to what term of imprisonment the judge will sentence your father, but it is certain beyond all doubt that he will take away his bookseller's licence.'

'His licence?' exclaimed Margaret. 'Do you mean that we shan't be able to sell any more books?'

Mr. Stone nodded his head.

'Not for as long as the licence is withdrawn.'

She looked at him in desperation. She had imagined—if the worst came to the worst and her father were found guilty—that she and Mrs. Neech would have been able to carry on the business until he returned to them.

'But how shall we live?' she asked starkly.

'That's why I want the catalogue. If I have your father's permission to value and take over his stock, you will at least be assured of some capital.'

Mrs. Neech brought in the tea, and their thoughts turned inevitably from Mr. Pargeter's business to Mr. Pargeter himself. The parlour was full of the intimate things that belonged to his daily life—the delft jar on the mantelpiece containing the spills for his cheroots; his bergamot in the window; his second pair of glasses on the escritoire; his chair by the table with its foot rail rubbed where he rested his shoe.

Mr. Stone sat down in his old friend's chair and turned suddenly to Robert.

'Your uncle is a Member of Parliament, is that not so, young man?'

'Yes, sir.'

'Then write to your father this afternoon,' said Mr. Stone. 'Carry the letter to Lombard Street yourself and see that it goes on the night mail. Tell your father to come to London immediately and to bespeak his brother to attend the court with him on Friday next. It is time that men whom the world consider wise and of good repute should speak in my old friend's defence.'

'Yes, sir, of course,' replied Robert with a puzzled air.

Though his father was Mr. Pargeter's godson, he could not see him defending the old man's radical beliefs in a court of law. The present order of things suited him too well for him to wish to see them changed.

'They'll do it if they've a spark of honour in them,' growled Mr. Stone.

Margaret and Robert looked at him in astonishment. There had been both anger and contempt in his voice. And he looked back at them grimly, noting their bewilderment.

'Your father, Margaret,' he said, 'saved this young man's father from a scrape—no, it was worse than a youthful scrape; it was a matter of downright disgrace. And it is just that Dr. Kerridge should now stand by him in his need. The reputation which your father saved should now be used in his defence.'

'What did he do?' asked Robert.

'Who?'

'My father.'

Mr. Stone smiled sardonically.

'No, my boy. It happened a long time ago and it is best forgot. When you are your father's age, there will perhaps be matters that *you* will not wish your son to know about. A man must keep faith with his generation.'

'But what can Dr. Kerridge and his brother *do*?' asked Margaret. 'Surely it's too late? The jury has given its verdict.'

'Before sentence is passed,' explained Mr. Stone, 'the defendant has still another chance to put his defence, and he may bring witnesses to testify to his good character.'

A few minutes later, Mr. Stone left with the catalogue that John had made, and Robert went up to his room to write to his father. Elijah had joined Mrs. Neech in the kitchen and was running his finger round the edge of a jar of preserve. The morning's grief had made him extraordinarily hungry.

Margaret, left to herself, stood in the dim bookshop looking up at the high shelves full of books.

The shop had been her nursery and her schoolroom, and the books themselves, that she had used in her infancy as building blocks for castles and medieval towers and later in childhood had read omnivorously, were as dear to her as Suzannah's dresses and love-letters were dear to Suzannah. They meant eveything to her. What would she do without her books? They were the food of her mind. She had long known this. But in the last two years she had come to realize that they were also the family's bread and butter. They could not live without selling books. Margaret could not imagine that she would know a worse grief than she felt as she stood alone in the shuttered shop that late, unhappy morning. Her father had been found guilty of publishing a seditious libel. John had walked out of their lives. And now the books were to go.

But worse was yet to come.

Late on that same afternoon, while Robert was down at the coach station and Mrs. Neech and Elijah were busying themselves with the evening meal and the hamper for her father, Margaret went upstairs to look through her own personal books, wondering sadly whether these should be added to the catalogue for Mr. Stone. Slowly into her consciousness, as she knelt by the shelf, crept the murmur of many voices. She heard the shuffling of many feet in the lane below her and the sound of other feet running towards them from Cheapside.

What could have happened? Was there a fire? Had there been an accident? She ran to the window to find out what was going on.

Immediately below her stretched a turbid sea of tousled heads. A crowd of about fifty men and women—all poor and many in rags—thronged the lane. They were standing on the steps of the chemist's shop; they were pressed against the warehouse wall farther down, and they were packed in the narrow entrance to Paternoster Row. The low murmur rose to an angry rumble. Yet no one moved. They stood where they were, staring at the shuttered bookshop windows—waiting. Waiting for what?

Margaret was too astonished to feel frightened. What could this lowering, waiting crowd be doing outside her father's shop?

With half her mind she saw Mr. Fisher and his apprentice creep out of the side door with the shutters of the chemist's shop. Mrs. Fisher closed the parlour windows on the first floor and barred and bolted the wooden slats inside.

Margaret leant out of her bedroom window.

'What do you want?' she called down in a clear, loud voice.

The dark heads looked up. She saw stupid faces, starved faces, cunning faces, sullen faces, all turned upwards towards her—staring dumbly.

'Why are you waiting outside my father's shop?'

The crowd kept its silence.

Then a man's voice suddenly shouted:

'It's his daughter. It's the bookseller's daughter.'

The words were hardly out of his mouth before a stone crashed through the window pane beside her, scattering glass over the floor behind her.

Appalled, Margaret pulled in her head and stood for a moment inside the window, wondering what had happened to her world. But when another stone and another and another came hurtling through the glass, she pulled the shutters across and bolted them and ran headlong down the stairs to the kitchen.

'They've gone mad, Mrs. Neech,' she gasped. 'They've gone quite mad.'

The housekeeper looked up from rolling out the pastry. Margaret was white-faced and bleeding. A splinter of flying glass had cut her arm.

'What's happened?' she cried in alarm.

'There are people in the lane. Dozens of them. They threw stones through my window.'

A deep, hollow banging suddenly echoed through the house. The crowd was pummelling the shop shutters with its fists.

'But why, why, why?' cried Margaret. '*Why* do they hate my father?'

'Never mind why,' snapped Mrs. Neech. 'There's no sense in a mob.'

With the breaking of glass, the mob had found its voice. The pummelling on the shutters was accompanied by catcalls and shouting. And then at the height of the hubbub, a voice louder than the rest rose above the tumult, ordering the rabble to another course. The fist blows stopped, and Margaret and Mrs. Neech and Elijah heard the sound of many feet running away towards Cheapside.

'They're going away,' murmured Margaret in relief.

'No, they're not,' cried Elijah, white with excitement. 'They're coming back again.'

His ears were attuned to the shouts and calls of the London rookeries and he had understood what the leader had shouted to the mob.

He suddenly ran out of the kitchen and tore up the stairs to Margaret's bedroom.

'What are you doing?' shouted Margaret after him.

'Going to look through the cracks,' he yelled.

They stood, Margaret above Elijah, peering through a wide crack in the bedroom shutter at what was going on at the end of the lane. The crowd was swarming over the mangled heap of the tenement ruins, milling round and round, stirring up the dust. Margaret felt suddenly sick. She saw that every man was arming himself with a plank or a brick.

'What are they doing?' asked Mrs. Neech behind them.

Margaret turned round and told her and, in the telling, her indignation suddenly drove out her fear. Those brutes were going to break down their door. They were going to sack her father's shop. Yes, they were brutes. Mad brutes. It was for people as poor and wretched as themselves that her father had published his pamphlet. It was for them that he was going to prison. And *this* was the way that they repaid his care!

John's jeer suddenly rang in her ears.

'Show them kindness,' he had said, 'and they'll bite your hand.'

John had been right.

'Mr. Stone is coming down the lane,' hissed Elijah.

Margaret put her eye to the crack and saw Mr. Stone; she saw, also, the reason for the child's hiss. The crowd was returning armed for the attack. Three men were directly below them. Mr. Stone was walking, undetected, by the side of a group of women carrying bricks.

She tore herself from the crack.

'We must let him in by the side alley,' she whispered urgently, and ran down the stairs.

8 *The Mob*

An emergency brings out the strangest qualities in the strangest people. Old Mr. Stone, who had spent half a century with his nose inside a book, knew exactly what to do and how to do it. He was like a general on a battlefield.

'There's not a moment to lose,' he told Margaret as he ran along the inside alley-way. 'They mean business all right, that rabble outside.'

'But *why*? What have we done?'

'It's your father's ideas about their children,' he panted.

'Their children?'

'That's it. That they shouldn't earn till they're fourteen.'

'But they don't understand . . .'

'Of course they don't. You couldn't expect them to, would you?' he barked. 'Ignorant fools like that can't distinguish between the real and the ideal. They think your father means to starve them.'

A deafening tattoo started up on the bookshop door.

Mr. Stone hurried Margaret and Mrs. Neech into the kitchen.

'Where's that boy?'

'Elijah?'

'Get him. We want every pair of hands we can lay hold on.'

While Elijah was being summoned, Mr. Stone opened John's catalogue and started quickly ticking the most valuable items in Mr. Pargeter's stock.

'Margaret,' he asked sharply. 'Can you lay your hands quickly on any book I should name?'

'Yes, I think so.'

'Good. Then to work. Mrs. Neech, is that old hen roost still there—the one over your neighbour's yard wall at the back?'

'Yes,' said Margaret promptly. 'It is.'

'Mrs. Neech, you must forget your years and climb on that yard wall and stay there. Margaret and I are going into the bookshop with the catalogue. You, boy, are going to run along the passage, through this kitchen and out across that yard to Mrs. Neech, carrying the books that I shall hand to you. Mrs. Neech, you are going to drop them gently over the wall into the roost. Understand?'

They all nodded.

The heavy oak door of the shop was groaning under the repeated blows of the crowd. The noise was appalling.

'Burton's *Anatomy of Melancholy*, 1621,' shouted Mr. Stone.

Margaret ran for the library ladder and climbed to the shelf under the ceiling.

'Caxton's *The Dictes and Sayings of the Philosophers*, 1477,' called out the old book-dealer. 'Constable's *Diana*; Dryden's *Annus Mirabilis*, signed by the poet; Hakluyt's *Voyages*, three volumes, 1600.'

Elijah ran along the passage, through the kitchen and out to the yard wall with the books and then back again at the double for more. His breath was coming in queer noisy spurts that made him want to laugh. He was almost enjoying himself.

'Marlowe's *Faust*, 1604,' shouted Mr. Stone.

Margaret flew from shelf to shelf.

'Plutarch's *Lives* translated by North, 1579.'

The noise in the lane outside grew every moment more savage and frightening. The mob had made a battering-ram and the thuds on the oak door shook the house.

'Spenser's *Faerie Queene*, second instalment of three books, 1596,' yelled Mr. Stone above the din.

Margaret knew the bookshop like her right hand. Despite the tumult and the running and climbing and the pulling down of tomes, she yet had mind enough to think of Robert.

'*Works of William Shakespeare*, Second Folio, 1632.'

Where was Robert? He should have been home by now.

'Swift's *Tale of a Tub*,' roared the book-dealer.

But Robert could not get back. The house was almost surrounded. What if he were wedged in that terrible, yelling mob outside, incapable either of coming to their help or of leaving them to their fate?

'Vaughan's *Pious Thoughts*,' bellowed Mr. Stone.

There was a splitting, rending crash, and half the bottom left-hand panel of the street door fell with a clatter to the floor.

'We'll have to abandon the shop,' shouted Mr. Stone.

A jagged shaft of light fell through the gash in the door and caught in the old-fashioned buckles of his shoes. They could see the torn breeches and stockings of the men outside.

'What's in the snuggery, Margaret!' he asked urgently. 'Any money? Manuscripts? Papers of value?'

She could not think. Her wits were leaving her. The roar of the mob swirled through the gaping hole.

'The till,' she shouted.

Mr. Stone tore open the till and emptied the petty cash into the large pockets of his coat.

'Authors' manuscripts?' he cried.

'I can't think. I can't think,' gasped Margaret.

The nearness of the mob and the sight of the men's feet kicking in the rest of the door had made her feel frightened again.

Why had not Robert come? What had happened to him?

'Margaret!' roared the book-dealer, shaking her by the shoulders. 'Were there any authors' manuscripts? It is important. Your father is responsible.'

'There's *The New Jerusalem*.'

'Good God! Not that! We'll leave that to the rabble.'

'And Mr. Love's new ballad.'

Margaret seized Frances Love's *Haunted Lake*, and she and the book-dealer ran back through the shop towards the house passage. A massive, nail-studded oak door separated the shop from the house, and they slammed this shut behind them at the very moment that the street door finally gave way and the mob streamed into the shop.

'Slam home the bolts,' shouted Mrs. Neech over their shoulders.

When Elijah's supply of books had ceased, she had left her

perch on the yard wall and had come to defend what was left of her master's property.

The great door was like a thick wall. They could hear the mob moving about in the shop, overturning the tables, wrenching down the books, tearing open the drawers, but the noise came to them indistinctly, as though from a long way off. In the sudden deadening of the pandemonium, Margaret felt momentarily drained of fortitude.

Robert was never coming. He was hurt. He was dead. The rabble had trampled him underfoot, she was sure of it. They had battered him to death as he had struggled to come to their help.

'Mr. Stone. Mr. Stone,' shrieked Elijah, half falling down the stairs in his excitement.

He had been up in his watch tower, peering through Margaret's bedroom shutter at the progress of the riot.

'Mr. Stone,' he shrieked. 'They're bringing pitch and wood and lighted rope ends.'

Even Mr. Stone's valour deserted him for a second. He looked at Margaret, white-faced and shocked. He had lived through the terrible week in 1780 when London had been ruled by the mob. He knew the worst to expect.

'Margaret,' he muttered hoarsely. 'They're going to set fire to the shop.'

'Why doesn't someone stop them?' she cried. 'Why haven't the magistrates been called? Why aren't the soldiers here?'

Mrs. Neech and Mr. Stone caught each other's glance. They knew very well why there was no one to stop the riot. The London magistrates were weak and cowardly and, besides, they had no physical force to control a lawless mob. As for the soldiers—these could be called only by the Government, and the Government—even if it were aware of the sacking of Mr. Pargeter's shop—would scarcely feel bounden to protect the property of a citizen whom the courts had just convicted of seditious libel.

Elijah's ears, which were far quicker than anyone else's, were suddenly pricked up like a dog's. He looked down at the flagged passage floor with a puzzled air, and then he turned sharply to Margaret.

'Someone's in the cellar,' he whispered.

Almost immediately, a terrible iron clanking and beating of metal sounded under the parlour floor.

Margaret looked at Mr. Stone in bewilderment.

'What is it?' she gasped.

'Breaking up the press,' he explained grimly.

'The cellar door!' cried Mrs. Neech. 'We must barricade the cellar door!'

They ran in a body to the kitchen.

There were two ways into Mr. Pargeter's cellars: one was through a trapdoor in the snuggery—the way that the rioters had entered; and the other was through a door in the kitchen wall and down a flight of steps. The door in the kitchen was locked, but it was not nearly so strong as the heavy oak door which separated the shop from the house.

'The brutes! The damned, verminous, thievish brutes!' cursed Mrs. Neech as she and Margaret and Mr. Stone and Elijah tugged the heavy kitchen table against the cellar door.

'The pest-ridden, gin-sodden, filthy beasts!' she cried, as she banged down the coal hods against the table.

Distraught though she was, Margaret gasped at the stream of invective. She had no idea that the sedate Mrs. Neech knew such words.

'Gin!' panted Mr. Stone. 'Gin! Is there any gin in the cellar?'

'Gin?' repeated the bewildered Margaret.

'There's the master's port and his Madeira. And that new cask of rum. And there's the brandy, too. There's that brandy that Captain Leggatt sent him from the *Hebe*.'

Surprisingly, Mr. Stone smiled a thin, wintry smile.

'The spirits may save us,' he said. 'A drunk mob soon becomes dead drunk. And when they're dead drunk the danger is past.'

The four of them stood in the middle of the kitchen listening breathlessly to the sounds about them. They heard laughter and shouts and the breaking of glass beneath them; the rioters were clearly ransacking the wine bins. And from the bookshop along the passage came the muffled thud of books being hurled to the ground. Every thud caught at Margaret's heart. It was all too terrible to think about. Everything that she knew and loved in her home was being desecrated by the mob. And it was not only her own grief that shook her. There was her father's. And John's. How would her father ever survive this ignorant vengeance of the men and women he had tried to help? How could he ever excuse their brutal savagery? And how could John ever forgive himself for having left them alone at such a time? He would feel shamed for life. It was too great a punishment—even for John.

Suddenly the doorway into the yard darkened, and Robert stood hatless and dishevelled before them.

'Robert!' cried Margaret. 'Thank God you're safe!'

But if he was safe, he was hardly sound. One of his coat sleeves had been wrenched from its armhole, his breeches were torn at the knees, and blood was flowing from an angry gash on the back of his hand.

'Your hand!' she gasped. 'What happened?'

'It's nothing. Nothing. They threw a brick as I climbed the warehouse wall.'

'And your clothes!' exclaimed Mrs. Neech.

The mob had clearly tried to lynch him before he had escaped over the neighbouring roofs.

A ground swirl of smoke drifted under the door from the shop. Elijah smelt it first.

'They've lit the fire!' he bawled and ran out into the passage to watch the swirl change into a billow and the billow into a great cloud of choking fumes.

Through the thick wood they could hear the crackle of flames devouring the paper in the books.

'Quick!' cried Margaret. 'We must save what we can from the bedrooms.'

The four principal bedrooms of the house lay directly over the shop and the snuggery and the parlour.

Robert and Margaret tore up the stairs side by side.

'Your microscope,' she panted. 'And Mother's jewels. And the things in Father's room.'

She looked quickly at Robert as she ran. He looked wonderfully eager and alive in the rags of his fine clothes, and she almost smiled. Everything seemed far less horrible now that he had come.

'Don't try to save everything,' he shouted. There isn't time.'

Margaret ran into her room, wrapped the little bag of jewels in her best batiste gown, stuffed them into the crown of her new poke bonnet and ran into John's room, which overlooked the yard, and dropped her bundle on to the dahlias. Meanwhile Robert had run up to his room and down to the kitchen with his microscope, his new trousers, two books of anatomy, and some shirts and a coat.

The upstairs rooms were now heavy with smoke, for it was seeping up through the cracks in the floorboards, and Margaret, as she dashed into her father's room, could hear the roar of the flames in the shop below.

She should have come here first. There was so much to save. There was Rembrandt's little painting of the old woman that hung over her father's bed; there were her mother's letters that he kept somewhere in his chest of drawers; there were his clothes, his best boots, and Tyndale's translation of the New Testament which he kept by his bedside. She had left it almost too late. A tongue of flame shot up by the wardrobe. She grabbed the picture and the New Testament and put them out in the passage, and then she ran back into the room.

'Margaret, come back,' shouted Robert from the stairs.

'No. No,' she said over and over again to herself as she tore frantically through her father's shirts and waistcoats in his chest of drawers.

'Margaret,' ordered Robert urgently from the door. 'Leave

it. It's too late.'

She went on tossing out the cravats and lawn handkerchiefs, almost sobbing with frustration. Where *were* the letters? She knelt on the floor and groped under the chest.

'Margaret,' he shouted in her ear. 'Come at once.'

He was beside her, lifting her up.

'No, Robert,' she cried as she struggled free. 'I must find the letters.'

The flames were now licking along the floorboards in a long line at the farther end of the room.

'No,' he cried, tearing at her arm.

'It's all he's got of her,' she sobbed angrily.

The room was stiflingly hot. Everything in it was about to burst into flames.

'It's *you* he wants. Not the letters,' he cried, seizing her round the waist and carrying her struggling across the room.

The floorboards groaned; the wardrobe lurched, and suddenly the inferno in the bookshop below leapt up into Mr. Pargeter's bedroom. The far wall danced with flames.

'It's *you* he wants,' shouted Robert over their roar.

Margaret beat at his chest with her fists—powerless, angry, distraught.

He put her down in the yard beside the dahlias, and they stood looking at each other in wonder, their chests heaving with the smoke and the heat and their struggle in the burning room.

'Robert,' Margaret panted at last, part in tears, part in laughter, 'you're half-killed by the weight of me.'

But Robert was not half-killed at all. He suddenly caught her to him and kissed her firmly on her smoke-grimed, tear-stained cheek.

9 *Picking up the Bits*

Margaret tossed feverishly all night, re-enacting in her dreams the horror of the last few hours. The faces of the people in the street forced themselves so close to her that their hot, angry eyes seemed to blaze through her brain. They shouted incomprehensible words at her—angry words, which they spat out of their mouth as though they were a poison that their bodies longed to be rid of. She was distraught that she could not understand either the meaning of these venomous words or yet why she had deserved the people's rage. The same sequence of faces—broken-toothed, unshaven, repulsive in their mad fury— threatened and shouted and leered at her in endless pursuit; and she awoke in a panic only to fall asleep again in her exhaustion to dream of the same faces, the same blazing eyes, and the same incomprehensible shouts. She awoke finally at nine o'clock in the morning, drained of all hope for herself—damned for ever by these angry people for the nameless and terrible crimes she had committed. None of her own anger at the sacking of her father's shop and the burning of her home had survived the night's ordeal. It had been destroyed by this fierce delusion of her own appalling guilt.

She lay inert and stupid and miserable, staring at the sunshine fitfully dappling the unfamiliar patchwork quilt. Then she sat up, still dazed and uncomprehending, gazing dully at the empty grate filled with fir cones and the strange wardrobe and at every other detail of the drab, impersonal room in which she had spent the night.

Where was she?

She remembered now.

Mr. Stone had brought them to the booksellers' coffee house off St. Paul's Churchyard late at night when the flames from the bookshop had threatened the parlour and the kitchen and the tiny yard. Realizing that there was nothing left that they could do, they had escaped over the back wall with their few bits of salvage—the first editions from the hen roost and the microscope and the clothes' bundle with the jewels and a hamper of food got together by Mrs. Neech from the larder shelves. Yes, she remembered more now: her question to the people waiting in the lane; the stones through the window; the pummelling on the street door; the shouts; the laughter; the crackle of fire. And the more she recalled, the farther the morbid fog of her dreams receded into limbo. She had done nothing wrong. Nor had her father. They were guiltless. They had neither of them deserved the horrible things that had happened last night.

And then, as the bedroom curtain bulged out in a blast of autumn wind and its rings twitched back across their wooden rod, letting the sunlight stream into the room, Margaret remembered Robert. Robert had kissed her. This was not a dream. It was a fact. The wonder and surprise of it flooded over her at the very moment that the sunlight, at last freed from the flapping curtain, poured its radiance full on her face and arms. The warmth and joy of it flushed up in her cheeks and sparkled in her eyes.

She jumped out of bed and dressed quickly in her poor, tumbled, smoke-smirched clothes. Everything about her—her hair, her hands, even the air she breathed out—seemed to smell of acrid, choking smoke. So she splashed her face with the cold water in the bedroom jug and stood by the open window and filled her lungs with great gulps of fresh air, almost laughing to herself at the clean joyous wind that was blowing through her world. She let it blow over her bare arms and feet and through her hair and down her neck, her happiness all the time growing fresher and brighter and more urgent inside her. She must find Robert. She must look at him again. It was a whole long night since she had last seen him.

Half-way down the stairs, she remembered her father. No one had told him yet of the fire. It had been too late last night. The prison had been locked and barred. Realizing that she had forgotten him all this time, she stopped dead in her tracks, profoundly shocked that he should have come to take second place in her thoughts. She must go to him immediately—Robert must go with her—and together they would break the news of the fire to him and try to comfort him for the savagery of the mob.

But Robert was not in the breakfast room when she came down.

'He's gone out,' mumbled Elijah cavernously from the bottom of his porringer.

Gone out?

'He was out down the street before the boy and I were dressed,' confirmed Mrs. Neech.

Robert had left without seeing her! Margaret was so disappointed that she somersaulted straight out of joy into despair.

'Elijah!' she sighed. 'You're eating disgustingly. Use a spoon.'

His going depressed her unreasonably. He had treated the morning like every other morning in the year. He had gone off to his lecture at the hospital as though nothing had happened. He had allowed the humdrum world to swallow them both up. How could he have done such a thing?

'No, don't wipe your mouth with the back of your hand,' she said irritably. 'Use the napkin. That's what it's for.'

'Leave the child alone, Miss Margaret,' said Mrs. Neech quietly. 'You're at sixes and sevens with yourself. It's no wonder after such a night.'

Margaret sat down feeling wretched, measuring how badly she was behaving by the mildness of Mrs. Neech's reproach. Not even having one's home burnt down quite forgave one for being unkind to Elijah. She looked sadly across the table into the child's resentful eyes and tried to smile, but she felt hollow and empty inside. She wondered achingly whether she had dreamed the kiss or whether Robert had been carried away by the excitement of the fire and had meant nothing at all. That was it. He was ashamed of his outburst and had hurried away to avoid her. It was her own fault. She had had no right to expect such happiness to come to her out of a day and a night of such family grief.

'You'll feel better when you've taken some food,' said Mrs. Neech, pouring her out a bowl of coffee. 'And when you've put yourself to rights, you must think what you're going to tell your father.'

'Is there anything to tell but the truth?' she asked bleakly.

Life seemed suddenly as bitter as ashes.

Five minutes later she was herself again.

Robert and Mr. Stone stood in the doorway of the breakfast room, laden with books, Mrs. Neech's sewing-box, a picture, and her father's favourite pot of scented geraniums. Robert had not gone to the hospital; he had returned to Holly Lane to see what else he could fetch from the wreck of the Pargeters' home, and here he had met the old book-dealer, who had returned to the bookshop even earlier in the morning with the same thought in mind.

'There,' he said, putting down the little Rembrandt portrait and the heavy Tyndale New Testament on the tablecloth beside her, 'I thought you'd like these, since you went to such danger to save them.'

She looked up at him searchingly as she spoke her thanks, and he returned her look with the same amused, friendly smile that he had so often given her, his eyes travelling over her flushed face and new-brushed hair and her crumpled, smoke-stained dress with an expression, half mocking, half affectionately concerned.

'Well, you don't look much the worse for it all,' he said.

'And nor do you,' she forced herself to laugh back at him.

But her heart felt heavy as lead. Nothing was changed, she thought. He was the same Robert. And the kiss had meant nothing at all.

Mrs. Neech, meanwhile, was staring at the portrait and the book in astonishment.

'They're very wet,' she exclaimed. 'What have you done to them?'

The Rembrandt was glistening with water and the edges of

the leaves of the New Testament were stained with damp.

'You've your fine neighbours to thank for that,' said Mr. Stone dourly.

'The Fishers?' asked Mr. Neech in surprise.

It appeared that the Fishers, on seeing that Mr. Pargeter's bookshop was ablaze, had taken alarm for their own safety. The chemist knew that both premises were insured by the same company, so he had climbed over the wall at the back of his storehouse and run for help to Wood Street, where the Sun Fire Insurance had its office. By the time that the fire engine arrived, the rioters, having sated their lust for violence, were reeling home, not so befuddled by Mr. Pargeter's brandy as to be entirely oblivious of the consequences to themselves if they loitered near the fire and were arrested for the damage they had caused. No one had offered the firemen resistance and, in consequence, they had set up their pumps and hoses and proceeded to drown what remained of the bookseller's property in a flood of water.

'But I suppose the firemen at least stopped the fire,' said Mrs. Neech, trying to leave herself with one charitable thought for their neighbours. 'If it hadn't have been for Mr. Fisher, everything would have been burnt to the ground.'

'He might have come to our rescue much earlier in the night,' growled Mr. Stone. 'There was little left to burn by the time that the firemen came.'

'How was it that the Rembrandt and the New Testament weren't burnt?' asked Margaret.

'The floor of your father's room fell into the shop,' explained Robert. 'That must have saved the passage and the stairs and your room and John's. Mine went the way of your father's. I saw the charred frame of the bed sagging through the parlour ceiling.'

'Is the parlour gutted too?' she asked, swallowing hard to keep back the tears.

Robert nodded and turned away his face. The return to the Pargeters' house had been more terrible than he could ever tell

Margaret. She must never go back and learn the full horror of the night.

'But if my room is not burnt I can go back with Mrs. Neech and fetch more of my things.'

'No,' said Robert and Mr. Stone in one breath.

'But why not?' cried Margaret, startled by their tone.

'It is no place for women,' replied Mr. Stone grimly.

'But it is our home,' protested Margaret. 'We must save what we can of our possessions.'

'And my room, sir? And the boy's attic? Were they burnt, too?'

'No, Mrs. Neech. The kitchen and the rooms above are undamaged save for the smoke and the water.'

'Then there's much that we can bring away,' exclaimed Margaret excitedly.

'Myself and Mr. Kerridge will engage a carrier,' said Mr. Stone hastily.

Mrs. Neech looked narrowly first at Robert and then at the old book-dealer. Then she cleared her throat.

'It's time you went to your father, Miss Margaret.'

'And it's time you went to the hospital and had that hand of yours dressed,' said the book-dealer to Robert.

Margaret had noticed that he had wrapt it in a clean napkin.

'Does it hurt you?' she asked quickly.

'No,' he laughed. 'But it needs a stitch, I think. I'll leave you at the Compter on my way to St. Xavier's.'

During that sunlit, gusty walk to the prison, Margaret had time to get used to the new order of things or, at least, to learn to live with it without making a fool of herself. Suzannah had been wrong about kisses, she thought. They really meant nothing at all. She drove the excitement with which she had jumped out of bed that morning to the back of her mind and locked fast the door. Robert had been carried away in an upsurge of excitement or pity—or, perhaps, even kindness. And now, today, underneath all his charming, thoughtful care of her, he must be feeling embarrassed or ashamed. She was sure of it. She could not believe that he could be feeling nothing at all. He was not heartless. For both their sakes, she must try to steer back to the quiet waters of their friendship.

The people in the streets were a help. They looked so ordinary, so dull, so pre-occupied with their own affairs.

'Strange, isn't it?' she exclaimed.

'What's strange?' Robert asked her, leaning over her protectively for a moment as five ragged little boys jostled past them.

'Why, that nobody seems to know or care about all the things that happened to us last night.'

The court's verdict and the mob and the sacking of the shop, the fire and Robert's embrace were all so extraordinary that she felt that they must be written up in huge letters in a banner held over her head. And yet no one that they had met had stopped to look at them twice.

'They've got their own troubles, Meg. Everyone has his own troubles. And they're always so much more important than anyone else's.'

He gave her a quick, amused glance.

'Besides, we don't look as odd as all that!'

'Odd?'

'I feel a bit of a mess, and your dress could be cleaner. But we don't look as though we'd been through fire and rout. We look quite ordinary, you know.'

Ordinary. Ordinary.

The word suddenly maddened her. She did not *feel* ordinary at all. No one ever felt ordinary, she was sure. They felt lonely or lost or happy or sad or frightened or full of love—always something unusual and personal, that they were longing to share with someone else. And, instead, they found themselves shut up inside a dungeon of ordinariness; their faces masked by this dreadful word 'ordinary'; their tongues held fast in a scold's bridle of ordinary speech.

For all her resolution, she longed to speak without fetters to Robert; and she longed for him to tear aside his mask. But he was walking beside her in silence now, his face thoughtful and sad.

The prison stood grimly at the end of the street.

Outside the Poultry Compter, waiting for the porter to fetch his keys, Margaret found herself staring numbly at the rounded heads of the iron nails driven into the prison gate and smelling the loathsome prison smell that came to them through the iron grating level with their heads. It was a bitter return to her father's fate.

She was glad that she had held her peace. This was no time to think of anyone but her father.

'Let me go with you,' Robert urged. 'It's too much for you alone.'

She turned to him with anxious, everyday eyes. The white napkin that he had wrapped round his hand was now stained in the centre with blood where he must have knocked himself as they went along. The wound had opened again.

'But your hand,' she said.

'It can wait,' he replied, looking down dully at the widening stain. 'But your father can't, Meg. We've left him far too long.'

He had been alone, without them, ever since the trial. He knew nothing of the riot and the fire. He must have been in anguish all night, wondering why they had not come to him at this terrible time in his life. Margaret could not bear to think of it. He might have thought that she had deserted him as John had done—that everyone had deserted him.

'Please come with me, Robert,' she said.

They found him sitting on a stone bench out of the wind in a corner of the central court, and from their first sight of him they were sure that he already knew the worst.

'Father,' cried Margaret, running towards him.

Hearing her voice, he threw down the newspaper that had lain on his knees and stood up, looking towards her through his reading glasses, smiling tremulously at the vague figures that swam and blurred before him.

95

'Margaret! Robert!' he cried, snatching off the glasses and seeing them both, clear and distinct, at last.

He raised his arms and caught them to him as though they were both his children.

'Thank God you are safe. Thank God. Thank God.'

He smelled the ordeal of the fire in their hair and their clothing and saw it all in the strain of their looks.

'You know about it, Father?'

He nodded.

'It is in the morning paper,' he said.

'You didn't think we had deserted you?'

'My dear. My dear. Do you think I have so little trust?' he asked simply.

He held Margaret's face in his two hands and looked lovingly into her eyes.

'It is a great joy to me, Meg, that my greatest treasure is left to me. I thank God for it with all my heart.'

And then he turned quickly to her companion.

'And the others, Robert? Mrs. Neech and the boy? They are safe? The newspapers speaks only of the poor wretches in the cellars.'

'Who?' asked Margaret. 'What do you mean?'

'Why, Meg, the poor fellows who were burned to death.'

Margaret turned in horror to Robert.

'Who does he mean, Robert?'

'They were trapped in the cellars, Meg, and when the shop was burnt to the ground, the floor beams gave way and fell through on top of them.'

'How horrible!' she gasped.

They stood for a moment, shattered and numbed by the misery and futility of that unhappy night.

'I tried to bring them hope and life,' the bookseller said painfully. 'And I have brought them nothing but shame and death.'

'But they were drunk, Father,' protested Margaret angrily. 'They were laughing as they threw down the books—laughing as they set light to the house. They enjoyed what they were doing.'

'Then that is the measure of my failure towards them,' he replied quietly, without bitterness.

They sat down, the three of them, on the long stone bench, and Robert told Mr. Pargeter of what Mr. Stone had advised them to do and of how he had written to Herringsby and asked his father and his uncle to speak for him in court when the judge came to pronounce sentence.

'My character and my acts should not need their defence,' said Mr. Pargeter sadly. 'But I thank you, Robert, for your kindness.'

And then Margaret told him of Mr. Stone's saving of the first edition and of how they had carried them from the hen roost to the coffee house in the middle of the night.

'The Caxton is safe, you say?' he asked. 'And the Shakespeare folio?'

'Yes, Father, and Burton's *Anatomy*.'

'And Margaret saved the Rembrandt and your New Testament,' put in Robert.

'Bless you, my dear,' he said, turning to his daughter. 'It was like you to have remembered what was most precious to me.'

Margaret marvelled at her father's gentleness, for though she had known and loved him for seventeen years it was only now, when she had learned how bitter and unjust life could be, that she realized quite how fine and humble a man he was, and how indomitable in the face of defeat. He had often been angry when provoked in little things, and yet when the whole neighbourhood conspired to do him wrong he met its blows with quietness and humility, as though it were he who had failed his neighbours, not they who had failed him.

His gratitude to her at such a time moved her almost to tears.

10 *Dr. Kerridge*

Dr. Kerridge arrived in London on the overnight mail on Tuesday morning and went straight to St. Xavier's Hospital to meet his son. In justice to him, Margaret had to admit that he had come as soon as he could. He had not shirked his duty to his old friend. Yet his manner in performing that duty at once alienated her affections. She wanted to revere Robert's father and she could not. Something in his address filled her with dismay. He came into the family room at the coffee house that night with the air of a man much pressed for time and to whom the performance of the duty laid upon him entailed a tiresome interruption in the pursuance of more important affairs. Yet he was polished enough to attempt to cloak the impatience he felt.

'It is a bad business, Miss Pargeter. A bad business. I pity your father with all my heart.'

Margaret dropped a curtsy and swallowed a desire to spurn his pity.

'I came as soon as I could. Duties were pressing at Herringsby, I confess. But my old friend comes first. Indeed he does. I have discussed with Robert what is best to be done. He has gone with a letter to my brother's chambers in Westminster and, if he is still in Town, we shall meet tomorrow and decide what pressure can be brought to bear upon the judge to mitigate the harshness of the law. Believe me, we shall do all we can to help him.'

His sentiments were unexceptionable, yet Margaret felt no warm, compelling gratitude in hearing them; she felt only an aching unhappiness that Robert's father seemed so remote and unknown to her. He was a stranger where she longed for a friend. She knew that Dr. Kerridge had visited in Holly Lane quite often when she was a small child and that he had come again when Robert had first come to lodge with them, but Margaret had been barely fifteen on that last occasion and was so deeply lost in the world of books that the acquaintances who came and went in her father's life were as vague and formless to her as shadows passing along a wall at night. The extraordinary fact that this masterful, uncomfortable man was her father's godson had not distinguished him in her mind from the rest. And now, suddenly, this shadow from the past was Robert's father—the man, whom next to Robert and her own father, she wanted most in all the world to please. And yet, looking at him as she now did, frankly and openly in a long, unconscious stare, she felt repelled, anxious, discouraged—quite unlike her naturally hopeful self.

He was a tall man, exquisitely dressed, with more than a hint in the way he held his head that he knew what a splendid figure he cut. He was intelligent and alert, with Robert's Roman nose and his bright eyes and the same high back to his head. Yet, how different he was from his son! Success had made him arrogant; one could see it in the hard lines round his mouth; and, at the same time, it had made him somehow lax and sleek, as though he had shed his scruples as he had passed through life and had equipped himself instead with a more worldly and comfortable set of rules. Margaret's eyes fastened almost with relief on the grizzled hair, the heavy lines under the chin, and the hard creases round his mouth, for she could not bear to contemplate those likenesses of feature that he shared with his son. They seemed to her a travesty of the laws of inheritance.

Why did Robert have to be born with parents?

Her ill manners in staring at her guest were perhaps excused by the fact that Dr. Kerridge was engaged in the same occupation. She had offered him a chair and, while they waited for Mrs. Neech to bring in the tea things, he looked Margaret up and down with an almost equal dismay.

'You have changed a great deal in the last two years, Miss Pargeter,' he said at last.

'Yes, sir. I have grown up.'

'So I see,' he said, with a twitch of a smile.

The smile startled her. For a moment she saw Robert mocking her from the cobbles of Holly Lane. And then it was gone—brilliant but past—like the flash of a kingfisher along a brook.

And when she glanced up again, he was frowning at the top of her head.

'How old are you now?'

'Seventeen.'

He looked her sharply straight in the eyes.

'And the young men have begun paying you court? That is so, is it not?'

Margaret flushed with confusion. It was as though he had seen that moment during the fire in the little courtyard by the dahlias. Yet that was absurd. The moment had meant nothing. Was it, then, her own affection for Robert that was so plainly stamped on her face? Then, suddenly, she felt the impertinence of the question. It had been prompted not by gallantry but by something hostile and hard. She was sure of it. The cold intelligence in his watchful blue eyes told her as much; and the knowledge stung her to anger.

'I think, sir, you have come to London to speak for my father, not to question his daughter on her private affairs.'

This time it was the physician who looked startled.

'Do you always answer your father's old friends so tartly?'

'No, sir. They usually ask me questions about books, and when I know what they want, I tell them.'

'But for questions concerning the heart you give them a box on the ears?'

'I am no longer a child, sir.'

At this moment Mrs. Neech came in with the tea things and saw Margaret's angry flush and the nettled expression on Dr. Kerridge's face.

'It is kind of you to come, sir,' she said quickly, putting down the tray. 'Mr. Pargeter is in great trouble and we need your help.'

'I hope, indeed, Mrs. Neech, that my brother and I can assist our old friend.'

'He's not seditious, sir. Not like they say. He's not a traitor. He doesn't deserve the terrible things they've done to him.'

'I know he does not,' said the doctor gently.

Margaret could bear the room no longer. She loved her father and for her he needed no defence—not even Mrs. Neech's halting, loving apology. And he certainly did not need the assistance of this stranger who said he was Robert's father. She fled from the room, confused by her distress, knowing clearly that she had been rude and ungracious and unjust where she should have been nothing but grateful, and yet quite sure that Dr. Kerridge was an enemy, if not to her father, then to herself.

Mrs. Neech looked after her anxiously, and then turned to their guest.

'You mustn't mind Miss Margaret, sir,' she said. 'I don't know what she's been saying to you, but she always was one for speaking out, and she's moithered—as we all are—by the troubles that have come to her father. You must excuse her, sir, I beg of you.'

The doctor flashed her his bewitching smile.

'I have treated the young lady as a child, Mrs. Neech,' he explained. 'And I have very properly been snubbed for my pains.'

Margaret slept badly again.

She had waited above in her bedroom for nearly an hour, longing for Robert to return from Westminster, for she thought that, if only she could see Robert and his father together, this mysterious enmity that seemed to exist between them might disappear. She would come to see the doctor in a better light—as a father who was proud of his son; a parent who had given Robert everything that he had most wanted; someone who had been both generous and understanding. She waited and waited till she heard their guest bid Mrs. Neech good night and leave the coffee house and walk away towards St. Paul's Churchyard; and then, overburdened by the sheer multiplicity of things that had happened to her in the last few weeks, she undressed dispiritedly and got into bed and lay with her eyes wide open, thinking miserably of the change in all their lives.

It was scarcely a month since that bright early morning in August when she had caught Robert admiring his new hat in the Fishers' window—scarcely a month since she had looked out with a child's eyes on a child's sure world.

Now, nothing was sure.

It was not the physical facts of imprisonment and fire and homelessness that shocked her so much. These things, like illnesses and bereavement, were misfortunes that one had to face with what courage one could muster. Her father's fortitude had shown her that they need not damage a man's best nature; they might even refine and ennoble it. No. It was not misfortune in itself that kept her sleepless and anguished. It was the coldness and callousness and hatred that she had found in other people and the resentfulness that she knew was growing up inside herself that shook her so much. John's desertion, the indifference of the lawyers in the court, the crowd's rage, and, now, the hostility she sensed in Robert's father and her own hostility to him —all these things seemed extraordinary to her. Nothing that her father had taught her or that she had read about in books had led her to expect such a lack of kindness in the world.

In the watches of the night, she clung desperately to the thought of Robert. She knew now in her heart that she loved him; that she wanted to be his wife. She did not know whether he returned her love or whether he would ever come to do so, but the thought of him—friendly and sure and calm—brought her comfort, whatever the end might be.

Next morning she had an opportunity of seeing father and son together.

Robert had risen late and was breakfasting with Margaret and Elijah and Mrs. Neech, having given himself a holiday from his studies to accompany his father to his uncle's chambers. The three of them were to return later to the City—to the Poultry Compter—to acquaint her father with what they had decided to do. He was wearing his arm in a sling, but in other respects he looked rested and confident and well—quite unlike the torn and sleeveless Robert who had appeared over the back roofs only four nights ago. There was something gay and almost debonair about him that breakfast time, as though he had come to a great decision in the middle of the night and viewing it again in daylight had seen that it was good. He seemed full of strength and purpose and hope.

'We'll lunch with you here afterwards,' he said, turning eagerly to Margaret. 'And tell you all that they have planned. My uncle knows so many influential people in the Government that I know they will release your father on Friday. I'm sure of it, Meg.'

Margaret loved him for his hopefulness, even though she did not believe it was well-founded.

'Besides,' he continued, 'he has the sympathy of all good men. Everyone is ashamed of what happened in Holly Lane.'

'Sympathy? Ashamed?'

'Why, yes. Didn't you see the papers yesterday? Stimpson made some cuttings for me at the hospital. I was too late to show them to you last night. Look, here they are.'

He fumbled in his pocket and pulled out some fluttering columns of newsprint.

Margaret almost snatched them. When she had finished with one cutting she passed it on to Mrs. Neech and started reading the next.

On Friday night a mob gathered in Holly Lane and sacked and burnt the shop of a poor bookseller awaiting sentence at the Old Bailey. This despicable act is yet another example of the lawlessness of the London poor and its contempt for the proper course of justice.

Where were our City magistrates? asked another editor.

Yet another crime against property! exclaimed a third.

When she had finished she sighed and looked at Robert in a sad, puzzled way. The sympathy and shame appeared to her very wide of the mark. The writers of the articles knew very little about the father she loved and had not understood at all the nature of the crime that had been committed against him by the mob. It had not been a crime against property, but a crime against his faith and hope. But for what the writers had intended, she supposed she should feel grateful.

'Thank you, Robert,' she said quietly. 'It was good of you to have saved these for me.'

'Saved what, Miss Pargeter?' asked a voice from the doorway.

Everyone looked up in surprise.

Dr. Kerridge had entered unannounced and was scrutinizing the family party from Holly Lane with shrewd, searching eyes.

'Good morning, Father,' Robert greeted him, smiling and rising to his feet. 'Meg was reading the cuttings that I showed you yesterday.'

'Meg?' repeated the doctor quizzically. 'Miss Pargeter? And who, pray, is this?'

Dr. Kerridge's eyes had come to rest on Elijah, who, seeing the distaste in his expression, seized the table-napkin which Mrs. Neech had tucked into his collar and started vigorously wiping his mouth. Margaret could not help smiling. The boy was trying so earnestly to live up to the superior good-breeding of their guest.

'Mr. Pargeter's apprentice, sir,' replied Mrs. Neech quickly.

'An apprentice!' he exclaimed. 'What does your father want with an apprentice?'

Margaret could not explain to Dr. Kerridge in front of the child that it was the apprentice who had need of her father, and Mrs. Neech, seeing her difficulty, rose to take the boy out into the yard.

'We'll leave you alone, sir, with Miss Margaret and Master Robert. You will have matters that you will wish to talk with them.'

'What do you do with the child all day in a place like this?' asked the doctor when the housekeeper had left with the boy.

'Margaret is teaching him to read and write,' replied Robert proudly. 'She makes the most splendid school-ma'am you can imagine. Not too strict and full of ideas.'

The doctor brushed aside his son's enthusiasm.

'Does he work for his keep?' he asked.

'He is rather young, sir,' replied Margaret. 'He is not yet nine.'

'Nonsense!' exclaimed the doctor. 'A boy of eight should not idle his days with women. You will ruin him.'

'I am teaching him the first lessons of his trade, sir. A printer finds it hard to set up type if he cannot read.'

'So it is a printer the child is to be? Do you think your father will ever print again after what has happened?'

'I hope so,' replied Margaret resolutely.

She was determined not to be bullied by his catechism.

The doctor strode to the window and gazed thoughtfully out into the yard, where Elijah and the pot boy were floating chips of wood in the horse-trough.

'Would it not be better for all of you that he went back to the parish?' he said more gently.

'No!' exclaimed Margaret and Robert at once.

'No?' asked the doctor, swinging round on his heel and facing them both. 'Why not?'

Margaret looked desperately to Robert for help. She could not explain to this stranger something which she could not entirely comprehend herself. It was too large and complicated a thing—and far too near to her heart. Elijah was all that remained to her father from the hopes and ideals that had gone into the writing of *The New Jerusalem*. Everything else lay in ashes. He was someone that they had both saved—and John and Robert, too—from the unutterable misery of destitution, which was the plight of hundreds and hundreds of lonely, deserted London orphans. To abandon him now when they had taken him to their hearts was unthinkable. It would be a crime against humanity.

'Because Mr. Pargeter has pledged his word for his well-being,' replied Robert quickly. 'Because Mrs. Neech has grown fond of the boy and because Margaret would never consent to such a thing.'

He spoke with such finality that his father looked at him in astonishment.

He was clearly not used to these tones of authority from his son.

'As you will,' he said at last, shrugging his shoulders. 'Even with an acquittal it will be hard to keep the articles of apprenticeship, but with a sentence of imprisonment and perhaps a fine, too, neither Miss Pargeter nor her father will be in a position to indulge in philanthropy.'

He pulled out his watch and regarded the time with the same air of busy self-importance with which he had greeted Margaret yesterday.

'Come, Robert, we should already be on our way to Westminster.'

11 *In Court Again*

In court on Friday, Margaret saw the uses of worldly success. Dr. Kerridge and his brother, Sir Maurice, made a far more favourable impression on their hearers than her father had done a week ago, for they looked and spoke like men of consequence. The Crown lawyers, who had been content to doze or to whisper and smile among themselves while her father had read them *The New Jerusalem*, gave the physician and the Member of Parliament a respectful hearing; and the judge, to whom they addressed their eloquence, favoured them with his full attention. Watching their immediate effect upon their audience, Margaret felt grieved that her father, who seemed to her so much more worthy of regard, should have been so slighted by the court. And sadly—with a disillusionment beyond her years—she came to understand one of those shabby truths which belong to the adult world: most people accept you at your own valuation; think modestly of yourself, and the world will write you down a man of nought; consider yourself someone of importance and announce the fact in tones of authority, and it will accord you the respect that you regard as your due.

Sir Maurice Kerridge spoke first. He was a large-built, ponderous man, with a delivery that suited his appearance. He said that Stephen Pargeter, the prisoner awaiting sentence, was the son of the Reverend Doctor Percival Pargeter, a clergyman much respected in his time, not only as a scholar and a parish priest, but also as a friend of Sir Lionel Peake and a lifelong correspondent with the Duke of Godstowe on the subject of the scientific improvement of West Country grasslands.

Margaret did not quite understand what her grandfather's experiments in grass-sowing in his Devonshire glebe had to do with her father's case, but she noted the satisfaction with which Robert's uncle rolled out the names of the Duke and Sir Lionel Peake and the respectful buzz with which these were received.

'The late noble duke,' continued Sir Maurice, 'once gave it as his opinion that Dr. Pargeter's investigations into the properties of grasses might well come to be considered among the most beneficial to mankind of all the experiments in the sciences that were undertaken during the last century. The good doctor, my lord, was a gentleman of inestimable worth; a true patriot; a fine theologian; a bold investigator; a devoted shepherd of his flock; a true father. But in one respect, I submit, my lord, he was in part responsible for the sad occasion which has demanded our presence here in court today.'

Margaret caught a look of startled anger on her father's face. What could Sir Maurice mean?

Dr. Pargeter, he explained, had been an unworldly scholar and, like others of his kind, had been too absorbed in his studies and his parochial duties to pay a proper attention to his pecuniary affairs. Death had come suddenly to him in middle life. He had worked one hot hay harvest with greater zest than wisdom in collecting specimens of grass-seed in his glebe and had caught a chill and died. His improvidence had tragic results. His widow and son were left in poverty with a bare three hundred pounds to face the world.

Margaret glanced swiftly at Robert and saw that he looked almost as angry and embarrassed as her father. This public disclosure of family affairs seemed to her as pointless as it was humiliating. What could it possibly have to do with the writing of *The New Jerusalem*? She felt that Robert's uncle had in some way betrayed a trust; he must have learnt these facts from his father—facts that had been divulged only in the confidence of great friendship by her own father when he was young.

'This son,' continued Sir Maurice suavely, 'so fitted by intellect to have pursued a distinguished career at the University had his inheritance been less meagre, was apprenticed instead to a Plymouth printer and from the age of twenty-one had, by his own exertions, not only supported his mother in an honourable condition but had also begun to lay the foundations of a scholarship so wide and various that when he came to London in middle life and opened a bookshop in Holly Lane, men as eminent for their learning as the late Dr. Johnson and the late Mr. Edmund Burke had sought his acquaintance.'

The Member of Parliament lingered over the famous names with unctuous care.

'Fiddlesticks and bunkum!' Margaret heard Mr. Stone mutter behind her.

She turned round, and he whispered angrily in her ear:

'A baronet. A duke. And now Johnson and Burke. He'll call down the Archangel Michael next.'

Sir Maurice frowned across the court in their direction, then turned back towards the judge, cleared his throat, and began his peroration.

'Here, my lord, in this sad case before us, we see the results of a fine intellect and a noble heart lacking that discipline which should have been theirs by inheritance—I mean, the moderation and good judgement which a University instils into its sons. My old friend, I make bold to submit, stands convicted not so much of sedition as of an ungoverned enthusiasm—a want of political good sense. He is a gentleman. The son of a gentleman. The friend of some of the most eminent scholars of an earlier generation. Can I say more, my lord, to persuade you to show him mercy?'

Mr. Pargeter could scarcely control his indignation. His angry eyes blazed his scorn of so insulting a defence. Even to Margaret's untutored ears it sounded nonsense, and humiliating nonsense, at that. Sir Maurice had suggested that her father's most treasured ideals were the product of an ill-educated mind and that they were to be pardoned, it seems, because her grandfather had been an improvident friend of a baronet and had written letters on agriculture to a duke—and because her father, himself, had known Johnson and Burke. No wonder Mr. Stone was muttering 'Bunkum!' 'Fiddlesticks!' 'Pshaw!' into the back of her poke bonnet.

It was with relief that she watched Robert's father rise to his feet, for there was a briskness in his manner that promised speed and commonsense.

'My Lord,' he began, 'I have only three points to add to my brother's plea. First, my late father, James Kerridge, a City magistrate at the time of the anti-papist riots in 1780, often told me how much the parishes round St. Paul's owed to the wisdom and courage of Mr. Stephen Pargeter. During that terrible week, Mr. Pargeter went daily among the people, endeavouring to persuade them of the folly and criminality of their acts and, at great risk to his life, dissuaded them from still worse excesses of violence. Many, hearing his words, returned quietly to their homes.'

Margaret had never heard of this passage in her father's life, and she looked first at her father and then at Dr. Kerridge, her heart flooding with warmth and gratitude for the revelation.

'My father's old friend,' he continued, 'now stands convicted of having published a pamphlet with the intention of inciting that same mob to revolt. Such an intention, my lord, I submit is not in his character. He is a gentleman of ideas—a man of peace.'

Mr. Stone made a grunting noise of approval behind her.

'Secondly, I would deny those rumours which I have heard circulated in the City that Mr. Pargeter is a member of a Corresponding Society—one of those groups of disaffected citizens who combine to undermine the nation's strength in its war against the French. Mr. Pargeter's ideas are his own. He speaks for himself. Had he been a member of such a society, funds would have been forthcoming to fee a counsel; but, as your lordship knows, he has come before you as a poor man, pleading his own case.'

Dr. Kerridge threw back his fine head and, with the gesture of the most accomplished actor, collected the eyes of everyone in the court.

'Thirdly,' he said, turning again to the judge, 'I would remind you, my lord, that Mr. Pargeter has already suffered most grievously at the hands of those very people that he has been convicted of inciting to rebellion. His bookshop has been burnt, his house destroyed, and his family rendered homeless. This, I submit, is punishment enough for the writing of a pamphlet which, though innocent in intention, has justly received the condemnation of the court.'

The doctor sat down amid a buzz of appreciative whispers.

'A spare speech and a good one,' rumbled Mr. Stone in Margaret's ear.

The judge adjourned the court for three hours while he considered the submissions that had just been made to him.

It was a difficult three hours.

They spent them quietly and heroically, Margaret and her father, in a small sunny yard at the back of the court, both knowing that these might be their last few hours alone together for many weeks and each wishing to make them as calm and happy for the other as it was possible for them to be. They could not look forward to the days ahead, for the judge held their future in the palm of his hand. So they looked back on the past —on the times that had been happiest.

Mr. Pargeter, smiling at his daughter's grave and gentle face, remembered suddenly another Margaret who had been neither grave nor gentle—an impulsive, laughing, headstrong child of five—the Margaret that had gone with her brother and himself to the Frost Fair at Putney in 1789.

'Do you remember the Frost Fair, Meg?' he asked.

The Thames had frozen over to such a depth that people had set up booths on the ice, and roundabouts and puppet shows, and had roasted an ox and baited a bear far out in the middle of the stream.

Margaret wrinkled up her brow in remembrance.

'Yes, I remember,' she replied, her eyes catching again some of that magic of long ago.

The coloured flares from the booths had repeated themselves in the ice so that one did not know which was flame and which its reflection. It was a wonderful nonsense world of upside-down. In their reflections, people were walking the wrong way

111

up. And the cold and the brilliance and the iron ringing of skates on the ice and the loud hallooing in the winter air had intoxicated her so much that she had broken away from her father and run, laughing and wild, in and out among the booths, stooping to pick up the lights out of the frozen river.

'I slipped and bumped my head,' she smiled. 'And yelled and yelled.'

She remembered clearly now the magic and excitement of the shimmering scene and the surprise and anger of the bump. The lights in the ice had seemed to her a cruel cheat—not lights at all, but something hard and flat coming up out of the river to give her a staggering blow.

'It was the delight that I remembered, not the tears,' said her father gently. 'You enjoyed things so boldly, my dear.'

Margaret's memory glanced away to John at the Frost Fair. She saw him standing on the ice, a defiant, tousled boy of eight, his legs apart, his fists up ready to continue the fight that he had already lost, an angry bruise swelling to close his left eye.

'John fought a fight with a man, didn't he, Father?'

'Not a man. It was a boy. But a boy much bigger than himself—a great bully who had been thrashing his dog.'

'Poor Father,' smiled Margaret. 'What a day it must have been for you!'

'No. It was a good day, Meg. One does not mind drying the tears of the brave.'

They fell silent, thinking of John, slowly remembering the whole of him.

The yard was full of sparrows, for Margaret had crumbled up some of the bread and cheese which Mrs. Neech had sent in to them for their lunch, and the birds had gathered in a flurry from the roof eaves to peck the crumbs at her feet.

He had left them—sullen, confused, afraid. He had written no letter. Sent them no message. And yet he had once been brave!

Margaret's heart ached for her brother as she stared at the

birds and at their little, dark eyes, darting to right and left, sensing danger in every movement of her hand and in every shifting glance of the sunbeams playing on the paving stones. Their eyes and their heads were never still; they were pulsing with fear. Yet they continued to strut and peck and squabble all about her in the yard.

Mr. Pargeter had not spoken of his son since he had left him. He turned now to Margaret, taking her hand in his own.

'You must forgive him, Meg. And try to understand.'

'But I can't,' she said miserably. 'Can you?'

'Of course,' he said quietly. 'I know that John will come back to us one day. He will come back as himself—as resolute and unconquered as that boy on the ice.'

Though Mr. Pargeter was so hopeful about his son, he held no great hopes of his own immediate release.

He heard the sentence pronounced upon him with quiet resignation.

'Six months!' gasped Margaret.

She turned to Robert, hardly believing the words that she had heard.

All the humiliation of Sir Maurice's defence had been in vain!

Robert tried to steady her. He took her hand quickly. His understanding of her poured out of his eyes in a blue blaze, commanding her to be brave and accept this injustice.

'So, *this* is what courage means,' she thought. 'Enduring something that can't be endured.'

'It might have been worse,' rumbled Mr. Stone behind her. 'It might have been a year and a fine and his licence gone.'

Instead, it was six months in the county gaol at Ipswich and a curt order from the court that the bookseller 'henceforth keep silent and mind his own business'.

12 *Outward Bound*

Since the night of the fire, Margaret had turned more and more to Mr. Stone for advice and help in dealing with the practical matter of winding up her father's business. It was this gruff, sardonic old friend who had visited the offices of the fire insurance, who had sold Mr. Pargeter's few shares in Smith and Rawsthorne's paper mills, and who, with the money so raised, had paid his debts with the publishers and with the bookbindery behind Ludgate Hill. He had arranged for the storing of the kitchen furniture and the battered press and, with her father's consent, was in treaty with a brewery for the smouldering site of the shop.

It was he, moreover, who had told Margaret roundly that her childhood was now over. Whether or no her father went to prison, there was to be no more of her profitless dreaming over books. She would have to work.

'Dreaming's been the bane of the lot of you, Margaret,' he had barked.

'What shall I do for a living, Mr. Stone?' she had asked, perplexed. 'I have no accomplishments and I cannot sew.'

'Start a dame's school, girl,' had come the prompt reply. 'Set Mrs. Neech baking those beefsteak pies of hers and get Elijah to sell them round the streets. And heaven help you all.'

Dr. Kerridge, however, had other ideas.

On the afternoon of the day on which the judge passed sentence on her father, the doctor came to the booksellers' coffee house where they lodged and told her brusquely that she and Mrs. Neech and the boy had better spend the six months of her father's imprisonment at Herringsby. They would be but twenty miles from Ipswich and so would be able to visit him every week. And, since winter was approaching, a time when few visitors came to Herringsby, he—the doctor—would be able to procure rooms for them at no cost to themselves.

'It will not be a gay six months, Miss Pargeter,' he explained. 'In your circumstances you will scarcely feel like attending the winter assemblies. But we have a library in our little resort and some fine walks.'

'Can the three of us afford such a lazy life, sir? Mr. Stone thinks I should start a school.'

The doctor shrugged his shoulders.

'That idle young apprentice of your father's can pick up a penny or two with the fisherfolk,' he replied. 'And Mrs. Neech, if she has a mind, can get plain sewing in the houses in Montpellier Crescent.'

'And me? What can I do?'

Dr. Kerridge considered the matter a full thirty seconds with his back turned to her, staring out of the window.

'Young ladies, Miss Pargeter, are not expected to do anything in such cases,' he said at last. 'Apply yourself to your needle, worship your Maker, and keep yourself in health. That is all that your father can expect of you in the next few months.'

He turned towards her, unsmiling, with the same cold gleam in his eyes that she had seen the first night that they had met.

The gleam repelled her.

'Well?' he asked almost sharply. 'What do you think of my plan?'

Poor Margaret!

She had left the court that morning feeling full of gratitude towards him for his able defence of her father, and had she met him immediately afterwards she would have thanked him with all the flowing warmth of her warm heart. But now—now when the moment had come for a sober acknowledgement of her debt to him—the words stuck in her throat. Dr. Kerridge seemed quite different from the dazzling figure in the witness-box, and she knew that it was herself—she, Margaret—that had brought about this change. His cold 'Miss Pargeter' froze her. He had made a sensible suggestion and a kind one in inviting them to Herringsby. Yet she felt rejected and hurt. She sensed his antagonism towards her and could not understand it. She had never met anyone who actively disliked her before, and the shock of it numbed her.

'Thank you, sir, for your suggestion,' she heard herself say stiffly. 'I will ask my father tonight if he wishes us to accept it.'

He bowed and took his leave.

She watched him pass along the street outside the window and wondered why it was that he could not accept her as his old friend's daughter—as just seventeen and in trouble and needing the warmth of a friendly smile.

'Perhaps Mr. Stone is right,' she thought bleakly. 'My childhood is over, and he's treating me as one grown-up treats another.'

It was scarcely a cheerful foretaste of adult life.

She made up her mind to refuse Dr. Kerridge's offer, for she hated to be beholden to such a man. Yet, when she broached the matter with her father, she found that it was not nearly so easy to refuse as she had thought. His enthusiasm for the plan should not have surprised her. For all his courage, he felt lonely, old, and shamed. He was about to set out for Ipswich alone, cut off from his family, bereft of his home, his reputation gone. He needed her desperately. And the prospect of seeing her every week during his imprisonment so raised his spirits that Margaret had not the heart to tell him her misgivings.

'He is a good man, Margaret,' he exclaimed. 'He is paying his debt of friendship a hundredfold. A hundredfold!'

'But ought we to accept his money, Father?'

'To the extent of the rent? Why not?'

Why not, indeed? Money meant very little to her father, as she well knew. And his morality in money matters matched the unimportance that he attached to it. If one had money, one gave it to one's friends in need, and if one had no money, one accepted it from the friends who offered it. It was as simple as that.

'But, Father, we shall lie in his debt!'

'We all lie in one another's debt, Meg,' he said cheerfully. 'That's the beauty of life.'

The more he thought of the plan, the more pleasure it gave

him.

'Herringsby is capital, my dear! It will put the roses back in your cheeks. You will grow plump and pink in the sea air. And think of Elijah! He will grow so stout and strong that I shall not recognize him in six months' time.'

Margaret felt trapped. Trapped by her love for her father. Trapped by his need for her. Trapped by the common sense of Dr. Kerridge's suggestion.

Yet, she did not give in without a struggle. She could not ask Robert for help; it seemed unfair to ask Mrs. Neech to settle her trouble; so she went to Mr. Stone.

He heard her out with attention.

'He pays the rent, you say?' he asked.

She nodded.

'He can well afford it,' he barked.

'But, I don't like him, Mr. Stone,' she said miserably. 'And I don't want to sit idly by for six months and do nothing to help. I'd much rather work here in London as you suggested that I should.'

The book-dealer brushed aside her protest.

'And it's twenty miles from your father, you say?'

Margaret nodded again.

'And they'll take you to see him?'

'So he says.'

'Then there's nothing for you to do but accept.'

The crusty old man looked down almost gently into her rebellious, unhappy face.

'Your father has little else left to him but you, Margaret,' he said. 'It's your duty to go where you're near him.'

Then he chuckled softly as he rubbed his dry hands together.

'Especially when it's his precious godson that's put you in the way of it,' he smiled.

Elijah was all agog for the countryside and the sea; like Margaret, he had never seen a stretch of water wider than a reach of the Thames. And even Mrs. Neech found a sound, practical reason to approve of the scheme.

'I don't hold with the sea myself, Miss Margaret. But you can live very cheap off fish, they say. And it's money we'll be having to think of till your father comes home.'

Robert alone of all their little circle frowned when Margaret told him the news. They were walking, as was their custom, in the little churchyard beside the coffee house late in the evening, before they went to bed.

'My father suggested it himself?' he asked her sharply.

'Yes.'

He walked on in silence beside her, his face in the shadows taut with dismay and disappointment and with a mounting fear for the future rising in his heart. He knew his father. He knew the courage that was needed to stand against him. He wanted to shout aloud, 'Meg, don't go. Stay here in London. I don't want you to go.' But he had no right to command where she went. He knew that he had no right. And he knew, too, that it was her duty to go where she was near her father—her loving duty. If she did not perform that duty she would come to despise herself and despise him, too, for persuading her to stay.

The longer he kept silent the more distressed Margaret grew. Robert had never been one to be short for words before. Indeed, it was his quickness of thought and word that she loved. Yet now, when it was so easy for him to protest or to say, 'Meg, I shall miss you,' or 'Meg, we must write,' he said nothing at all. He just frowned and clenched tight his fists.

'You'll be down there for Christmas, won't you?' she asked bleakly, her mind's eye surveying the arid waste of the autumn weeks.

'Yes, Meg,' he sighed at last, joyless and grey. 'I'll be at Herringsby for Christmas.'

Suddenly she could bear it no longer. She turned from him quickly and ran out of the churchyard and up to her room. She felt bitterly hurt and angry with Robert.

Why could he not say that he loved her?

. . . . . .

Throughout the week in which Mr. Pargeter had awaited sentence, the rumours of peace negotiations with France grew more and more circumstantial, and a few days after Mr. Pargeter was taken down to Suffolk, late on the evening of October 1st, Mr. Stone hurried in from the Strand with news that the preliminaries for a treaty had been signed that night at Lord Hawkesbury's office in Downing Street.

'Pray God the price of bread goes down!' exclaimed Mrs. Neech.

Next morning, the poorer people of London did not stop at pious hope. They were certain that the coming peace would bring better times for them and they thronged the streets in tumultuous rout, singing, shouting, many of them drunk, rejoicing that the long winters of starvation were at an end.

'So Father was right and John was wrong,' Margaret thought. 'Poor John! He won't get his glory after all.'

Nothing had turned out as the Pargeters had planned. Her father's *New Jerusalem* had landed him in prison. John had run away to a stupid life of drills and dress parades. And she was off to Herringsby without knowing whether Robert wanted their close friendship to continue.

Yet, life went on. The history of nations continued to be written.

At noon on October 10th, while Margaret and Elijah and Mrs. Neech were packing the last of their belongings for the sea passage to Herringsby, the crowd in Bond Street took out the horses of General Lauriston's carriage and drew Napoleon's envoy in triumph to Downing Street. In the afternoon, as the three of them sat in the cart which was taking them to Wapping, they heard the boom of the guns in the Park and at the Tower.

'It's signed,' smiled Mrs. Neech with satisfaction.

And, as the brig *Marianna* of Aldeburgh slipped down the great river with the ebb tide, the night sky was suddenly pierced with rockets and bursting stars.

'Look! Look!' exclaimed Elijah in astonished joy. 'Look at the flowers in the sky!'

There had been few occasions for rejoicing in his short life, and he had never seen fireworks before.

Looking down into his eager, upturned face, Margaret suddenly ached with envy at his happiness. She wished that she could re-awaken her own faculty for such self-forgetting joy.

Two days later they awaited their first sight of Herringsby.

All morning the brig had tacked laboriously up a sluggish river lying parallel with the sea; only a narrow ridge of shingle and sandy beach, indeed, separated them from the grey sweep of the North Sea, while inland on their left the marsh stretched away flat and treeless to a long, low height. The two masts of the brig were the tallest things in all that level scene, so that in some strange way the vessel seemed to dominate the land—as the sea and the things of the sea have always dominated this eastern English outpost.

Margaret and Elijah were disappointed with the river. It was no proper way to approach a sea resort, they thought. They had expected rocks and cliffs and a lighthouse and a harbour bar; and, instead, they were slowly winding through a grey-green marshy waste that was more like the featureless sea of the last few days than any English countryside they had ever dreamed about.

'Did you ever see such a coast as this?' exclaimed Margaret in exasperation. 'It's nothing but pebbles and water and reeds.'

How *could* Robert love his Suffolk so?

As she stood on the deck of the brig looking right over the top of the shingle strand at the sea, she felt bleak and exposed and far too tall.

'I wish there were some people about,' said Elijah, his teeth chattering in the north wind.

An hour ago, they had passed two men in a low punt dredging for oysters and, a little later, a child waving to them from a deserted, grass-grown staithe; on the low height they could see cows and a farmhouse and a man ploughing a wide field. But to their London eyes, Suffolk looked absolutely empty.

'Where do you think they've all gone to?' Elijah asked.

'Perhaps it's dinner time.'

Margaret knew this was a silly remark; it was only ten o'clock. She knew, too, that she had said it to cheat herself. It was a great shock to her that the countryside was so large and lacking in people.

Mrs. Neech's opinion of Suffolk was confined to her tempered relief that the *Marianna* had left the high sea and was now beating up the quieter waters of the river. She lay in the low cabin of the brig with her eyes closed, trying to forget the indignity of her recent seasickness and to summon up the courage needed to face their new mode of life. In this she was not being very successful, for her physical discomfort and her fears for the future combined to depress her exceedingly and to give her a headache. The closeness of the narrow cabin stifled her, and the slight shifting of the bales of cotton and the crates of china in the hold each time the *Marianna* changed its tack filled her with alarm; she felt sure that at any moment the vessel would heel over and capsize. She resented being frightened in this way; she resented feeling unwell; but, most of all, she resented the shame of the coming months at Herringsby. In Holly Lane she had been Mr. Pargeter's housekeeper—a woman of character and purpose—with a duty to perform; she had known her worth, and her neighbours had known it, too. In Suffolk, she and Margaret and Elijah would be objects of pity—the helpless dependants of a man who had been sent to prison. Every nobody in Herringsby would have the right to look down upon them. It was a terrible prospect for anyone as proud as Mrs. Neech.

Margaret and Elijah watched her prostration of the last two days with wonder and concern. Margaret had held a bowl for her and had cooled her head with damp cloths and had done everything she could think of to make her more comfortable, marvelling all the time that the gentle motion of the sea should so quickly change the stern mentor of her childhood into someone as humanly vulnerable as herself. It gave her a fresh pang of remorse that she had taken so long to discover that Mrs. Neech must be very much like everyone else; and she vowed that in future things should be different between them.

Elijah's astonishment had been of shorter life. So many extraordinary things had happened to him in the last few weeks that Mrs. Neech's sudden collapse soon found its place among the other queer surprises that were stored away in his mind. In the cabin he had done what Margaret had told him to do, and then he had gone up on deck and stared at something which was infinitely more astonishing to him—the unbelievably vast and heaving *dullness* of the sea. Its huge monotony had not only amazed him; it had made him want to howl.

On its next port tack, the brig entered another reach of the river where two sloops and a hoy were bearing down on them, sailing fast before the wind. Margaret and Elijah had watched their sails approaching for the last quarter of an hour, winding slowly towards them across the green marsh, as though they were gliding over the land. Now, as they rounded the corner, the foremost vessel was suddenly upon them, not twenty yards away, its prow cleaving a deep furrow in the water and its sails spread wide across the channel.

'We're going to crash,' screeched Elijah in joy.

Someone shouted a warning, and the brig swung sharply into the wind, so that its sails emptied and hung loose and flapped. The noises about them were startling; ropes rattled in cleats; a crate of crockery lurched over below decks, and everyone on the river either shouted or cursed or laughed. As the *Marianna* drifted sideways into the reeds and the down-coming vessels ploughed heavily past, their crews greeted the crew of the brig in strange, broad cries that ended abruptly high up in the scale. Margaret could not understand a word they said, but she caught the racy tang of that intimate world from which women are always shut out—the rough fraternity of men following the same hard trade. Elijah caught it, too, and he watched the stern of the hoy disappearing downstream in the wake of the sloops, suddenly homesick for the raucous cries of the London streets.

He hated the emptiness of the sea and the silence of the marsh.

Ahead of them, however, the landscape was filling with sails, and as they beat upstream against the wind and tide they met every kind of small coastal craft coming down the river. They were all bound for London, a seaman said, with their holds full of cheeses and barley and wheat.

'That's Herringsby,' he told them just before noon, pointing to a low cliff nearly two miles away.

Margaret followed the line of the shingle till she came to a lighthouse.

'Why, it's got a lighthouse, after all.'

'Aye, Miss, and a shipyard and a fishing fleet and a great church.'

'And big houses, too,' exclaimed Elijah, catching the glint of sunshine in large window-panes along the top of the cliff.

'Aye, boy, and the grand folk ha'e builded themselves a prom'nade.'

'What's that for?'

The seaman scratched his head.

'That's the wonder, boy. They just walks on it—up and down, up and down—slow and stately-like—as grand folk do.'

'Don't they do anything else?'

The seaman thought for a little, his brow puckering up in bewildered amusement as he considered the pastimes of the rich.

'Well,' he said slowly, 'the ladies puts their children up on Sam Tillett's donkey and pays him for takin' 'em for a ride. And the gentlemen—the gentlemen walks to Aldemere Cove and takes off all their fine clothes and splashes naked in the sea.'

With each tack in their slow approach, the features of Herringsby became more and more distinct. Margaret could see quite plainly now the roofs of the new Crescent built on the cliff above the huddled little river port; and through the newly planted shrubberies on the height she caught a glimpse every now and again of gleaming stucco façades, fine bow windows, and imposing porticos. This was Dr. Kerridge's Herringsby, she thought. The houses bore his easy grace; they were the kind of houses in which a Kerridge should be born.

Seventy feet below, about the ancient quay, stretched the warehouses and timber yards and coal heaps of quite a different world—a world dominated by the two great ships perched high in the air on stocks, their long keels level with the roofs of the shipwrights' shacks and their half-completed bulwarks towering above the little port. The smell of the place came to them across the water—a compound of new-sawn wood and tar and burning lime. The smell, more than anything else, filled her with a dreadful sense of foreboding. It was a good smell of its kind: an honest, working smell. But it could never belong to the people on the cliff. Herringsby was a town of two nations: the two nations that her father had so often talked about. And here, in Suffolk, seventy feet of sandy cliff stood between them.

'Where is it that you're stayin' in Herrin'sby, Miss?' asked the seaman who had talked to them before.

'We have rooms with Mrs. Dunnett in the Rope Walk.'

He looked at her in surprise.

'I thought you'd be for the grand houses in the Crescent,' he said.

Margaret smiled as she shook her head.

Yet, under the smile, the most painful thoughts were assailing her. She had never really understood the social distinctions before. Her father's bookshop had been a true democracy. But now, in this river view of Herringsby, she saw with perfect clarity the physical fact of the two nations and the physical barrier that stood between them. Robert and his family belonged to the new town at the top of the cliff. Dr. Kerridge had placed her firmly in the little port and humble fishing village at its foot. He had seen to it that seventy feet of sandstone—an insurmountable wall of social difference—stood between them. And, remembering his attitude to her in London, she could not believe that this had been done without design. He had brought her down to Suffolk to show her the gulf that lay between herself and his son—and the impossibility of a closer friendship between them than the one he had already suspected.

Margaret winced with pain, for with a cruel twist of memory she had suddenly recalled Robert's strained, unhappy face that evening in the churchyard.

Was this cliff, then, the cause of his silence and his drawing away?

Twenty minutes later, as she waited on the quay for the doctor to come to them, she was sure that she had interpreted that gentleman's intentions aright. He had wanted to take her away from Robert, to put the whole of Essex and half Suffolk between them; and he had also wanted to humiliate her—to show her how presumptuous had been her dreams.

Dr. Kerridge had left his carriage on the road above the quay and, seeing them waiting for him, had raised his hat. Then he had stopped to talk to a harbour official and then walked slowly on and stopped again, this time dragging out the minutes in easy conversation with a red-faced farmer in a stout frieze coat. Then he was lost to sight behind the casks of butter and piles of hard, yellow cheeses awaiting shipment, and a little later emerged quite close beside them busily engaged with yet a third acquaintance. He was clearly in no hurry to come to them. He was taking his time—as one can with people of no account.

Margaret blushed with pain. His insufferable dawdling had forcefully brought home to her the humiliating penalties of 'not being in society'.

'Don't poke your head down, Miss Margaret,' hissed Mrs. Neech sharply. 'No Pargeter ever poked.'

Now that she was on dry land again, Mrs. Neech was ready for Herringsby. It looked a poor sort of place, she thought, after London. And, feeling so much more herself, she glared at the scene in front of her, determined to out-snub the whole of Suffolk, should the need arise.

Margaret looked at her and smiled through a blur of tears.

Then she stuck out her chin, like her father, and walked across the quay to Dr. Kerridge.

'Mrs. Neech is tired,' she said, interrupting his conversation. 'We should be grateful to you, sir, if you would take us to our lodgings without delay.'

The colour stood high in her cheeks.

13 *Herringsby*

After such a reception, Margaret and Mrs. Neech expected nothing but humiliation to await them in Herringsby. But here they were wrong, for Suffolk was neither kinder nor more cruel than the London that they had left behind. Indeed, like the great city, it was completely indifferent to their fate. If Margaret and the housekeeper and the boy from the tenement brought their past with them, that was their affair—not Herringsby's.

Herringsby had far worse troubles on its mind.

Dr. Kerridge drove them past the new fortifications and the great flint church and the row of old shops and *The Royal George*, where the assemblies were held, and out along the causeway to that part of the town which is oldest and poorest and most at the mercy of the winter storms, where the masts of the fishing-boats drawn up on the beach rise from behind the roofs of the fishermen's shacks and where the sea seems to climb like a wall up into the sky.

The coachman reined in his horses half-way down the Rope Walk.

'Well, Miss Pargeter,' said the doctor, 'here we are. You will find Mrs. Dunnett a good, honest woman. A widow. Husband killed last year in an accident on the beach. Not a lively lodging for you; but it is clean.'

Margaret thanked him.

They had stopped in front of a neat, white-washed cottage with a pile of pale driftwood spars heaped up beside the step, and the coachman had jumped down and opened the carriage door for Mrs. Neech to step out on to the pavement, but before Margaret could follow suit, the doctor detained her for a moment with his hand.

'It will be a week or so before you receive word from your father,' he said in a low voice. 'And a month, perhaps, before you

127

are allowed to visit him in prison. New regulations, I'm told.'

Margaret nodded, and he let her go.

'Mrs. Kerridge will call upon you within the next few days, Miss Pargeter,' he said in clear, cold, ringing tones, as the carriage drew away.

Standing in the windy street, she sighed with relief that he was gone.

A sad, brown-eyed woman had opened the cottage door and was standing on her step, looking down at her guests.

'Are there no more of your things to come from the *Marianna*?' their landlady asked, seeing only the five small bundles at their feet.

The quiet voice sounded more resigned than curious.

'Mr. Pargeter's home was burnt down,' said Mrs. Neech.

Mrs. Dunnett gave the faintest of troubled sighs.

'You'll be tired then, and wanting a dish of tea.'

It was such a strangely insufficient reply that Margaret wondered at first whether the landlady had understood what Mrs. Neech had said. Was a dish of tea the answer to a lost home?

And yet, why not?

What else could this poor, defeated woman do to comfort them?

'I'll show you the rooms and the parlour,' she said, 'and then leave you to yourselves.'

The cottage inside was as small and neat as the living-quarters on board a ship, the rooms upstairs being more like ships' berths than bedrooms and the parlour below no bigger or higher than the *Marianna*'s cabin. But, unlike the brig, Mrs. Dunnett's home was filled with a peculiarly hard, brilliant daylight. It rippled on the low ceiling of the parlour in such a strange way that Elijah stared up at it with his mouth open.

'It's the waves,' the landlady explained, taking the boy to the window.

And there, not twenty yards away, the latest wave of the wide ocean was breaking gently on the foreshore. As they watched, it licked slowly forward and then withdrew with a faint rattle of tiny stones. All the view was taken up with the sky and the glinting sea and the narrow strip of beach.

'How lovely!' murmured Margaret, watching the next wave and the next and the next slowly rolling forward and bursting softly on the shingle.

It was not lovely. That was not the right word. The scene was too huge and empty and sad—too sudden an extension of the mind for someone who had spent her life in Holly Lane. But its vastness and the brilliance of the light filled her with an aching pleasure that was almost pain. Here was something, she thought, that she would live with day and night for the next six months. Here was something that Robert loved.

'It's pretty enough now, Miss Pargeter,' said the quiet voice at her elbow, 'but it's not always like this.'

'No?'

'There's the fogs and the winter storms.'

A new quality of resignation had come into Mrs. Dunnett's voice.

'Terrible times for the men at sea,' she said.

Margaret looked quickly into her patient, careworn face.

'There's nights, my dear, when one knows what the preacher means when he speaks of the Wrath of God.'

Mrs. Neech shuddered. She had had enough of the sea in the last few days and, pride or no pride, she felt tired and dejected and ill.

'Come along both of you,' she said sharply when Mrs. Dunnett had brought in the tray and left them alone. 'Leave mooning there and come to your tea.'

Unlike Margaret and Elijah, who were still staring out of the window, Mrs. Neech had sat down heavily in the only armchair, with her back turned resolutely upon the beach.

'Wouldn't it be nicer to look at the view?' asked Margaret, taking some sugar, too full of the wonder of the breaking waves to have noticed the expression on the housekeeper's face.

'What view?'

'Why, the sea.'

'That's not a view,' snapped Mrs. Neech. 'It's just salt water. And it's far too close for my comfort.'

Margaret, however, in those first few days found the nearness of the sea a great solace to her. That same evening, as she and Elijah ran along the wet sand at the waves' edge, she learned the savour of the sea's salt tang and laughed at the taste of salt in her mouth. And that first night, as she lay awake in her narrow bed, listening to the soft thud of the waves on the shore and the quiet sifting and jingling of the small stones as the water drew back, she felt calmed and soothed by the mighty rhythm that had come into her life. Faintly, in the dawn, the sounds of the boats setting out for the fishing grounds entered her dreams, and she heard, through the mists of sleep, the shouts of the men, the squeak of the oars in the rowlocks, and the splash of their blades in the sea. They consoled her in some odd way for the loss of all those familiar, early-morning noises that she had loved so much in Holly Lane.

Next morning, Elijah dragged her not unwillingly to the stretch of beach north of the Rope Walk, where the roadway petered out in a sweep of shingle littered with fish baskets, torn nets, rejected spars, broken oars, and the battered hulks of old boats—all the castaway outworn gear of a people too strenuously occupied in scraping a living from the sea to notice the rubbish they left about them on the shore. Here, the neat cottages gave way to shaggy, round, turf huts, in front of which the fishwives stood, gutting the morning catch.

It was a squalid, smelly scene, and Elijah, hearing the raucous shouts of the women and the high shrieks of the boys as they ran in and out among the huts, let go of Margaret's hand and ran forward by himself. His eyes were bright. He stopped by the water's edge and stared in wonder at the boys jumping in and out of little boats and rowing themselves round and round in small circles, laughing and shouting and knocking up the water with the flat of the oars to wet their friends. He watched, too, when a high-pitched cry warned them that a fisherman had left

The Old Ship and was coming to reclaim his boat. Then they rowed hard for the beach, grinding the keels deep into the shingle, dropped the oars, and fled pell-mell among the turf huts, the shrieks of the fishwives pursuing them as they knocked over baskets and scattered the stinking heaps of fish-heads.

Margaret sighed and turned away. It was Elijah's world; not hers. She could never find forgetfulness in Elijah's childish joys.

As she walked back along the Rope Walk, she held her head high, with an expression in her eyes that seemed to say 'Here I am and I feel perfectly at ease'. But, inwardly, she was beset with a heaviness such as she had never known before. She felt numb and hollow and utterly cast down, the true nature of her plight, now that the excitement of the voyage was over, having at last come home to her.

Her father was in prison; John, goodness knew where; Robert silent and in London; Mrs. Neech shut away in the fastnesses of middle-age; and Elijah but a child. She was alone, entirely alone, in her distress—a distress that was personal and private and peculiar to herself.

She saw it all clearly now.

In her lowest moments, that dreary second day, she was torn with terrible doubts, wondering wretchedly whether the doctor were not right: that there was no hope for her happy dream. She saw Robert faced at Christmastide with the Herringsby cliff and drawing farther and farther away from her. Her love for him had been too sudden, too rash; she had never considered his career or thought of his family or of the world to which he had been born. Then, having reached the bottom of despair—with no letter from him and no visit from his mother— she struggled painfully to the surface again, reproaching herself bitterly for her lack of courage and sick at heart at the utter selfishness of her grief.

She remembered her father.

How could she ever forget his cold, lonely vigil in Ipswich Gaol?

Her distress was nothing to his.

Full of compunction, she sat down and wrote him a letter, giving him the most cheerful account of their situation that she could manage. Mrs. Dunnett was kind, she wrote, and the rooms were both comfortable and clean. Elijah had spent most of the day playing with the boys on the beach and had come home with his pockets full of winkles, which they had eaten for supper—pulling them out of their shells with a pin. Mrs. Neech was putting a patch in one of the landlady's sheets. They were all in good health and longed for news. Please would he write as soon as he could.

During the night, lying awake listening to the thudding of the waves, she remembered her despair and, to give herself courage, she tried to cling to the knowledge that she was living in Robert's Suffolk and to the belief that if she could only come to love this bleak, inhospitable land which was so much a part of him, then she would be able to find something to comfort her in the harshness of her plight.

She listened gratefully to the rhythmic pounding of the waves and knew that it was not enough to love the sea.

She must learn to accept Herringsby itself.

Next day, full of determination, she walked back to the river port and watched two pleasure skiffs sailing upstream towards Snape and tried to imagine Robert's delight as a boy, sailing on these quiet, inland waters. He had loved sailing. He had loved riding on the heath, too, so he had once said. So she climbed the steep cliff path to the open land behind the upper town and brushed through the dying heather, her dress catching in the stiff fronds of bracken and ling.

But, everywhere, Robert eluded her. She could think only of the London Robert—the Robert whom she had come to love in Holly Lane.

The heath meant nothing to her. It was cold and gaunt and grey; the dead heather bells rattled mournfully in the light wind; and the whole wide sweep of country seemed desolate with the dying year.

She could not understand why his Suffolk had so little to say to her.

On the fourth day—still waiting for a letter from London and for the visit from Mrs. Kerridge—Margaret decided to face the worst that Herringsby had to show. In the early dusk, she walked up the carriage road to the upper town. At that hour the place would be deserted, Mrs. Dunnett had told her, because the grand folk dined at half-past four.

It was a dull evening, for a sea scud muffled the shore and dropped dolefully from the laurels on the height and, as she stood on the edge of the pavement in the middle of the Crescent, she shivered in her thin dress and cloak. Mrs. Dunnett had been right. There was no one about. She could stand and stare at this fashionable upper town for as long as she liked.

They were fine houses. They were new and elegant and clean. The justness of their proportions, the height of their windows, the generous width of the front doors, their whole air of quiet good-breeding pleased her in spite of herself. People in those beautiful houses, she thought, must live very ordered, sheltered lives. The ladies belonging to those upstairs drawing-rooms, now shuttered against the night, could know nothing of rubbing orchid root and serving saloop or hiding the *Rights of Man* behind the sermons. They had never seen a London bread riot or listened for the daily cry of *Dust O! Bring out your Dust!*

As she stood quite still, letting the sounds of the place come to her, she could hear nothing but the distant murmur of the sea and the ceaseless soft dripping of mist in the shrubberies.

The very silence of the upper town set it apart from the life that she had known in Holly Lane.

Despondently, she completed the curve of Montpellier Crescent and entered King's Parade. This was where the Kerridges lived. Many of the houses were older here, and they stood back in their own gardens, among low trees blown crooked by the east wind. She caught sight of the words *The Grove*, lettered on a

133

stone gate-post and, with her heart beating quicker, she looked up the carriage sweep at a solid, four-square gentleman's residence. So *this* was where the Doctor lived! *This* was where Robert had spent his childhood! She looked numbly across the green carpet of lawn and imagined herself walking up the stone steps and standing under the high, pillared porch, waiting for a butler to open the door. Then she hurried past the gateway, afraid of being seen. A second later, however, she stopped by the garden railings and looked over the top of the low bushes at the upstairs windows. Robert's bedroom must have been there, she thought. As a child, he must have gazed out of one of those high, chill windows and looked at the sea.

Trying to recapture what he must have seen, she turned her back to the house and looked in the same direction. The sky and the sea were merged in a single, indistinguishable, grey blur. As she stood there, with the width of the road between herself and the edge of the cliff, she gasped at the emptiness of the view. She suddenly realized that she could see nothing of the Rope Walk or the shacks or the boats drawn up on the beach. They were too directly below her.

She realized, too, what the emptiness meant.

It meant that for the people who lived in King's Parade the fishing-village of Herringsby might never have existed. Out of sight, out of mind. The two nations did not even share the same landscape.

It seemed to her, at that moment, that she knew the worst.

And, sensibly, having learnt and understood the worst, she gathered her cloak more tightly about her and walked thoughtfully home.

14 *A Wet Afternoon*

'Handsome is as handsome does!' ejaculated Mrs. Neech a week later, pursing up her lips in an expression of extreme severity.

Robert's mother still had not called upon Margaret, and she interpreted this not only as an insult to the Pargeters but also as an indictment of the entire Suffolk gentry.

'Stiff-necked, narrow-minded, purse-proud, country nobodies!' she muttered angrily under her breath, seized afresh with a passionate loyalty to the old bookseller whom she had served so long and still understood so little.

'I don't hold with folks,' she continued aloud, jabbing her needle viciously into her sewing, 'who promise one thing and do another.'

Margaret, however, to whom these words were largely addressed, sat watching the spurts and flares of the driftwood fire, a smile of complete abstraction playing over her face, singularly unmoved by the insult that had been offered to her family. Indeed, it was clear to the least observant of companions that she had heard scarcely anything that the housekeeper had said. Her thoughts were miles away. Outside, the waves were thundering on the shore, and squalls of rain smacked against the window panes and rattled the frames. If she were conscious at all of her surroundings, it was to know that it was good to be inside, warm and quiet, hugging the happiness that the day's post had brought.

Robert had written at last.

The single sheet of his letter creaked stiffly in her bodice whenever she breathed, and its crackle and bulge so close to her heart made her want to laugh with joy.

Robert was there—as close as he could possibly be.

'Within the week, the doctor said,' burst out Mrs. Neech, as she returned to the attack, 'and it's near a fortnight since we came. It's not right, Miss Margaret. Not kind. Nor just.'

'Perhaps she has a cold,' murmured Margaret at last, dragged back unwillingly from Robert to the little parlour in the Rope Walk.

'She could send you a note, then.'

Poor Mrs. Neech had washed and ironed Margaret's best dress and steamed out the dents in the poke bonnet which it had received when it had been thrown out of the window on the night of the fire; she had even washed and curled the child's hair, in an excess of concern for her outward appearance— something she had never much bothered herself about before. And all had been in vain. Her bonny Miss Margaret was to be rejected.

'She could have sent you a message,' she continued bitterly. 'They've got five servants inside the house, Mrs. Dunnett says, and a coachman and a gardener and a boy. Don't tell me she couldn't have spared *someone* to bring you a civil word!'

Margaret sighed very softly. If she kept absolutely quiet, she thought, perhaps Mrs. Neech would stop.

She wanted to repeat the words of Robert's hurried, un-studied note over and over again to herself—imagine Robert speaking them, and the expression on his face as he spoke the words.

Dearest Meg,

I miss you so much. Please write. Try to forgive me for parting with you as I did.

Robert.

It was so little that he had said. And yet, surely, surely it was enough to give her hope?

She lost herself in happy thought.

Very slowly, the sounds of that autumn afternoon crept back into her hearing: the stray sputter of the dying rain against the window; the low boom of the sea; the crackle of the fire; the soft rasping of Mrs. Neech's thread as she pulled it through the stout cloth of the curtain she was sewing. And, shaking herself from her dream, she was back in Herringsby in Mrs. Dunnett's cabin parlour.

'She might even have sent the Doctor himself,' declared the housekeeper.

'Who might?' asked Margaret, puzzled.

'Mrs. Kerridge, of course,' snapped Mrs. Neech. 'I do believe you haven't been listening to a word I've said.'

'Yes, I have,' replied Margaret quickly. 'At least, I think I have.'

'Then, you've no proper pride,' cried the housekeeper with a sudden break in her voice. 'No pride at all.'

Margaret looked at her in consternation. Mrs. Neech's face was crumpling up in grief.

'You've forgotten your father and your mother were born as good as them,' she choked.

Margaret jumped up and flung her arms round her neck.

'But it's barely more than a week, Mrs. Neech. It's not twelve days. She'll come in her good time. I know she will. She's Robert's mother, Mrs. Neech. I *know* she'll come.'

She pulled out her handkerchief clumsily and started drying the poor woman's tears.

'Don't grieve so,' she smiled. 'I don't.'

Mrs. Neech had never been caught in tears before. It was worse than the seasickness. And she snatched the damp handkerchief out of Margaret's hand and blew her nose fiercely as though it were a trumpet. Margaret went over to the window and stayed staring at the glistening beach till she heard the soft rasping of the thread being pulled through the cloth again.

It was such an embarrassing reversal of their roles that Elijah's kicks on the parlour door and his sudden bursting into the room was the greatest relief to them both.

'It's from Ipswich,' he shouted, his voice still pitched for the beach, and thrust a letter into Margaret's hand. 'It came with the carrier that stops at *The Royal George*.'

It was a letter from Mr. Pargeter—the one thing in the world that could have made Mrs. Neech forget her humiliation.

Margaret hurriedly broke the seal and read it hungrily to herself. She had longed for news of her father almost as much as she had longed for news from Robert.

Ipswich County Gaol.   October 14th, 1801.

My dear child,

It is only today that I have been given permission to write to you, so I hasten to tell you that I am well and in good heart and that your letter of a week ago brought me great comfort and joy. My true grief on coming here was the fear that you and Mrs. Neech and Elijah were ill-provided-for at Herringsby, but what you have told me has put me more at ease. Should you find yourselves in need, you must spend your mother's money. Write to Mr. Baltimore; he will tell you what to do.

For the rest, we must all use this sentence passed upon us in the best way possible. For me, it is easy. This is one of Mr. Howard's new model prisons, and my cell is light and dry and airy. Best of all, it is mine alone. It is no bad thing, Meg, for a man to be shut up with himself for a few months of his life. It concentrates his thoughts and shows him that there are imperfections in his own company that he had not realized before. We are none of us idle. This, too, is Howard's doing. The other prisoners make baskets, pick oakum, or sew sacks. I am today allowed paper and pens, and think that I shall set about finishing that Booksellers' History that I began when you were seven years old.

It is less easy for you, this exile. But I want you all to use it well. Meg, I want you to take to your needle. A woman must sew her husband's shirts. Mrs. Neech will help you. And get her to teach you pastry-making, too. A girl who is only book-wise makes an unhandy wife. And Meg, I want you to teach Elijah not only to read, but also to write and to add and subtract. Teach him in the evenings or when it rains. When it is fine, push him out of doors to play with other boys. When I open my new bookshop, I want an apprentice who can stand up for himself like a man—not a scared waif who clutches at women's petticoats.

And being in so bold and demanding a mood, I have something to beg of Mrs. Neech, as well. Ask her, please, to knit me some stout stockings and a pair of mittens as soon as she can. It is not Mr. Howard's fault. It is my age. Old men need to be out and about to keep themselves warm, and that is not possible here.

The prison governor says I may receive a visitor here a month after my coming—so I shall look for you round All Souls.

Give my love to Mrs. Neech and Elijah.

Bless you, dearest child,
Your loving,
Father.

Margaret handed the letter to Mrs. Neech.

'He writes to us all, really,' she said gently. 'I'd like you to read it, too.'

Though the arrival of the two letters seemed to Margaret the most important events in those first days of their stay in Herringsby, other things had happened which, if less personal to the little party in the Rope Walk, were, in fact, to have a considerable effect upon the next few weeks of their lives.

Margaret, for instance, had met Lucy Moore.

She had seen her first on the day that she had walked on the heath, sitting very upright in an old cabbage cart beside a jolly, red-faced farmer, who was driving along the rough track that joined the carriage-way behind the upper town. The strange contrast between the beautiful girl and her shabby equipage had made Margaret want to smile. Erect and proud, in a blue pelisse and a new poke bonnet, her gloved hand disdainfully gripping the side of the cart, Lucy had looked more like a queen riding in state than a farmer's daughter driving to market with six dead geese and a sack of carrots on the floor behind her. And the way that she had maintained her brave dignity against the heavy lurching of the wheels had filled Margaret with delight.

'What sort of a girl was this?' she had wondered.

How had she come by such an exquisite grace?

Three days later, they had met at the circulating library. Margaret had come in to borrow Miss Burney's *Camilla*, and Lucy was standing at the table by the window, looking at the trinkets. In stretching to reach a china figure of a shepherd boy, she had dropped her parasol, and Margaret had stooped to pick it up.

Both seventeen, both lonely, and both baffled by the strange new course their lives were taking, they had shyly murmured their way into an acquaintance and, leaving the library at the same moment, had walked thoughtfully up and down the promenade together for an hour, Lucy telling Margaret that life in the finishing school at Woodbridge—which she had just left—was far more to her liking than the rough homeliness of the farm kitchen at home, and Margaret confessing that Herringsby was vastly different from Holly Lane and that she missed the bustle of the bookshop.

'Let us meet again,' Lucy had smiled when they were at last taking their leave of one another. 'Father drives to town at least twice a week, and we could meet at the library and repeat our walk.'

Elijah, too, had made friends of his own in Herringsby. He had climbed into a boat with Will and Gideon and Sam and Josh and, on seeing its owner returning to the beach, had yelled and shouted as loud as they, and had jumped ashore and run to hide among the shacks, kicking slyly at the piles of fish-heads on the way, as though this were a childish ritual that he had performed all his life.

One day, soon after their arrival, he came back from the

140

beach with a black eye and his clothes badly torn. He had spent the morning, he said, with his friends, shut up in a shed because of the rain.

'Josh said I was a furriner,' he burst out angrily. 'Said I was as furrin as th' French.'

'But, you're not a foreigner!' exclaimed Margaret. 'How could he say such a silly thing?'

'Ev'rybody born out a Suffolk's a furriner, he says.'

Margaret looked thoughtfully at his flushed, unhappy face.

'So you punched him?' she asked.

Elijah nodded his head.

'And then he punched you?'

Elijah nodded again.

'And what happened next?'

'Then all the others started kickin' and punchin' too.'

'You mean they all set upon you in a gang?' she asked in shocked surprise.

Elijah shook his head.

'No,' he said. 'Gid hit me and Will hit Josh. And then—don't know why—but I kicked Will and Josh kicked Gid. All on top of the other, we were—in a heap.'

'Goodness me! Do you always squabble like that?'

'It was the rain,' explained Elijah, more wisely than he knew.

'And how did it end?'

'Why, Sam, who'd done noth' at all but sit in th' corner, got a great bash on's nose and howled so that Dan Fiske came in and threw us all out—right out in the wet, he did.'

'Who's Dan Fiske?'

'Man on th' beach,' replied Elijah shortly.

He squinted ruminatively out of his bruised eye as he felt again the strong arms lifting him off his feet and flinging him far out on the wet shingle. Dan was a man to like. He kept his own boat and had let Elijah help him pitch its bottom only the day before. Besides, he was strong. He could down his brandy at a single swig.

'Called us a peevish set of mucks, he did,' the boy ended, a note of awe creeping into his voice.

Yet, within a week and in spite of being a 'furriner', Elijah came to know the life of the beach almost as intimately as he had once known that of the crowded alleys about Holly Lane. He could interpret the strange, high cries of the fishermen. He picked up the boys' slang and the curses of the fishwives. He learned to manage an oar and then a boat. And when he tumbled into the sea he fought his way back through the breaking waves to the land, without help.

Yet, far more important for the future welfare of them all in Mrs. Dunnett's parlour was the fact that—almost unconsciously —he breathed in the strange excitement and the dread and fear which even then, in the middle of October, were being handed on along the coast by a quick shrug of a shoulder; the fierce look in an eye; a whisper; a muttered oath. Without bothering to understand, he noticed the sudden silence of two fishermen when a stranger passed too close. Used as he was to the savage passions and ugly crimes of a London slum, he was neither surprised nor dismayed by the brooding secret that had gripped the place, and wisely, in the circumstances, he remained incurious.

It was only when Josh whispered something about 'runs' and Gideon told Will that the third riding-officer—the one that had come north from down Orford way—had not been seen for the last few days, that he began to prick up his sharp Cockney ears.

'What sort of talk was that?' he asked Margaret that night.

Margaret looked at him in a puzzled way.

'It's smugglers' talk, I think,' she replied slowly.

Smugglers' talk it certainly was. And the third riding-officer from down Orford way was, in fact, never going to be seen in Herringsby again.

On the afternoon that Elijah had handed Margaret her father's letter, Seth Fowler's men had dragged the riding-officer out of the disused hut where they had kept him imprisoned for the last week and had stabbed him to death.

They threw his body down an empty well.

This brutal murder seemed remote, indeed, from the lives of the family from Holly Lane, yet by one of the stranger twists of fortune, it altered the course of every one of them. Mr. Pargeter and Mrs. Neech, Margaret and Robert and Elijah—and even the unhappy, far-away John—were to be directly affected by the poor man's death.

15 *The Moores*

Early in the third week, Robert wrote again to her. He thanked her for her letter, was glad that she had had word from her father, and hoped that his mother had called upon her by now and was making her stay in Herringsby as pleasant as it could be. As for himself, he wrote, he had met with the most astounding piece of luck. The previous Monday, Mr. Barnaby Coke had watched his demonstration at St. Xavier's and immediately invited him to enter his household—'so please direct letters here at 10 New Broad Street and not to the hospital. He instructs me in morbid anatomy in the dissecting-room over his stable early in the morning before we begin at the hospital. I can't tell you, Meg, what a difference his kindness makes to my future. He says that I am ready to sit for my final examination now—that I need not wait the twelvemonth that I had supposed—and that if I acquit myself well enough he will take me as his dresser.'

In a postscript he added: 'Mr C. does not know my father, so it cannot be his influence. It is just luck.'

'Just luck,' exclaimed Margaret aloud.

Mr. Barnaby Coke, she knew, was one of the foremost surgeons of the day. And Robert was one of the ablest students. No wonder Mr. Coke had wanted him to join his household!

Yet, for all her pleasure in Robert's deserved good-fortune, there was an ache for Margaret in his letter. He was ambitious, she knew. And he was fulfilling his ambitions. He was doing all the things that his father most hoped of him. It was wonderful. It was heart-warming. It was what she most longed for him— for she could not imagine him other than bright with success.

But what of herself?

Here, in Herringsby, she was standing still. As she waited to go to her father, the days slipped by with nothing done; nothing achieved. She was learning to make pastry, it is true; and she had taken unwillingly to sewing a shift. But, oh, the aching waste of the hours! The frustrating, dutiful *waiting* in women's lives! She saw wretchedly that every tedious empty day that she passed in Herringsby and every new success of Robert's in London widened the distance between them.

'He's going to be another Barnaby Coke,' she thought, 'another Astley Cooper. He'll shoot right out of my life.'

And she looked down at her needle-pricked fingers and shabby dress with something bordering on despair.

Two days later, when Margaret had almost given up hope of Mrs. Kerridge calling upon her, a carriage drew up outside the cottage in the Rope Walk, and Margaret, dreaming her way through Dr. Johnson's *Lives of the Poets* in the parlour window-seat, heard a loud knock and then someone talking to Mrs. Dunnett outside the parlour door.

In a moment, Robert's mother was walking towards her with outstretched hand.

'So you are Miss Pargeter,' she said, smiling.

Margaret rose to her feet and curtsied and then looked up into the gentle grey eyes of the woman before her, too astonished to do herself justice.

'I am Mrs. Kerridge,' she continued quietly.

There was no doubt who she was, for though she resembled her son in nothing else, she had Robert's quick and charming smile—not the mocking gleam that he shared with his father—but the quick, affectionate responsiveness that he showed when things were going wrong. She asked Margaret if she were comfortable and if she had had word from her father. How was he? How was his health? She sat down on the window-seat and plied her questions with a kindness and sincerity that moved Margaret almost to tears.

'Thank you, ma'am. He is well.'

'Does he lack anything that we can supply?'

'He lacks nothing but warm stockings—which Mrs. Neech, our housekeeper, is knitting for him.'

As they spoke, each looked curiously at the other, surprised at what she saw. Mrs. Kerridge had been told to expect an unmannerly and sharp-tongued girl, and Margaret had long ago persuaded herself that Robert's mother must be as proud and cold as the doctor.

Mrs. Kerridge lowered her eyes, for Margaret's defencelessness confused her; she had unpleasant things to say.

'My husband tells me that he promised to take you to Ipswich.'

'Yes,' said Margaret eagerly. 'When can we go? My father expects me by November 1st.'

A faint flush appeared on Mrs. Kerridge's cheeks.

'It grieves me very much, my dear, that my husband can no longer honour his promise.'

'He can't take me?'

'No.'

'Why not?'

Margaret was trembling on the edge of angry tears.

Mrs. Kerridge seemed hardly happier than she.

'There is much sickness about. And in the past few days his affairs here in Herringsby have been thrown into the greatest disorder.'

'What affairs?'

It was an impertinent question, but Margaret was cruelly disappointed. She had been counting the days to her visit to Ipswich. Besides, it was part of the bargain between herself and the doctor; it was the reason why she had endured the frustration and wretchedness of this stay in Herringsby. It was cruel, wicked, dishonest of him to refuse her now.

Robert's mother laid her hand on Margaret's knee.

'One does not ask a man after his affairs,' she said, smiling sadly. 'But you must believe him when he says that he cannot leave the neighbourhood just now—even for a few hours.'

'It does not matter,' replied Margaret angrily, tossing her head. 'I can make arrangements with the carrier or travel on the mail.'

Underneath her anger, she felt hollow with consternation,

not at the prospect of a more difficult and inconvenient journey, but at learning that Robert's father was not a man of his word. It seemed to her a shocking thing.

'It is not as bad as that,' smiled Robert's mother. 'There is a farmer near here who drives into Ipswich once a week. He says he will take you and bring you back. Mr. Moore has a daughter of your age. I believe you have already met each other.'

'Lucy?'

Mrs. Kerridge nodded.

'Does Mr. Moore know that my father is in prison?'

'Yes.'

'And on what charge?'

'Don't worry, my dear,' she replied gently. 'I have explained everything.'

Mrs. Kerridge's visit left Margaret in a strange turmoil of emotion. She had made up her mind days ago that she would dislike Robert's mother as much as she disliked his father. Her neglect of them all had seemed hurting and hateful. Yet, one could not hate the gentle, considerate woman who had just called upon her. One could only feel grateful to her for her kindness—only wonder in pity that she had married such a man.

Mrs. Neech, however, when she heard of the visit, was not so favourably impressed.

'Did she tell you why she took so long to come?' she asked sharply.

Margaret shook her head.

'Has she asked you to call upon her at *The Grove*?'

Again Margaret shook her head.

'Did she say when she'd visit you again?'

Margaret frowned at the housekeeper and put a stop to her relentless questioning.

'She has arranged for me to visit my father,' she said firmly. 'That is all that I can ask of her, Mrs. Neech. And all that I want.'

It was *not* all that she wanted.

She wanted hope, affection, love. She wanted Mrs. Kerridge to open her arms to her as Robert's wife.

But there was no need for Mrs. Neech to know.

That night, under cover of the sea scud, the two remaining riding-officers in Herringsby rode quietly northward along the beach to Minsmere, turned inland behind the salt mere, tethered their horses in a wind-blown copse, and walked cautiously across the marsh to an empty well beside a deserted hut. One of them carried a long, stout rope.

Half an hour later, they returned to their horses.

The information that they had been given earlier that day had not proved false.

A week later, the storm still had not burst on the coast. The fishermen continued to fish; the fishwives still stood before their round, turf huts, gutting the morning catch; and Elijah and his friends still shrieked and yelled as they tore about the beach; while up on the cliff, in the beautiful houses in Montpellier Crescent and King's Parade, idle days followed one another in their customary, untroubled calm.

Lucy and Margaret set off across the heath in brilliant sunshine, lurching along the rough track in Mr. Moore's old cabbage cart and laughing at every jolt. They were happy, carefree, at ease with the world. Lucy had forgotten her queenliness, and Margaret had lost her despair.

She was on her way to her father. And she had heard again from Robert. What more could she ask of such a glorious day? The longer one thought about it, the better it was. Robert was to come, not at Christmas, but in less than a week's time, for Mr. Barnaby Coke had decided to take advantage of the peace between Britain and France to attend a surgeons' conference in Paris and had given Robert permission to go down to Suffolk during his absence. He would be here within days! That he could spare the time to travel down to Herringsby so soon before his examination must surely mean that he wanted to see her? It could not be for his parents' sake alone? He had not been in the habit of leaving his studies for his parents. Margaret tried to argue herself into sober thoughts—but they refused to come.

Robert's heath reflected her happy mood. The sun blazed in the rich, tawny brown of the dead bracken and the raindrops caught in the gorse bushes twinkling with golden light. It looked utterly different from the dreary waste she had trudged through less than three weeks ago.

Everything was changed.

Robert was coming down, and tomorrow she was to see her father again. She was to spend the night at Bush Farm and drive into Ipswich in the farmer's gig early in the morning.

'I've never seen a farm before,' said Margaret eagerly. 'And I've never driven in a gig.'

They had left the rough track and had entered a quiet country lane, where the cart no longer tossed them so violently about.

'It's not like London,' said Lucy shortly. 'Not grand and smart.'

Margaret glanced across at her companion. Lucy's laughter had fled, and she looked suddenly sullen and almost sad.

'But of course it isn't,' she exclaimed. 'Who'd want it to be?'

They were coming down now to the water meadows beside the river Ike.

'There's mud and muck in the yard.'

'That's natural, isn't it?'

But Lucy found no comfort in this.

'And the farm folk wipe their noses with the back of their hands,' she shuddered.

Margaret burst out laughing.

'But of course they do,' she cried.

'There's no "of course" about it,' snapped Lucy. 'It's disgusting.'

They crossed the river and rattled past a malting house as large as the flank of the Royal Exchange.

'Lots of London's disgusting,' said Margaret quietly, understanding at last the distress that Lucy's expensive education had brought her.

In silence, they drove through a fat land of tall elms and large fields bordered with hedges bright with hips and haws and, passing a newly-painted white fencing, turned suddenly into the drive of Bush Farm.

'It's beautiful, Lucy!' Margaret exclaimed, shaken out of her thoughts by the glowing warmth of the house before her.

It was built in old brick with curved, gracious gables—like the gables Margaret had once seen in a Dutch picture belonging to Mr. Stone. Its high-pitched roof was tiled with warm, curving, red tiles, and it had a great number of sash windows. Its front door was wide and sturdy and unencumbered with a porch.

'But where's the farm?' she asked.

In the first gasp of delight she could see only the last red apples glowing like balls of fire on the leafless orchard trees and the orchard grass sweeping up almost to the walls of the house.

'The cow byres are behind,' said Lucy dully. 'And the manure heaps and the mud. They're all there.'

The drive forked, and the cabbage cart, instead of turning right to the front door, lumbered left past a dovecot and a shed stacked with hurdles and apple skeps and ladders, straight into the farmyard at the back of the house. Margaret saw the mud and smelt the manure at once; but she saw and smelt and heard a dozen things besides. She saw a huge granary and a cloud of dust coming out from the wide doorway of a barn, a pump, a sleeping cat, and three cocks strutting proudly on a steaming dung heap. She caught the whiff of ripe apples and leather and hay, and heard, through the relentless thumping of the threshers in the barn, the distant lowing of the cows coming in from the fields. Despite her town-bred ignorance, she grasped immediately the robust rightness and dignity of all that Lucy had been born to. It came to her even in the dry prickling of the corn dust in her nose and the hard knobbles in the knotted wood of the cabbage cart under her hand, as she waited for the old farm hand to take the reins and help them down to the ground.

With a lightening of her heart and a strange sense of peace, she felt as though she were coming home—that these country things were not only Lucy's inheritance but also her own. She had not felt so securely herself since the hour before her father's arrest.

A minute later, Lucy and Margaret, carrying Margaret's small bundle between them, entered the farm-house scullery.

Everything was very quiet.

'Mother and Aunt Kitty and the maids must be at their rest,' muttered Lucy.

'At their rest?'

'Always take off their shoes after dinner and lie on their beds,' explained Lucy laconically, leading the way through the kitchen.

It was a large room—the centre of family life—with a settle by the fire and gleaming copper pans hanging on the walls and blackened hams in a rack over the hearth. It was drowsing now in its own warmth, with its floor so beautifully rippled with new-thrown sand that Margaret hated to spoil it.

At the foot of the broad, uncarpeted stairs, Lucy took off her shoes.

'Be careful,' she whispered. 'They're slippery.'

The oak boards were polished almost black and shone like ice.

Lucy stopped on the landing and waited for Margaret to come up to her, a sudden smile playing about her lips.

'That's my piano,' she whispered, pointing through an open door.

Margaret gazed long through the doorway, not knowing what to say.

'It's beautiful,' she said at last.

It was not, however, the piano to which she was referring but the room in which it stood. Her eyes had travelled slowly and in amazement over the priceless damask curtains, the costly chandelier, the cabinets crowded with china, the buhl tables, the chairs shrouded like ghosts in their white sheets, the walnut escritoire, the silver candlesticks, and had come to rest at last with even greater astonishment on the glass-like radiance of the polished oak floor. Mrs. Moore's drawing-room had all the lonely splendour of a state room.

'Father bought it in Ipswich,' smiled Lucy, tiptoe-ing cautiously across the floor. 'It's rosewood. You should hear its tone.'

She opened the lid and played a chord so softly that the sound lapped gently over the shrouded chairs and got lost in the damask curtains.

'Do you use it often?' asked Margaret.

'The piano? Of course. I play it every day.'

'I mean this lovely room.'

Lucy made a comical face.

'Once a year, perhaps. When Lord Chillesford takes tea with Papa. And at election time—when they want his vote.'

Margaret felt her stockinged feet slipping away under her.

'But this floor,' she gasped, saving herself from a skid. 'It must be polished at least twice a week.'

'It is,' laughed Lucy. 'Mama does it every Tuesday and Friday directly she's finished in the dairy.'

'Your mother?' exclaimed Margaret.

'It's far too precious to be left to the maids.'

'How odd!'

It was.

And poor Lucy, suddenly remembering the coarse blue apron her mother always tied round her waist and the ugly way her skirt humped over her back as she knelt on the floor to polish the boards, blushed with embarrassment.

'She's old-fashioned,' she frowned.

.   .   .   .   .

That evening, after the tea-things had been cleared away, Margaret sat on a stool in the shadows to the side of the hearth and looked at the kindly family that had offered her hospitality. They were all there: Lucy's mother; her father; her brother Dick; her Aunt Kitty; the three maids, seated behind their mistress, stitching away silently in the light of a single rush; and Lucy herself, playing with the end of a ribbon and staring into the fire.

The day's work was over, and it was time to talk.

Mr. Moore and his son talked in slow, end-of-the-day contentment of pheasant-shooting and the progress of the threshing, while Mrs. Moore and Lucy's Aunt Kitty chatted quietly about the three children whom Aunt Kitty had left at home with their father at Rushby. Uncle Henchman was a doctor, Lucy had said, and he had driven Aunt Kitty over to the farm a few days ago, telling her to rest and grow strong for the birth of the child that was to be born to them so soon.

It was a dull, homely, happy scene, and Margaret, longing for the return of such uneventful, peaceful evenings in her own family, invested everyone about her with more goodness and sweetness and wisdom than they possessed. This was the only family in Suffolk that had shown her unaffected kindness, and she turned from one member of it to the next with a heart full of gratitude.

Mr. Moore suddenly startled the company by slapping his leather breeches hard with his hand and exclaiming:

'Bless me, Loo, if I haven't forgotten to tell you the news!'

Up till now his head and shoulders had been lost in tobacco smoke, but he sat up straight as he spoke and his weather-beaten, rugged face emerged like the sun from a cloud and beamed at his daughter.

'Lord Chillesford's bringing a party to that ball of yours.'

'To the assembly ball in Herringsby?'

Lucy's face flushed with excitement.

'Then it's your white dress, not your blue,' announced her mother firmly, biting off a thread of her cotton.

'And the gig, not the cart, Papa,' laughed Dick.

Everyone was delighted with the news.

'Your first ball, too,' said Mrs. Moore with calm satisfaction. 'You couldn't be coming out at a better time.'

'Oh, Lucy, your first ball!' exclaimed Aunt Kitty, smiling happily. 'What a lovely thing!'

Margaret sighed with pleasure as she looked at Aunt Kitty. She was like the blue sky, or the sun on the sea, or the sand washed clean by the tide—something that you did not even have to think about but that you knew by instinct that you loved. She was calm and gentle—set apart from the vexations of life by the baby that was coming so soon. She was not handsome, like her brother, nor pretty, like her niece; nor even strong, like Mrs. Moore. Perhaps she was even a little plain. But she was at peace. And Margaret longed for Aunt Kitty's kind of peace.

'And the Grices and Fitzgeralds and Tovells are coming,' said Dick. 'And the Cobbolds, too.'

Once Lord Chillesford's intention of attending had been noised abroad, the farmer said, all the other big families in the neighbourhood had decided to drive into Herringsby for the first of the winter balls, and, doubtless several families from the upper town would soon send word of their coming, too.

'Dr. Kerridge and his lady'll be present, for sure,' he continued.

Lucy looked up quickly.

'Then their son will be there, too.'

'Robert?' laughed Dick. 'Not him.'

'Yes, he will,' pouted Lucy. 'Margaret here says he's coming down from London in a week's time.'

Margaret wished that she had never told Lucy of Robert's coming. It had been said in idleness—for something to say. It had nothing to do with the Moores.

But she was wrong. It had everything to do with the Moores —so it seemed.

'He may be in Herringsby, Loo,' argued her brother. 'But that don't mean he'll go to the ball.'

154

'Why not?'

'He's a biggerty young fellow, that's why,' snapped Mrs. Moore. 'It's London folk and London ways for him!'

Margaret's cheeks flamed with anger. It was untrue. Unjust. Mrs. Moore could not be speaking of Robert—the Robert she knew.

'It's his father more than the boy,' said the farmer mildly out his cloud of smoke. 'He's hopes of him—out of the common run.'

'So, make up your mind, Loo,' laughed her brother, 'he's not for you.'

'Robert Kerridge'll look higher than yeomen stock, my lass,' said her mother.

Margaret could not bear it. She could not bear his name on their lips; she could not bear their imputation that he was arrogant and conceited and proud. She wanted to stand up and tell them that they were seeing him only through his father's pride.

Unexpectedly, another voice was raised in Robert's defence.

'Betty, dear,' said Aunt Kitty, smiling gently at her sister-in-law. 'The young man is a student. He must work hard. One cannot expect him to have time to go fishing and shooting with Dick as he did when they were boys. And for the same reason, perhaps, he has no time to spare dancing at balls.'

The attack upon Robert petered out after a short rearguard action from Mrs. Moore.

'That's as may be, Kitty,' she said with a fierce, unyielding frown on her face, 'but he's clarred up out of our world and there's no blinking the fact.'

It was over and done with. She bent close to the rush light to thread her needle, dismissing the proud Kerridges from her kitchen with superb disdain.

In the quietness, Margaret's heart slowly hushed its beat. Aunt Kitty began turning the heel of the sock that she was knitting, Lucy returned to her dream in the glowing logs, and Dick and his father resumed the subject of pheasants.

16 *Ipswich Gaol*

Next morning, Margaret was very silent on the long drive to Ipswich. She sat in the gig beside Mr. Moore with a sad, abstracted look on her face, her mind revolving in some distress the small snobberies and hurt prides of country neighbours and the pain which Dr. Kerridge's inordinate ambition brought to her.

Mr. Moore, glancing across at her, caught the forlornness in her eyes and mistook its cause. The girl was on the way to her father. Here was reason enough for her grief.

'Now, don't you cruckle, lass,' he said in his clumsy, kindly way. 'He's a good father, and you're proud of him.'

Margaret, startled out of her thoughts, looked up at him without understanding—at first—the meaning of his words.

'He stood up for what he thought right,' continued the farmer.

Margaret flamed into life, realizing at last that Mr. Moore must think she was ashamed of her father.

'Of course he did what was right,' she whipped out. 'Do you think I'm ashamed of his being in prison?'

The yeoman looked into her proud, flushed face.

'No, lass,' he said with a slow, sad smile. 'You're not ashamed.'

The sun had risen by now, and they could see the dim stubble fields and the hedgerows slipping past on either hand and the farm folk setting out with great cartloads of muck.

'But, it's much for a lass to bear.'

'No, it isn't,' she flashed back. 'It's nothing to being shut up by oneself in a cell.'

They were driving past a park now with stately elms and a pond fringed with rushes and a scattering of cows, knee-deep in mist.

The farmer sighed.

'It's a grief for a good man to suffer for notions that are wrong,' he said.

'Wrong? What do you mean?'

'Of course, they're wrong. Property's property, lass, whether it's houses or land. "Give the houses to the parishes," says your father. "Give the land back to the people," says Thomas Spence. Why, where'd we be if I gave my land away to Hodge and Tim and those carters we passed back the on the road? We'd starve, lass. And so would they. And so would the country, too.'

Theories meant little to Margaret. She knew only that men had died in the London streets for lack of bread and that five families in Holly Lane had been wiped out because of their landlord's want of care.

She told Mr. Moore about both.

'You didn't see the bodies that were carried out of the tenement,' she ended, clenching her hands, feeling again the horror of it all.

'That was no sight for a child like you,' said the farmer looking at her in sharp concern.

'It was no sight for anyone,' she burst out. 'It was no sight for Elijah to see how his mother died.'

They drove on in silence, the ruins of the tenement in Holly Lane standing as a great barrier between them—for Mr. Moore, for all his kindness, would never understand the thoughts and feelings of those who had watched the tragedy of that August night.

And dimly, for the first time, Margaret began to realize that her father and herself and Robert—and even John—were ringed about by what they had witnessed, cut off, and set apart from the rest of the world.

An hour later, she was at Ipswich Gaol.

'Meg, my dear child!' cried her father, looking up from his table of books.

She put down her basket of presents and ran into his outstretched arms.

'Such a time it has been, dearest,' he murmured into her

hair. 'Such a long time without you.'

They looked at each other for a long time, smiling and beginning sentences and then stopping and then smiling again, so full of the pleasure of being together that they neither knew where to begin nor cared where they stopped. At last, with Mrs. Neech and Elijah inquired after and Mrs. Dunnett's cottage described anew and Mr. Moore's kindness in driving her to visit him fully recounted, Margaret called a halt and asked her father about himself.

'And you, Father, are you well?'

'Well?' he asked in a startled way. 'Why, yes, Meg. Of course I'm well.'

She could see for herself that he spoke the truth. There was healthy eagerness in every gesture that he made.

'And are you warmer, now?'

The old man rubbed his hands cheerfully and nodded towards a small fire burning dully in the hearth.

'They've allowed me coals at last.'

'I've brought the socks and mittens,' she said, unwrapping Mrs. Neech's present. 'And I've brought a great deal else.'

She began unpacking the rest of the presents and piling them among the books on the table. There were apples from Mr. Moore and a tiny bunch of the first violets, which Lucy had tied up with a grass-blade, and a dozen eggs from Mrs. Moore.

'They're good folk, Meg,' he said, much moved by their kindness. 'And it's all the kinder of them in that they cannot understand or sympathize with what I have tried to do.'

Margaret winced as she recalled the farmer's words in the gig and reached down in her basket for the last of the gifts. She pulled up a sea-smooth pebble with a hole through the middle, which Elijah had sent, a pint measure of shrimps from Mrs. Dunnett, and her own untidy-looking pork pie.

All were eagerly scanned and all admired.

'You've made it yourself?' exclaimed her father, poking his finger into the crumbling pastry.

She nodded.

'I couldn't wish for a nobler pie,' he said, smiling tenderly into her eyes.

With the presents unpacked, Margaret looked about her.

The cell was in Mr. Pargeter's own special kind of confusion: she had often seen the snuggery look just like this. The floor was littered with crumpled pieces of the coarsest and cheapest paper, scribbled across on both sides and then tossed away, and many of his books were piled on top of each other in drunken columns about the chair in which he sat.

'How is your book about the booksellers going?' she asked.

'I've given it up,' he laughed.

'Given it up?'

'There it is,' he said, pointing to a corner full of torn sheets of manuscript. 'And there and there and there.'

Every corner of the cell was littered with discarded work.

'But why?'

'Who's interested in the past, Meg? What *good* could the book do? It's the future we must look to—the ten glorious decades of this new century that's just begun.'

'What are you writing, then?' she asked with a kind of hollow foreboding, the ghost of another *New Jerusalem* rising up to haunt her.

'Why, a reading book, child. A book to teach men and women how to read. Something so sure and so simple that with a few weeks' study every ploughman and tinker in the land can master the written word.'

His face was alight with the joy of his new idea.

'Do ploughmen and tinkers *want* to read, Father?'

'Of course they do, Meg! Of course they do!' He thumped the table with all his old passion. 'Reading unmanacles a man. It sets him free.'

She saw now the reason for his vital, eager good health. He had a new cause to fight for.

'I cannot think why I never saw it before,' he added more quietly. 'I was in too much hurry to strike off his chains myself. But it's no use, Meg. It's no use at all. A man must cast aside his own manacles if he is ever to be free. And reading will do it. Reading alone. Once the poor and the dispossessed have read the Bible and Shakespeare and Milton and *The Rights of Man* they will know to what greatness they are heirs. They will no longer tolerate these unjust laws, these taxes designed to pinch the poor and let the rich go free, this system of government which gives them no vote.'

'Hush, Father, hush,' said Margaret urgently.

His voice was ringing in the gaunt, carpetless cell.

Mr. Pargeter laughed a happy, carefree laugh.

'Read it, Meg,' he said, picking up a sheaf of papers from the table. 'A reading manual. That's all. It is a file for prison bars, but it is not seditious. It is not a libel. No government can prosecute a man for teaching his neighbours how to read.'

His high spirits were infectious.

'And when I'm free of this,' he continued gaily, sweeping his hand to include the barred window and the bolted door and the sullen, smoking little fire, 'we'll mend that press of mine and print the thing. And we'll not only sell it in my new shop, but we'll teach it there, too. That's it, Meg. We'll run a school and call in all the men and women from the streets—the rag-and-bones man, the milk maid, "New brushes and brooms", and all the rest.'

She shook her head.

'It's a dream, Father,' she said gently.

'It certainly is not, my child,' he exclaimed forcefully. 'It is a humble step—a slow, practical, lowly step to better things. And with Robert's help we could make it something more.'

'Robert! Why, what is he to do?'

'Get himself qualified as quickly as he can,' came the prompt reply. 'And we'll open a sick people's dispensary in our shop as well. There's room for all in Holly Lane if we contrive it so.'

'In Holly Lane? But it's all burnt down!'

Mr. Pargeter shrugged away the difficulty.

'Well, if not there,' he said, waving his hand impatiently, 'then somewhere else. In Spital Fields. Or across the river in

Southwark. Wherever people are poor and hungry for knowledge and in need of help.'

Robert!

Margaret's thoughts had come full circle. The day had begun with Robert—with a desperate longing to have him beside her, assuring her that what she had heard last night meant nothing at all; that he himself was untouched by his father's hopes.

'Health of body and health of mind,' continued the old bookseller, shaking back his mane of white hair. 'That's what we'll offer them when I'm free again.'

Robert! Robert buried from fame in a London slum!

What different futures their two fathers had planned for him!

With a sigh, Margaret, sitting on the floor at Mr. Pargeter's feet, turned aside from the old man's dreams and the doctor's ambitions and stared the true problem that had always confronted her straight in the face.

What future had Robert planned for himself? Even if he loved her, was she the sort of girl who would make a suitable wife for the future that he had planned?

Sensing her ignorance of herself and baffled by the shortness of her knowledge both of Robert and the world, she looked up into her father's eager, happy eyes and longed for help.

'Father . . .' she faltered.

Mr. Pargeter caught the tremor in her voice and, looking down, saw the trouble in her face.

He banished his dreams.

'Meg?'

'Father . . . I love Robert.'

The bookseller nodded his head as though he had known all along.

'Does he love you?' he asked gently.

'I don't know,' she said, the colour flooding into her cheeks. 'I don't know, but . . . sometimes, I think he does.'

'Then, why so sad?'

She told him of Dr. Kerridge's coldness towards her; of his ambitions for his son; of the difference in their fortune; of Herringsby's conviction that the doctor would force Robert to seek a wife who could bring him worldly success. And Mr. Pargeter listened to her gravely and with patience until she had done.

'But he loves you, you say?' he asked again.

'Oh, Father, I don't know,' she said, pressing her burning cheek against his knees.

'Then leave it to him,' he said quietly, running his fingers through her hair. 'If he loves you, he'll find a way.'

It was as simple as that.

17 *The Camp on the Heath*

While Mr. Moore and Margaret were away in Ipswich, the arm of the law reached out at last to the Herringsby coast.

Mrs. Moore and Lucy and Dick could talk of nothing but the soldiers. They crowded round the gig in the farmyard in their hurry to tell them both the news.

'They're everywhere, Papa!' exclaimed Lucy excitedly.

'We heard the first clatter of their hooves not an hour after you left,' said Mrs. Moore.

'And after the horsemen came the foot soldiers and the baggage wagons. They streamed past all morning, didn't they, Mama?'

'But why've they come?' asked the farmer, jumping down from the gig, his brow wrinkled in concern. 'There's been no trouble on the coast to warrant a regiment of foot.'

'Yes, there has,' cried Dick, bursting into the conversation. 'A riding-officer killed up Minsmere way—near a fortnight ago.'

'Killed at Minsmere! A fortnight ago!' exclaimed his astonished father. 'But why haven't we heard of it before now?'

The excited party swept into the farmhouse kitchen.

'Hushed up, Ben Farrer says, till the soldiers arrived. They saw his body down Mr. Catchpole's old well over a week back. Left it there. Not a word said.'

Catching sight of Margaret's puzzled face, Lucy threw her an explanation.

'It's the smugglers,' she told her.

'Always been smugglers on this coast, Miss Pargeter,' added her brother. 'Always will.'

'And they killed the riding-officer?' Margaret asked.

But the family were too excited at the arrival of the soldiers to attend to her question.

'Damn it, Dick! It's shooting time!' groaned the farmer, his open face clouding with fears for his favourite sport. 'Where've they camped?'

'Up on the heath—over along the hundred wood.'

'Bloody noses, Dick,' he roared. 'The best covert of all! The best covert from miles around!'

Mr. Moore showed scant respect for the arm of the law.

'There'll not be a bird alive in it by morning,' he continued savagely. 'And by the end of the week there'll not be a hen or a goose or a duck either—not this side of Tunstall, there won't.'

He turned sharply on his wife.

'Your poultry, Bet!'

'Bless you, Tom,' she said calmly. 'You're not married to a fool. We've had the soldiery here before now. Ned brought them in from the home field so soon as we saw the baggage train.'

'But why did the smugglers kill the riding-officer?' asked Margaret again, this time in a clear, loud voice.

They all looked at her in surprise, a sudden silence falling upon the room.

Aunt Kitty who, alone in the family had stayed quiet by the kitchen hearth, at last gave her an answer.

'I expect he had learnt too much, my dear.'

'When one lives on a coast like this, lass,' explained the farmer grimly, 'it's best to know nothing at all of what passes 'twixt dusk and dawn. Nothing at all. That's my rule.'

Next morning, Margaret, anxious to be back with Mrs. Neech and Elijah in the Rope Walk, hurried out to Mr. Moore and the waiting cabbage cart and thanked the family most warmly for all their kindness to her.

Mrs. Moore gave her a brusque, friendly nod. Dick doffed his cap. Lucy shook her hand. And Aunt Kitty, in loving-kindness, took Margaret in her arms and kissed her on the forehead.

'Good-bye, dear Margaret,' she said. 'And God bless you. I shall not be here when you come again.'

And then, quite distinctly, while she still had her clasped in her embrace, she whispered:

'Have courage, my dear. Your Robert is worth the pain.'

Margaret could hardly believe her ears.

Aunt Kitty had understood.

The wonder of it flashed like summer lightning in the back of her mind, but she could only smile and nod and wave her hand, for Mr. Moore had hustled her up into the cabbage cart and was talking of potatoes and turbot and a keg of rum. He had three sacks of potatoes in the back of the cart for an old woman living on the edge of the heath—his mother's old dairymaid, he said. He must be in Herringsby early enough to choose the best of the morning's catch. And he must pick up the rum at *The Royal George*.

'One must lay in one's stores, lass, when the Military's about,' he said wryly as they swung down the drive. 'They'll soon have drunk the place dry.'

They immediately saw signs of yesterday's invasion, for the heavy army wagons had left deep ruts in the country road, and the grass along the hedges was dulled and scuffed with the tramping of many boots. At the great malting-house at Snape they saw an officer with a party of redcoats and a wagon, requisitioning barley, and as they crossed the river and mounted the hill to the heath, the noise and clang of the camp came to them through the still, dull air.

As they topped the rise, the great citadel of tents lay stretched before them. The whole broad heath was dotted with horses and tents and scarlet coats. Such a swift peopling of Robert's lonely kingdom made Margaret gasp, for here was the Army— John's army, she thought with a pang—wrenching up the ling wood for the camp fires, splicing down the lower branches of the windblown copse, digging trenches for latrines—desecrating this ancient place of peace. Close beside the track, six troopers were grooming their horses. They shouted and cursed and laughed and spat, unconscious of the beauty into which they had trespassed.

A heavy, lumbering young officer rode up, shouted an order, and the laughter stopped.

He might have been John, Margaret thought.

This was the life that he had chosen

Yet, though the tented camp and the memory of John were vivid to her, she saw them with her eyes and with her intellect rather than felt them in her heart. Her heart was too full of Robert.

'*Your* Robert,' Aunt Kitty had whispered.

Later, when the cart rattled through the upper town, she saw that many of the houses were shuttered and barred, as though their occupants had packed up hastily and gone away. And when they drove down the carriage-way into the Rope Walk, she imagined that the fishwives looked sullen and watchful and afraid. All these things she noted clearly and stored away for future thought. Yet, beneath her questing mind, she was filled with a silent, pulsing joy.

Robert would be with her in three days' time.

'Leave it to him,' her father had said. 'He'll find a way.'

As Mr. Moore stopped before Mrs. Dunnett's door, Dr. Kerridge rode past, touching his hat. But it was not her defiance of the doctor that had brought the light into her eyes. Nor yet the coming of the soldiers. Nor the murder on the coast.

Back in the cottage parlour, however, it was not so easy to push aside the struggle that had been joined between the smugglers and the law, for a platoon of redcoats was drawn up on the beach immediately below the window.

'They're going out in those boats,' explained Elijah over his shoulder, too excited at what he was watching to remark on her return.

A slim young officer ordered four fishermen to man the oars of the two boats; the redcoats stumbled clumsily aboard; and with three savage pulls, the surly Herringsby men drove their overladen craft out from the shore.

'What *can* they be doing?' asked Margaret.

It was a clear morning, and the wide sea was empty of ships. There seemed nothing that the two boat-loads of soldiers could possibly find.

Margaret and Elijah watched them for four or five minutes

moving heavily away, their sterns low in the water, the boats every now and then giving a dangerous lurch as a land-lubberly soldier shifted himself awkwardly on board.

'Look!' exclaimed Elijah. 'They're stopping.'

He was right. The two boats were now some three hundred yards from the beach and were bobbing idly up and down.

'They're over the sandbank,' whispered Mrs. Dunnett, who had come quietly into the parlour and was watching the scene over their shoulders.

The fishermen had their oars cocked up high above the waves with the handles gripped tight below their knees, and the soldiers were peering down through the water.

'What can they be looking for there?' Margaret asked her in wonder.

Every few minutes the boats were rowed a little further to the south, and the peering of the soldiers began again.

'The Lord knows what they're looking for, Miss Pargeter,' cried Mrs. Dunnett in angry defiance.

Margaret looked at her in astonishment, never having imagined so quiet a woman capable of such anger.

'Look!' shouted Elijah. 'One of them's coming back!'

Margaret and Mrs. Dunnett pressed close to the window-pane.

One of the boats was pulling back towards the shore. The other still bobbed up and down over the sandbank.

'They must have found something down there under the water,' said Margaret.

'And the boat's coming back for help to pull it up,' shouted Elijah.

He clutched excitedly at her skirt.

'Let's go. Let's go quickly and see what they pull up.'

By the time they were out on the beach, the fishwives had left gutting the catch and the fishermen scraping their boats lower down the strand and had gathered in a sullen, silent knot, awaiting the return of the approaching boat. Another party of soldiers had come down to the shore. And a half-frightened, half-delighted little group of young ladies from the upper town was whispering and giggling on the edge of the newly-paved promenade.

It was cold on the beach; and after the first excitement, nothing seemed to happen at all. The returning craft lumbered slowly to shore and, when its keel ground at last into the shingle, the soldiers jumped out and ran up the beach to report what they had found. The fishermen who had rowed the boat out shrugged their shoulders and walked up to the inn.

Elijah stood out in the cold with his legs wide apart, his hands buried deep in his breeches, and his dark hair blowing softly in the light wind, toughly content to wait for the slow dredging up of the sandbank's secret. Margaret, however, shivering and suddenly bored, walked briskly southward a little way to try to keep herself warm.

She did not understand Mrs. Dunnett's anger; she did not understand what was happening out to sea. The sullen looks of the fishing folk and the shuttered houses in the upper town all perplexed and bothered her—as though she were standing on the very edge of a discovery that she was too stupid or lazy to make on her own.

'When shall I stop just looking on at things?' she asked herself irritably. 'When shall I stop waiting and waiting and waiting to understand?'

And then she thought of Robert.

Only three more days, she sighed with relief. Only three more days.

With a quick gesture of impatience, she swung northwards again into the cold onslaught of the wind, shutting her eyes against the sharp particles of sand that stung her cheeks.

'Meg! Meg!'

The shouting came to her over the sounds of the beach.

'Meg!'

It was not Robert. Not Robert's voice.

It was John's.

Dashing away the blur of the wind's tears, Margaret looked in bewilderment towards the promenade.

A group of young officers stood on the paved way, surveying the operation at sea. One of them had detached himself from his companions and was running across the shingle towards her.

'Meg!' shouted John again.

Margaret stopped still and stared.

It was John all right—a sunbrowned, breathless, military John.

'Meg!' he gasped as he came up to her. 'I could not believe my eyes! I could not believe it was you!'

He took both her hands in his own.

'What are you doing here? Why aren't you at home in Holly Lane?'

'In Holly Lane?' she repeated dully. 'In Holly Lane?'

She was so winded with astonishment that she could do nothing but stare blankly into her brother's puzzled, manly, sunburnt face.

'Yes, in Holly Lane,' he said again.

'But haven't you heard?' she faltered. 'Don't you know?'

'Know what?'

'It's burnt to the ground.'

'The shop?' he exclaimed. 'The house?'

'Everything,' she said flatly.

She told him what had happened as calmly as she could, though every moment she felt herself fighting to keep the bitterness out of her voice. He had run away. He had left them. Yet, somehow, she must stifle her resentment.

She smiled wanly into his taut, anxious face and saw from his eyes that he was confused with pain.

She released her clenched fists and took his hands in her own. What had happened had happened, she thought. It was past. Over. Done with.

'And Father? Where's Father? Is he with you here in Herringsby?'

Margaret caught her breath. Was it possible that he could not know?

'Where should he be, John,' she said slowly, 'but in prison?'

She told him of the verdict and the sentence and of her visit to Ipswich Gaol the day before. Their father was well, she told him. He was busy with his writing, she said. And how was it, she asked in her turn, that he, John, was here in Suffolk? How had he got his commission? Why had he never written?

She asked it as gently as she could, but the sting of the question brought the blood up into his face.

He answered her thickly as though his thoughts were choking him as he spoke. The commission had been easy, he muttered. Uncle Allen was rich and he had no heir, and with his Oxfordshire influence he had been able to secure him a captaincy in the XXIVth—and had been glad to do it. The peace had knocked down the price of commissions and the exchange had been made and he had joined his regiment almost immediately. John could not explain why he had not written nor yet why he had failed to discover what had happened to his father. They had moved every fortnight, he stammered. Carlisle. York. Lincoln. They did not see newspapers when they were lodged in camp.

'The regiment's here to put down smugglers,' he said, with a little more ease. 'But why are you here, Meg? Why Herringsby?'

'Dr. Kerridge obtained cheap lodgings for us, that's why.'

'Robert's father?'

Margaret nodded.

'Didn't you remember he came from here? Look,' she said, pointing to the back of Mrs. Dunnett's cottage. 'That's where we live.'

'We?'

'Mrs. Neech and Elijah and myself. It's quite comfortable and nice. Come back with me and see them.'

John disengaged his hands and looked back over his shoulder at the group of officers on the promenade.

'I can't, Meg,' he said hoarsely. 'I'm on duty.'

There was something so wretched in the way he said it that she was sure that he was going to leave her—slip away, bury himself—before they had healed what had to be healed.

'John,' she said desperately. 'Don't go. Not for a minute. Wait just a minute before you do.'

She clutched him by his braided sleeve.

'We've got to begin again,' she said. 'Me. You. Father. All of us.'

He looked down upon her, waiting upon her words in abject misery.

'You must go to him at once,' she urged. 'Today. Tomorrow.'

He nodded his head.

'Do it quickly. Put the rest out of your mind. Don't think of anything but him.'

He gave her a faint smile before he turned on his heel.

'And come and see us, John,' she called after him. 'Come and see us on your way back.'

18 *Robert*

That afternoon the soldiers hauled up five barrels of brandy from the floor of the sandbank. They had seen them through the green water, roped together in a loose net and weighted with an anchor to withstand the drift of the tide. On a coast without rocks or caves or narrow coves, the sandbank was an obvious hiding-place for the smugglers to unload their goods— so obvious that one wondered that the riding-officers had not realized earlier where the contraband must have been stowed. Under cover of night and fog, any fisherman in Herringsby could row quietly out and collect his share of the loot.

Elijah stared entranced at the dark, sodden barrels being carried dripping ashore, but Margaret was too full of John to care much what she saw.

Her brother had come back.

She knew that standing there on the beach two hours ago, holding her hands, John had been confronted in a terrible way by the son that he had been and that he had clung to her for help as she—long ago in her childhood—had once clung to him. She knew by the wonderful lightening of her heart that his need for help had altered everything between them: that she had lost her hate; that she no longer felt angry and bitter, but only tired and at peace—as in the moment in the crisis of a long illness when one realizes that one has only to lie still to get well again. Memories of Holly Lane and of her father welled up in her mind, flooding her with quietness and calm. She knew beyond all certainly that she would never despise John again. They had been children together. He was her brother.

It was as well that something brought comfort to Margaret in those last few hours before the lightning flashed and the thunder rolled, for what followed on the eve of that great winter storm was to be unimaginably painful and humiliating to her.

Hardly had she returned to the cottage parlour and drawn the curtains on that cold November dusk when she and Mrs. Neech heard a carriage pull up outside in the Rope Walk and the thud of boots as the coachman jumped down from the box on to the pavement beneath the window. He knocked with his knuckles on Mrs. Dunnett's door.

Dr. Kerridge had sent Margaret a note.

Yes, an answer was expected, the coachman said. He would wait for Miss Pargeter to fetch her pelisse.

Dr. Kerridge summoned Margaret immediately to *The Grove*. There were matters, he wrote, that it was urgent that they should discuss together. The carriage would drive her to the Upper Town, and Tomlins would wait with the horses to take her home again in an hour's time.

The peremptoriness of the note and the lateness of the hour filled her with alarm. What *could* have happened?

As she sat swaying in the draughty carriage while the horses plodded slowly up the steep roadway to the Upper Town, she stared miserably at the broad laurel leaves lit by the sputtering street lights, and longed for the safety of Holly Lane. The laurel bushes were tossing and bridling in the freshening north wind and their shiny leaves caught and threw down the yellow lights just as the ripples did under Blackfriar's Bridge on a stormy night. She longed for her father. She longed for Robert. Most of all for Robert.

She was shown into the library where, to her surprise, she was met not by the doctor but by Robert's mother.

'Miss Pargeter,' she began in some distress, drawing her gently to a settee close to the fire. 'You must forgive our seeming haste. . . .'

The room was sombrely lit, and the expression in Mrs. Kerridge's eyes was impelling enough to hold Margaret's whole attention. She was both embarrassed and tortured with anxiety.

'What has happened?'

'Our son comes tomorrow.'

'Tomorrow?'

Mr. Coke had set off for Paris earlier than had originally been planned, she explained, and Robert had taken the night coach. He would be in Herringsby by dawn.

'Miss Pargeter,' she continued, a faint blush spreading over her pale cheeks, 'we understand from our son's letter that matters stand more closely between you than we had thought.'

Margaret looked up, startled.

What did she mean?

What had Robert said? What could he possibly have said that he had not said to herself?

Yet, as she stood there puzzled and at a loss, she suddenly felt as though she were being swept along on the crest of a huge wave.

'I do not know ... what he has ... written ... Ma'am,' she heard herself reply breathlessly.

'You deny that an affection exists between you?'

An affection? A deep friendship? A true regard?

'No.'

'And that you wish to marry?'

Was *that* what Robert had said? Could it really be so?

'Is that what he writes?' she gasped.

Someone stirred in the shadows of the long curtain by the window and Margaret, coming back to her senses, realized with a shock that they were not alone in the room. The doctor had been standing with his back to them, looking out into the dusk.

'But marriage is *your* intention, Miss Pargeter,' he said sharply, turning and striding out of the darkness towards them.

'Intention? *My* intention?' she repeated stupidly, so dazed by astonishment at this whole fantastic scene that she seemed even to herself to have lost her wits. Dimly, she understood by his tone that he had said something crudely insulting, but the true nature of the insult eluded her.

Dr. Kerridge smiled down at her contemptuously.

'Come, come, you are not a child. You have told us that you

think you love him. And you are ambitious enough, I know, to value his prospects of worldly success.'

Ambitious? Worldly success?

The meaning of his words suddenly struck her like a blow. Robert's father thought that she was as cynical as himself! He thought that she loved Robert only for the brightness of his future—in fact, that she did not love him at all: that she was merely out to make a good match. She felt stifled with indignation, for it was not only an insult to herself; it was an insult to Robert.

'Can you not believe that I love Robert for himself?' she flashed, her anger flooding hotly up into her face. 'Have you so little pride in your own son?'

The doctor scowled fiercely, for Margaret had hit more closely than she knew. His overweening ambitions for Robert's career had long outsoared his simple, fatherly, loving pride in Robert himself.

'Pride that he should be loved by you, Miss Pargeter?' he flashed back, purposely mistaking her meaning.

'No,' cried Margaret. 'Pride that he is fine and lovable *now*! Now—before he has earned his fame.'

The words tumbled out of her in a rush. She felt so excited and outraged that a demon of anger seemed to have taken charge of her.

And then, at the height of her rage, she knew that Robert's mother was beside her, gentle and distressed, and feeling the anguish of it all as achingly as herself.

She turned to her, on the edge of tears.

'I have not been brought up to look for worldly success, Mrs. Kerridge,' she said, her lips trembling.

'Then, do not jeopardize our son's,' rapped out the doctor. 'My son is able, clever, and well-connected. With a prudent marriage he should rise to the highest ranks in his profession. If you love him as sincerely as you protest, give him up. Do everything in your power to see that he does not fail.'

'If he marries me,' cried Margaret, stung with pain, 'then

he fails?'

'Of course.'

So, she was fighting for Robert—really fighting.

'But why? I love him.'

'Then, give him up.'

'No—not if he wants to marry me.'

Mrs. Kerridge stretched out her hand and put it gently on Margaret's knee. 'This matter is too serious for us all, my dear, for us to lose ourselves in anger.'

Her gentleness commanded a hearing.

'I believe that you love our son truly: that you love him only for himself.'

She paused for a moment to let her words sink in.

'We all love him, Margaret,' she said sadly. 'That is why we must be calm. That is why we must see quite clearly what your marriage would mean to him.'

Quietly, she described Robert's childhood and upbringing and their circle of friends here in Suffolk—the Chillesfords and Grices and Robert's uncle the baronet. Then she reminded Margaret of his success at the medical school, his acceptance by Mr. Coke, and the whole bright promise of his future. And lastly—as gently as she could—she told her of his need of a wife who could bring him wealth and a position in the world.

'It is not your fault, my dear,' she said almost tenderly. 'Had things been otherwise, I should have welcomed a brave, intelligent girl like yourself as a daughter.'

It was harder for Margaret to fight against Robert's mother, but she brushed aside the comfort.

'What things?' she asked hoarsely. 'If what things had been otherwise?'

Mrs. Kerridge looked down unhappily at her pink satin slippers, and her husband sighed impatiently and turned away to the window.

The silence became unbearable. In it, Margaret became uncomfortably aware of her shabby dress and of the darn in her stocking; for the first time she felt acutely embarrassed by her own cleverness, independence, and self will. She knew that her whole upbringing and experience of life unfitted her for being the daughter of this elegant, charming, defenceless woman beside her on the settee.

'You mean . . .,' she faltered, 'that I know absurd things . . . like Latin . . . and book-keeping . . . and the price of books . . . and how to make saloop . . . and serve in a shop?'

Mrs. Kerridge shook her head and then raised her eyes and looked at her, compelling her to be brave—just as Robert had done in the courtroom.

'No, Margaret,' she said quietly. 'I mean your father's imprisonment.'

Their true reason for spurning her was so surprising that Margaret could not at first believe her ears.

'His imprisonment!' she gasped in astonishment. 'But surely you know . . . surely Dr. Kerridge has told you—that my father has done nothing wrong?'

In the silence that followed, Margaret waited desperately for some answer to her words.

'Bunyan was imprisoned once,' she burst out bitterly, 'and Milton was arrested and fined. All sorts of good people are punished wrongly by the law.'

She turned in blind anguish first to one and then to the other. But Robert's mother had turned away her head, too wretched to face her, and the doctor stood again in the window with his back to the room.

She hated the cruel set of his shoulders—the whole arrogant heartlessness of the man.

'You defended him,' she said to him, searingly. 'When you spoke in his defence you said that he was a man of peace; that he was a patriot; that he was innocent.'

The doctor whipped round on his heel and gave full rein to his exasperation.

'Fulfilling a debt of honour to a foolish old friend,' he cried, 'and allowing one's only son to marry his daughter are two quite different things.'

Margaret sprang up out of the settee, beside herself with anger. How dared this hateful, dishonest man think her father foolish?

'Margaret! Margaret!' Mrs. Kerridge called out in despair.

But Margaret was deaf to the world. She ran across the room to the hanging cord handle of the bell and tugged it hard.

'Please call for your carriage, Mrs. Kerridge. I want to go home.'

She stood there, erect and proud, and for the first time in her life, entirely grown up.

'It is Robert who must decide if we are to marry—not you; not me. He is twenty-one. He is a man. He must decide for himself what is best.'

Margaret made a splendid exit from *The Grove*. But there was nothing splendid about the turmoil of mind in which she tossed all that night in her narrow bed—for there is nothing more feverish than hope, nothing more oppressive than despair, and nothing more calculated to keep one energetically awake than well-founded rage. The scene in the library given her high reasons for hope—puzzled, incredulous, breath-taking hope. Had Robert really written to his parents and told them that he wanted to marry her? But why had he not written to her himself? What did it mean? Perhaps it was not true. Perhaps they had misunderstood what he had written. Wilfully misunderstood! That was it! For some obscurely cruel reason the doctor was torturing her or testing her—or just playing with her affection for Robert. And she turned from hope to the deepest despondency. She had no right to expect such happiness; no right to imagine that life would be so good to her; she had been foolish and presumptuous and worse to love Robert. Then, just as her head was sinking deep into the torpor of despair and she might have slept, she remembered the doctor again and her anger yanked her wide awake and she lay flat on her back and stared up at the darkness, cursing him for his heartless betrayal of her father. A foolish old friend, indeed? What a coarse-grained, hateful man he was!

Aeons of time later, her hope came back. If the doctor had behaved so badly it was because he was afraid. And why was he afraid? Why, because of what Robert had said in his letter.

What *had* Robert written?

Just after breakfast next morning, as Margaret was sitting heavy-headed and leaden-eyed in the parlour, wondering how she was going to endure Mrs. Neech's questioning one moment longer, Robert ran headlong down the zigzag carriageway from the Upper Town to tell her what he had written.

'Meg! Meg!' he exclaimed, directly they were alone together. 'You must marry me. You must marry me at once.'

He was still out of breath from his running, and his words, as he held her in his arms, shot out of him now loud, now soft, like the sound of a voice carried onwards in a gale.

'I don't know what they've said to you. I can't bear to think what they've said. But it's you that I want. Nothing but you.'

'Oh, Robert, Robert, is it really what you want?'

She felt like bursting into tears with relief and happiness and flinging her arms round his neck. But she did nothing of the kind. Instead, she disengaged herself from his embrace and sat down soberly in Mrs. Neech's rocking-chair and propped up her aching head by cupping her chin in her hands.

'Dear Robert,' she said quietly. 'We must think; we must be calm; we must try to see how it will be.'

'You don't *want* to marry me?' he shot at her in anguished incredulity.

Margaret shook her head, the tears gathering in her eyes.

'I want to marry you with all my heart.'

'Then what do you mean? Why do you say . . .'

'Marriage is for life. It's for ever and ever and ever. It alters everything that happens to you.'

'Of course,' he urged. 'That's why I want you.'

'You're clever, Robert. You have a great future. You may

become one of the greatest surgeons of the day—if I don't hold you back.'

'Hold me back?' he exploded.

He flung himself away from her in anger.

'You've been listening to my father.'

'No, I haven't!' she exclaimed indignantly. And then, she added more quietly: 'I've been listening to your mother.'

She stared miserably down at the floor.

'She loves you. She knows you. She may be right.'

'Of course she's not right!' he shouted. 'You're a fool, Meg. My mother's a fool.'

Robert towered above her in Mrs. Dunnett's cabin-like parlour, proud, angry, handsome, compelling.

'It's not my parents that I'm marrying, nor the Chillesfords, nor the county of Suffolk. It's you. I don't want their snobbery, their petty prides, their cheap success. It's you I want.'

She looked up at him, with her scruples gone; and he caught the joy in her eyes.

'Let's have an end, Meg,' he said, suddenly smiling his mocking, happy smile. 'Let's leave the shaking of heads to our parents.'

Margaret thought of her father. He was a parent, too, she supposed.

'Father won't be shaking his head.'

'Why, of course not,' Robert laughed. 'He's not a greybeard. He's a child. He's younger than we are.'

Their laughter brought them back to their naturally happy selves, for thinking of the old bookseller and recalling the life that they had all led together in Holly Lane somehow blurred the bitterness and anguish that they had both endured in Robert's home.

It also brought Robert back to his good fortune in London.

'Meg,' he said suddenly. 'Mr. Coke's seen to it that I'm to be elected a demonstrator next term.'

'A demonstrator? What's that?'

'It means that I shall help a little with the teaching.'

'*You* teach the other students? Oh, Robert, how wonderful! How well he must think of you!'

'It's better than that,' he said gaily. 'It's the reason why I can ask you to marry me.'

'What do you mean?'

'Why, they pay me. It's not much. But I think it's just enough. It means that I am independent. I can support you.'

Robert's simple account of his money affairs suddenly opened up for Margaret a whole new vista of a man's world and of a man's thoughts. How stupid she had been! Of course, it was independence that he had waited for. He could not have talked to her of love when they parted in the churchyard. It would have been impossible for him. He was still dependent on his father.

While Margaret was following this train of thought, Robert was following another. He had come back smartly to the quarrel he had had with his father not half an hour ago and to his realization of what Margaret must have been through the night before. Both had been a bitter sequence to his vaunted independence.

'Meg,' he said humbly, 'you must try to forgive me for what happened last night.'

Margaret flushed in spite of herself as she recalled the scene.

'Forgive you, Robert? But it was not your fault.'

'Yes, it was. I should never have written to them in the way I that I did.'

'Why, what did you tell them?'

'I thought it was such a fine and dashing and honest way to write. Honest, that was it. I could not bear not to be open with them.'

'You told them that you wanted to marry me?'

He nodded his head.

'I told them about my being elected a demonstrator. I thanked them warmly for all their love and help. I should have achieved nothing without them, Meg. They have been good parents to me—generous and kind. . . .'

'And then?'

'Why, then . . . I told them that through their kindness and encouragement I had been able to earn my independence. That it was good for me, and that I hoped they felt proud.'

'And then?'

He turned towards her, his face clouded with pain.

'That I wanted to marry you.'

He had sat down on the box by the fire and held his head in his hands.

'I'm so sorry, Meg. I did not mean it to be a cruel letter to them. And I never saw what it would do for you. Please forgive me. It was blind of me—stupidly blind. I don't know why I was so stupid.'

Margaret tried to comfort him as best she could. She told him that it was past. Over. Done with. That yesterday was yesterday —not today. That it was far worse for him: he had quarrelled with his parents because of her, while she came to him with her father's love.

'It will give my father such happiness,' she said. 'Now he has all of us back with him in his life.'

'All?'

'Yes, all.'

And she told him of her meeting with John on the beach the afternoon before and of his shame at hearing of his father's sentence and his horror at learning what had happened to the shop in Holly Lane.

'He's riding over to Ipswich today. It'll be all right between them; I know it will.'

'And he's in the army, you say?'

Margaret smiled as she thought of John looking so splendidly martial in his scarlet uniform.

'A captain,' she said.

'But what is he doing here in Herringsby?'

'Why, putting down the smugglers, of course. His regiment marched in and camped on the heath the day that I visited Father.'

'The smugglers? Are they in trouble again?'

She told him of the murder of the riding-officer at Minsmere and of the Moores' belief that it was the work of Seth Fowler and his gang.

'But why did you say "again"? Has there been trouble on the coast before?'

'There are always smugglers, Meg,' he laughed. 'And there's trouble whenever an outside gang of them moves down the coast and poaches in the home preserves.'

Margaret wrinkled up her brow in bewilderment. This was such a new view of life on the English seaboard that she was puzzled at first and did not understand.

'Do you mean that there have always smugglers here in Herringsby?'

Robert shrugged his shoulders.

'So Father says.'

'Do you know any of them?'

'Of course not, Meg. It's no concern of ours. Smuggling is so common among fishermen and so much a matter of everyday life that it just goes on about one and one takes no notice. One just does not *see* what's going on. It's like pickpocketing in London. One does not think about it till one finds one's own money filched and one starts a hue and cry.'

'So smuggling just goes quietly on—with nothing said?'

'The riding-officers and the revenue cutters do their best, but it's little they can do against a community that's watchful and careful and loyal to itself.'

'And Seth Fowler?'

'I've never heard of him. But I suspect he's come south from Lowestoft or Yarmouth and is working a stretch of coast that the Herringsby folk consider theirs.'

He lowered his voice a little.

'There was trouble a year ago near Minsmere when Joe Dunnett was knocked on the head and thrown into the sea.'

'Joe Dunnett?' whispered Margaret, aghast. 'Do you mean Mrs. Dunnett's husband? But your father said it was an accident.'

'That was the verdict—but no one believed it.'

Margaret suddenly understood the cause of Mrs. Dunnett's empty wretchedness and the reason for her sudden spurt of anger when the soldiers searched the sandbank. So much of what had been happening about her was now made plain.

Robert, seeing the thoughtful, solemn look in her eyes, took her hand and brought her back to the present hour.

'Don't grieve and fret, Meg,' he smiled. 'It's nothing to do with us. We are happy. We have each other. Besides, I must go within the hour.'

'Go?' she exclaimed, appalled.

'Yes, Meg,' he laughed. 'To your father. I can't take you away from him without his blessing and love.'

He caught her to him.

'Oh Meg, Meg, Meg,' he laughed again, incapable of controlling his joy, 'a whole new world begins for us today.'

'It's begun already,' she smiled back at him, her eyes shining with happiness. 'It began ten minutes ago. And now I can't remember what the old world was like.'

The clock ticked. The new-made fire sputtered in the hearth and the sounds from the beach came to them muffled and slow —as though from a long way off.

'I wonder what on earth we did with ourselves before we loved,' she said.

19 *The Storm*

Robert hired a cob from *The Royal George* and set off for Ipswich in a flurry of wind and rain, and Margaret, standing at the entrance of the inn yard, waved after him with the first fierce gusts of the coming storm tossing back her hair and spattering her face and cloak. Robert clutched at his hat as he turned to smile, and then he was away behind the church and galloping along the river road towards Snape and the turnpike, with his face streaming with rain and his heart leaping forward with the joyous, carefree motions of his horse.

He had told Margaret that he would come back in two or three days' time. He did not know how long—for he must inquire in Ipswich how one obtained a special marriage licence. He was ignorant of these things. Perhaps he and her father had but to sign a form and pay a fee, in which case he would return to Herringsby that night. But, whatever the delay, she must be brave and patient.

'It is such a little time, Meg,' he had said, smiling down at her from the height of the cob. 'Such a little time longer for us to wait.'

She returned to the little parlour so many fathoms deep in love that not even Mrs. Neech's worried questions about how they were to prepare for the wedding in such a mighty haste had power to draw her up to the surface of life.

'But what can you wear, Miss Margaret?' she asked almost irritably.

From where she was standing, by the street window, she could see the swollen runnels of water pouring off the Rope Walk and the shutters going up on the pastry shops across the way.

'Where can we buy the bonnet and gowns and linen in a place like this?' she continued. 'Where can we buy cakes for the breakfast and the flowers?'

'Does it matter?' Margaret asked dreamily, her thoughts far

away down the valley road, following Robert's progress to the turnpike. She saw him galloping past the great malting-house, and now he was coming to the white fence of Bush Farm.

'Of course it matters!' exclaimed the housekeeper in shocked surprise. 'A girl to go to her husband in her old gown! With no chest of linen!'

'Aren't you happy?' smiled Margaret, suddenly coming out of her dreams and understanding what Mrs. Neech was saying. 'Aren't you happy that Robert and I are to marry?'

With so much wealth of love, she was prodigal with her riches. She put her arms gently round the poor woman and whispered:

'Don't worry. Please don't worry. It's our happiness that matters. Not the linen.'

Two hours later, when Margaret was alone, rubbing the mist off the window overlooking the beach and peering through the spatters of rain at the crests of the waves breaking white and foaming far out to sea, John strode into the room, shaking the water from his military cloak.

'John!' she exclaimed, running to him.

'Meg,' he smiled.

There was no need to ask whether he had been to their father. His whole bearing proclaimed that he was free—free from his burden of shame.

'He was well?' she asked.

John nodded.

'He sends you his love,' he said.

Margaret pulled him to the fireside and made him take off his jacket and took out her handkerchief and wiped down his streaming face, too shy at first to express her thankfulness in words.

'I'm so glad,' she said at last.

'So am I,' mumbled John, staring down at the floor.

Then, when they were more at ease, she told him of Robert, of their engagement, of his parents' refusal to accept her, and of Robert's ride to Ipswich to see their father and to get a marriage licence.

'So you are to marry him, after all,' he smiled thoughtfully, when she had done.

'After all?'

'I thought you might,' he said hesitantly. 'In Holly Lane—before the trouble came. He was always looking at you while you read your books.'

He tried to meet her joy. But she sensed a doubt or fear beneath his laugh.

'Aren't you pleased?' she darted at him, knowing him too well from of old not to catch his mood.

'Please?' he stalled. 'I like Robert. He's a good fellow. You'll be happy, I think.'

'Then what?'

Her brother turned away his face, not knowing how to tell her his fears.

'John,' she urged, 'please tell me what is the matter.'

'It's Herringsby,' he burst out at last. 'It's what's happening here in Herringsby, Meg.'

'The smugglers? The murder?'

John nodded miserably and turned away again, frowning.

'But, they've got nothing to do with Robert and me,' she exclaimed.

He began, then, in his awkward, incoherent way to tumble out what troubled him. Herringsby was a hot-bed of smuggling, he said. Probably always had been. It was true that the fishermen here had had nothing to do with the murder of the riding-officer. That was the work of the Fowler gang, and yesterday three of them had been rounded up and arrested. But in investigating the crime, Colonel Foster had uncovered a vast organization of smuggling centred in Herringsby itself.

'They're all in it, Meg, Colonel Foster says. The fishermen. The fishwives. Even the shopkeepers and the warehousemen at the river port.'

John's frown grew deeper. They had a network of agents, he

continued, that carried the brandy and tea and the bales of lace thirty miles inland and more.

'It's not a guess, Meg. It's a fact. The customs men have traced a consignment of tea at Bury back across the county to this stretch of coast.'

Margaret looked at him, puzzled.

'I believe you, John,' she said. 'But what of it? Supposing everyone is in league with the smugglers—supposing they have their agents and their carters—what difference does that make to Robert and me?'

John's face became even heavier and more flushed with his trouble, for he had come now to the hardest part of all.

'It's too large; it's too well-run for the work of ignorant men,' he said hoarsely.

'What do you mean?'

Colonel Foster and the riding-officers, he explained, were looking for the brains behind this vast organization of illicit trade. Looking for a group of men or, more likely, for a single man of quick intelligence, whose lawful occupation took him about the county visiting at farms, at cottages, at personages, at country seats—who knew fishermen and landowners alike. Someone whose comings and goings attracted no attention, asked for no explanation beyond the practice of his calling.

Margaret was so stupid with love for Robert that her wits had lost their edge. She went on looking at her brother, waiting for him to explain himself.

'Colonel Foster has been posted to this sort of work before,' he blundered on. 'Up in Northumberland, he found that it was the village physician that had organized the smugglers.'

Margaret understood at last and she went white in the face.

'So here in Herringsby he thinks that it's Robert's father that runs the trade?'

John nodded wretchedly.

'We've just posted guards in the upper town.'

'But you've no proof?' she asked. 'How can you know?'

John shrugged his shoulders.

'We don't.'

But he begged Margaret to take Mrs. Neech and Elijah inland.

'Get lodgings in Tunstall or Snape or one of those towns on the turnpike,' he urged. 'There's trouble coming here, Meg. And you'd best be out of it.'

'No,' she said firmly.

'Why not?'

Why not? Why should they not leave Herringsby to its fate? It had nothing to do with them.

Margaret raised her head slowly and looked her brother full in the eyes.

'Because I don't believe your Colonel Foster, John,' she said resolutely. 'Robert's father has nothing to do with the smugglers. It's absurd. If you knew him better, you would know yourself how absurd it is for anyone to think such a thing.'

Left to herself, Margaret considered again what John had told her—this time dispassionately, in the cold light of reason.

She despised Robert's father; he was a ruthless, dishonest man. But she thought him more likely to be dishonest in breaking faith with his friends than in breaking the law of the land. He was too proud to stoop to such dangerous shifts; too eager to stand well with the world; too ambitious for his son. She remembered his splendid mien in the courtroom when he spoke in her father's defence and the murmur of approval that his able plea had won from the lawyers and Mr. Stone, and she could not bring herself to believe for a moment that Dr. Kerridge was the man for whom Colonel Foster was looking. The doctor was too clever and already too successful to risk all that he had won in so nefarious a trade as smuggling.

And yet, even while she was convincing herself of all this, little draughts of doubt were blowing under the doors in her mind. She remembered now that Mr. Stone had once told them that Dr. Kerridge had done something shameful in his youth and that her father had saved him from disgrace; and she wondered desperately what his crime had been. Some youthful extravagance, no doubt. Gambling. Debts. A drunken brawl. But not wholesale smuggling, planned over many years—surely, not that!

And then she remembered with an uncomfortable jolt that of all the lodgings that he might have chosen for them in Herringsby, the doctor had picked on Mrs. Dunnett's—Mrs. Dunnett, a smuggler's widow! If he were really the mind behind the trade perhaps he had wanted to recompense her for her loss.

And yet, equally, if he were a kind and observant physician and had seen her poverty, perhaps he had wanted to help her in her need.

But Dr. Kerridge was not kind!

Troubled and restless, Margaret listened to the growing clamour of the storm. The wind was now blowing in fearful gusts, and the old houses in the Rope Walk shook in its fury as though they were clutched in some giant hand.

Elijah, driven in from the shacks, burst into the room, his hair wild, his clothes askew, and even his limbs held unnaturally apart—like a shipwrecked man thrown up on the rocks.

Angry and surprised, he struggled with his breath.

'It's awful,' he panted. 'There's nothin' to breathe; it blows it all away.'

Margaret pulled off his soaking coat and his shoes and socks and stood what was left of him as close to the fire as she dared and pummelled him dry with a towel. She longed to ask him what was being said on the beach, what he knew about the smugglers, and whether he had ever heard the doctor's name on the fishermen's lips. But the boy seemed only conscious of the dreadfulness of the wind; his teeth chattered and his eyes were so inflamed that he kept drying the tears off his cheeks with the back of his hand.

'It's awful,' he complained again. 'How long will it go on?'

Margaret shook her head. She did not know.

And then, suddenly and unasked, Elijah yielded up the sum of his knowledge.

'Dan Fiske says the soldiers won't never put down the smuggling here.'

'Why not?' she asked quickly.

'They're too clever, he says, that's why.'

Margaret racked her brains to think how she could keep him talking and then, having thought of a way, framed her question with care.

'Do you know, Elijah, that they've posted guards in the upper town?' she asked.

The boy nodded his head.

'Does Dan Fiske know?'

Again Elijah nodded his head.

'Does he mind? Does it worry him at all?'

The boy looked inquiringly into her face. It seemed an odd sort of question to ask. But he considered it for a few moments, frowning with thought, and then shrugged his shoulders.

'Didn't say,' he said. 'Didn't say nothing about it.'

'Nothing at all?'

'No,' said Elijah, quite sure in his mind. 'Josh and I told him as he was finishin' the boat, and he just looked up and nodded and told Josh to pass him the pitch. Don't think he cares much where the soldiers go.'

The wind howled for a day and a night and then for another day. Margaret and Mrs. Neech had never known such a wind. They could hear it roaring above them in the middle air and they could see it ploughing the sea up into great valleys and hills and driving the ragged clouds, stampeding southwards, over the tops of the heaving waves. A little before the height of the storm, Mrs. Dunnett insisted that they struggled out to put up the outside shutters.

'It'll hurl up the shingle and smash in the windows,' she explained.

And all the time, through the din and the roar, Margaret waited longingly for Robert and pondered miserably the mystery of the beach.

The wind died down on the second night.

Margaret, lying in bed listening to the sounds from the shore, still heard the waves pounding upon the shingle and the sharp rasp of the undertow pulling back, but the fury had gone out of the sky; the windows no longer rattled, and the old cottage stood safe and firm. Surprised by the calm, she held her breath to catch the least noise from the Rope Walk below her window: the squeak of a shop sign swinging in the air, or a banging door or the thud of running feet. But everything in Herringsby was quiet. Not a soul stirred. The silence came to her with such relief that she let go her breath in one long, happy sigh, snuggled deep into her bed and, feeling suddenly drowsy with peace, fell into a profound and mindless sleep.

She did not wake up till ten in the morning and she would not have awoken then, had not Elijah run into her room and pulled her by the arm.

'Come and look,' he shouted. 'Come and look at what's happened.'

He dragged her downstairs to the parlour window.

'Look,' he said. 'Look at that!'

He pointed out to sea—though there was little need, for there, two hundred yards from the shore, for all to see, stretched a long, thin island of sand, shining wet and new in the morning light, over which the seagulls wheeled and swooped, filling the air with their harsh, discordant cries.

'What is it?' she gasped. 'What's happened?'

It was the storm. It had scooped up the shallow bed of the sea and left its secrets exposed to the neighbouring beach and the wide sky.

Secrets there certainly were, for sticking up out of the glistening surface of the new island were dark, heavy objects that looked like the ends of kegs and barrels and crates of wood.

The storm had revealed and laid bare in a single night what the army might have failed to unearth after weeks of patient search.

20 *The Night of the Assembly*

Robert returned to Herringsby on the night of the assembly ball. He clattered down the High Street at the very moment that Lord Chillesford's carriage drew up outside *The Royal George*. For an instant, he heard the strains of the violins and the hum of voices and a gay laugh; and then, urging on his horse for the final hundred yards, he trotted quickly down the darker, quieter Rope Walk, his face already smiling with the joy of his journey's end, his left hand holding tightly the small dress box balanced on the pommel of his saddle.

Margaret and Elijah had been at the parlour window overlooking the street for an hour or more, watching the lights of the carriages from Montpellier Crescent and King's Parade swinging down the looping carriageway from the upper town. In spite of everything: the murder, the soldiers, the rumours, the fear, and the casks of brandy on the new island staring unwinkingly up at the stars, a ball was still a ball. And even Mrs. Dunnett and Mrs. Neech had come out on the step and were looking down the Rope Walk to the entrance of the inn and counting the lights of the country gigs.

As he trotted out of the darkness, Margaret gave a cry of joy and ran from the window to the front door.

'Robert,' she cried. 'It's you. It's you at last.'

He jumped down from his cob, gave the reins to Elijah, and with a gay smile and a nod to the two women, swept Margaret with him back through the hall and into the parlour again.

'All's well,' he said triumphantly, drawing her more closely to him and kissing her on the forehead.

'My father?'

'He gives us his blessing,' he smiled.

He told her all that had passed between them: the old man's joy; his trust in them both; his faith in the future; and his earnest desire that they should come to him directly they were married.

'And the licence?'

'It's here,' he laughed, patting his pocket. 'It's here, at last!'

And he told her of the complications of the law, of his running hither and thither through the streets of Ipswich from one office to another, of his return to the prison with the forms, of his journey back to Bush Farm.

'To Bush Farm? To the Moores?'

'Dearest Meg,' he laughed. 'Even with a marriage licence we still need a parson and a wedding.'

It had all been arranged, he said. The Moores had offered to help them and he had accepted their kindness. He had driven over to the Vicar of St. Mary's at Ikenthorpe with Mrs. Moore and settled upon the time of the service. They were to be married in two days' time in Mrs. Moore's drawing-room.

'The day after tomorrow?' she gasped happily. 'And in that wonderful room?'

Margaret's lips suddenly twitched with laughter.

'Oh, Robert, have you seen it? The room? It's like a palace of ice. It's full of the ghosts of chairs in ghost-white shrouds.'

And then she went back in her mind to the peculiar slipperiness of its slippery floor.

'Goodness, it'll be Saturday! Mrs. Moore will have polished it only the day before. Oh, Robert,' she laughed, 'I do hope I won't disgrace you and fall flat on my face.'

She was so happy and so glad that he was back with her and so excited about the wedding that she was gabbling the first nonsense that came into her head.

Robert put his fingers on her lips and laughingly bade her be quiet. She must let him tell her the rest of their plans. There was so much for them to do. He was to take her to Bush Farm in the morning, and Dick was to drive over in the cart and bring Mrs. Neech and Elijah and Mrs. Dunnett. They were to spend the night at a neighbouring farm, for the marriage was to be early in the day—at half-past ten—so that they could be with her father in the afternoon at least an hour before the prison

194

gates were locked at dusk.

'We must find John,' Meg,' he said urgently. 'We must find him tonight. He must ask for leave of absence to give you away.'

'He'll be up at the camp.'

'And there's this,' said Robert, picking up the neat dress-maker's box that he had brought with him.

He looked, for the first time in his life, a little self-conscious.

'What is it?' she asked in astonishment.

'It's a dress,' he said, deftly undoing the ribbon. 'I hope it's what you like. I know nothing about dresses, Meg. But it looked pretty on the stand.'

He lifted out a charming, high-waisted, white muslin dress with a low-cut neck-line and a fichu.

'Robert, it's beautiful!' she exclaimed.

It was the dress of her dreams.

She took it from him and lifted it high in the air so that its soft folds swept downwards and she could admire the sheer whiteness and delicacy and charm of the thing.

'Robert, it's lovely. It's a joy of a dress.'

'Put it against you,' he said happily. 'And see if it fits.'

Everything was perfect; it might have been especially made for her.

'Where did you get it?' she asked wonderingly. And then, in a sudden panic: 'Oh, Robert, I do hope it didn't cost too much.'

She looked enchanting, holding the dress up against her shoulders, with her happy face and cloud of chestnut hair coming out at the top. He did not want to tell her that, seeing that Lucy Moore was the same height as Margaret, he had borrowed one of her latest cotton gowns and ridden over to Ipswich to the best mantua-maker in the country and told them to copy it in the finest Indian muslin.

'And now, for John,' he said.

John.

In the midst of her joy, Margaret thought of John and the terrible suspicions that his colonel had planted in both their minds.

'Must you go tonight?' she asked, clutching Robert's hand hard in her own.

'But why not, Meg?' he laughed. 'The sooner the better.'

Nothing had happened in the last few days either to confirm or to allay their fears. The townsfolk of Herringsby had gathered on the beach and stared aghast at the new island and the evidence of their guilt; and the soldiers had gathered on the cliff's edge and stared at it, too. Even the young men from the inland farms had ridden over to gape at the extraordinary sight. But nothing had emerged. The murderers of the riding-officer were safely locked up in Woodbridge Gaol, and the doctor still rode about the country visiting the sick.

'Oh, Robert,' she sighed, 'I wish you could take me away tonight to Bush Farm. I wish we were married already and away from here.'

'But it's only two days, Meg,' he laughed. 'By the end of the week we'll be Mr. and Mrs. Kerridge. An old married couple. Married one whole day!'

He looked happily into her flushed and anxious face.

'Mrs. Kerridge. How does it sound?'

Margaret smiled to match his mood, but deep inside, even her new name brought an ache to her heart. Mrs. Kerridge. The name belonged to another. It belonged to Robert's mother. To someone she longed to love and longed to be loved by in return.

As she stood there, still holding his hand, she knew what she wanted. She wanted Robert to go to his mother and ask her to come to their wedding. Surely, his father need not know?

'Robert . . .' she began falteringly. . . .

The thought remained to be spoken another time, for at that very moment a musket was fired not a dozen feet away, and the Rope Walk was suddenly filled with shouts and cries and the heavy clumping of army boots.

196

Robert ran to the window and threw up the sash, and the acrid smell of musket smoke and the receding shouts of the runners drifted into the room with the cold November night.

'What is it?' asked Margaret, running to his side. 'What's happening?'

They stood leaning out of the window and straining their ears through the frightened whinnying of Robert's cob to the sound of the boots ringing along the paved way northward to the shacks and the fishing-boats on the shore till, coming to the end of the roadway, their clamour was swallowed up in the sand. Except for the horse, the street was deserted. And as their eyes became used to the darkness, they looked across at the shadowy houses over the way and saw that, for all the noise and rout of the last half minute, not a door had been opened, not a shutter cautiously pushed ajar. It was as though every family in the Rope Walk had expected and feared this ear-splitting clash in the night.

'Some poor devil resisting arrest,' said Robert, frowning into the dark.

Margaret shivered. She hated the obstinate silence of the place. She was angry that even Mrs. Dunnett and Mrs. Neech and Elijah had kept themselves shut up in the kitchen. That someone in Herringsby was running for his life and that no one in the Rope Walk made a move to help him.

The last sound of the running feet had died away and the low thudding of the sea and the strains of the music from the ball came softly into her ears again.

'They're even *dancing*,' she exclaimed in disgust.

Suddenly the musket-firing began again—not a single shot, but a long spattering of flashes and bangs—in among the fish-wives' huts and the fishing smacks. The noise was appalling. The whole coast had blazed into life.

This was not a runaway smuggler. It was a battle.

Someone was knocking on the parlour door.

'Is the boy all right, Miss Margaret?' shouted Mrs. Neech through the panels. 'Shall I have him with me?'

The boy?

'Elijah?' shouted Margaret. 'But he's not here!'

Mrs. Neech flung open the door.

'Then where is he?'

They shouted up the stairs over the noise from the beach and, receiving no answer, Margaret ran up to his room to make sure that he was not already in bed and fast asleep; the bed was untouched.

'I thought he was with you. I thought he was with you,' cried Mrs. Neech over and over again, her fear mounting each time she said it.

'He must be with Josh or Gideon or at home with Dan Fiske.'

'Not Dan!' exclaimed Mrs. Dunnett from the kitchen door. 'Not Dan Fiske! Pray heaven not with him!'

Her voice was taut with alarm.

'I'll go to look for him,' said Robert, catching up his coat and making for the door.

'No,' cried Margaret. 'Where can you look? We don't know where he is.'

The firing had risen to a crescendo and was now dying away to the northward a mile or two up the coast towards Minsmere.

'I'll go to Dan's shed,' shouted Robert, tearing himself free.

'No, don't,' cried Margaret, running after him.

They ran along the Rope Walk, one behind the other, looking now to left, now to right, down the narrow alleys between the buildings and calling Elijah's name. Far behind them, the music had stopped at *The Royal George* and the dancers were out in the street; they could hear them shouting and calling to one another to look at the light from the firing far up the coast. But, beside them in the Rope Walk, the houses frowned down upon them, silent and dark, while the frightened women inside awaited in agony the outcome of the night.

Yet, even here, there was the faintest murmur of little sounds. As she passed close to a door, Margaret heard someone furtively pulling back the bolt and unlatching the lock.

'Elijah. Elijah,' Robert called down a darkened lane.

As they came to the last house, a shadow limped painfully along the side of the wall and then, leaning against the un-latched door, fell noiselessly inwards into outstretched arms. On the paving stones, where he had walked, the man's footsteps gleamed wetly in the faint night glimmer.

'Robert!' Margaret whispered in astonishment. 'He's been in the sea!'

They had no time to think why such a thing should be; they could think of no one but Elijah.

'Elijah. Elijah,' Robert shouted, running across the end of the paved way to the first of the fishermen's shacks.

The place was deserted. The soldiers had started firing again at the fugitive fishermen running inland by the mere into the cover of the reeds.

Robert and Margaret had come out at last on to the beach, where the hint of light from the night sky was reflected up at them from the sand and the wet shingle and the silver edge of the waves, and saw before them the dark mounds of the fish-wives' huts and the slender masts of the boats pointing upwards to the stars.

The musket-firing had grown in intensity.

'Elijah. Elijah,' they called desperately as they ran in and out among the huts.

Suddenly, Margaret stumbled over a heap on the sand.

'Robert!' she gasped in horror. The heap was wet and it was faintly warm.

They stooped over the body of a fisherman shot in the head.

Robert slipped his hand through his coat and shirt to his heart and then lifted an eyelid.

'He's dead,' he said quickly. 'There's nothing we can do.'

They ran on together holding each other's hand, Margaret aching with pain for the dead and sick with fear for the child.

And then—of all blessed and merciful things—a small shadow ran to them across the sand. And Elijah threw himself round

Robert's legs. His face was streaming with tears.

'Elijah!' panted Margaret, kneeling breathlessly by his side.

The boy turned to her and flung his arms round her neck. Then, drawing himself away a little, he sobbed out his message.

'Go for the doctor,' he said. 'Fetch him quick.'

'My father?'

Elijah nodded.

'Who's hurt?' asked Margaret. 'Who, Elijah? Where?'

The boy, who was standing farther off, suddenly turned and ran away from them, back through the maze of turf huts.

Robert overtook him.

'Elijah, who is it that's hurt?'

But the boy shook his head vigorously as he struggled free.

'Said not to tell,' he wept.

'Where is he?'

'In his shed—lyin' aside his boat.'

'It's Dan Fiske,' said Margaret. 'I know it is.'

Elijah, hearing her give the man his name, ran back and clutched her hand and started dragging her in and out between the heaps of gear towards Dan's shed.

They found the young fisherman lying beside his boat with his knees bent up almost to his chin, and he was threshing the air with his uppermost arm, his mouth and chin contorted in pain.

'Dan, it's me. Robert Kerridge.'

'It's not you that I want,' the man groaned angrily, speaking his words with dreadful effort. 'Go away, Master Robert. Go away, quick ... afore the soldiers ketch yer. You've no hold ... to be ...'

Robert rolled Dan over on to his back and saw the great wound in his chest.

'Take that cloth off his eyes, Meg,' he said sharply. 'And give it me quick.'

But, as Margaret stooped to lift the rag with which he had tried to hide his face, Dan clutched at it feverishly.

'You're a fool, Master Robert,' he panted, choking terribly

as he spoke. 'If . . . you don't know who I am . . . they can't tek you.'

'They're not going to take me in any case, Dan. Give it Meg, and keep quiet.'

With the rag, Robert did what he could to staunch the bleeding, but it was all up with Dan. The bullet had gone right into his lung close to his heart. He was choking with blood, and his pulse was already failing. Yet Robert could at least ease his pain a little by sitting him up.

'I'm going to prop you up, Dan, against your boat,' he said. 'It'll make it more comfortable for you to breathe.'

Between them, they lifted him up so that he was sitting up straight, and his choking lessened.

'Fetch the doctor,' he murmured. 'Fetch the doctor.'

There was nothing that Robert's father could do that Robert himself had not already done, but the young fisherman begged them again and again to bring Doctor Kerridge to him.

'I'll go,' whispered Margaret.

Robert shook his head.

'Not you,' he said. 'I'll go. I'll back in five minutes. Keep him upright. Try to lean him forward a little if it gets worse than this.'

Robert found his father pacing up and down the inn yard of *The Royal George* with their old friend, Mr. Grice, in a fever of anger and exasperation.

'The fools and rogues,' he was saying, 'they've been out to the sandbank, I suppose, to recover their damned kegs of rum. And now the whole place has gone up in smoke. It'll be in the London papers, very like. And then where shall we be? What happens to our season here next year? What happens to those precious summer visitors of ours?'

'They were certainly very unwise,' Mr. Grice replied dryly, 'with the military so close at hand'.

Robert caught his father's attention and made a sign for him to draw aside.

'You're wanted on the beach, Father,' he whispered. 'You're wanted at once. A man's dying.'

His father looked at him sharply.

'A smuggler?'

'A fisherman. He's shot in the chest.'

'Shot? Then he's a smuggler. Don't lie to me. No. I'll not come.'

'Not come?' exclaimed Robert in horror. 'Not come? But he's asked for you, Father. The man's dying. You *must* go to him.'

'There's no "must" about it,' he lashed out savagely. 'The man's a felon. He's wanted by the law. Let the law take care of him then.'

'But Father, he's dying.'

Dr. Kerridge looked at his son in a cold fury.

'It's unlawful for a physician to help a felon to escape from the law. They know it. I know it. And so do you.'

'But he's not escaping, Father. I've told you that he's dying. He won't last the hour.'

'I'll not come, Robert. It's a priest the fellow wants. Not me.'

And his father turned on his heel and walked into the inn.

By the time Robert got back to the shed, Dan had nearly gone. His eyes were closed and his breathing came quick and faint. Margaret and Elijah were on either side of him, holding him up.

Margaret looked at him across the darkness of the shed, wordlessly asking him why he was alone.

He shook his head.

And, five minutes later, it was all over. Dan was dead.

Robert laid him gently out straight beside his boat and folded his hands over his breast.

Then the three of them went out of the shed and stood by the sea.

Robert's wretchedness was beyond compare.

'He's a doctor, Meg,' he said brokenly. 'He's taken his oath.'

Margaret did not know how to comfort him.

'He's sworn to help the sick and the dying.'

She stared on at the heaving tops of the night waves and reached out her hands for his. She knew that, though she was not yet married to Robert, this was the first grief of their married selves: that he had found shame in his father.

'One does such dreadful things when one's afraid,' she said slowly. 'We all do, Robert. Every one of us.'

A small wave broke gently at their feet, and then another, and then another, while the silence lengthened between them.

'But he was not afraid,' Robert said at last. 'It was worse than that.'

A fourth and a fifth wave broke.

'He just didn't care.'

21 *All's Well*

In the early dawn of her wedding day, Margaret opened her eyes with a sigh of happiness and lay staring at the light paling the darkness beyond the window panes. It had come at last! The great day had come! She could hear Mrs. Moore calling to the maid in the dairy and the sharp clop of feet in the farmyard behind the house as the ploughmen set off for the fields. But the bustle of Bush Farm was not for her. It could wait. Everything could wait, while she lay and thought of the happiness that had come to her. In five hours' time, the wedding would be over. She and Robert would be sitting up high in Mr. Moore's gig, bowling along the turnpike to Ipswich. Only five hours more, and they would be married—and alone!

Someone knocked gently on her door and, before she had time to answer, Lucy slipped noiselessly into the room with bare feet. She was still in her night-dress.

'May I come in?' she whispered, smiling and shivering close to the bed. 'May I come into bed with you just for this once?'

Lucy's cold feet slipped down beside Margaret's shins and the cold tip of her nose pressed into Margaret's warm cheek as she gave her a kiss.

'How excited you must be!' she said, laughing quietly into Margaret's neck. 'What's it like? What's it like to be as happy as you are?'

Margaret thought for a moment, with her face half buried in Lucy's fair hair.

What *was* it like?

'I can't tell you,' she replied at last, the laughter brimming up in her eyes. 'I can't tell you, Lucy. I haven't the words.'

But Lucy had not expected to be told Margaret's joy. Margaret's future was settled and clear. It was her own that she had brought with her into Margaret's bed.

'You're so lucky,' she sighed.

Margaret knew how lucky she was, and there seemed nothing

to say.

'You've grown up,' she continued. 'You've left me behind.'

'You'll follow me on,' Margaret laughed gently. 'I know you will, Lucy—in no time at all.'

'No, I shan't,' said Lucy, a little petulant in her reply. 'Who is there to marry in a place like this?'

'But the ball—you enjoyed the ball. There'll be other balls.'

'Yes,' she sighed bitterly, 'but they'll all have left before the next one, Meg.'

'Who will?'

'The officers, of course.'

Lucy suddenly kicked up the bed-clothes in a gesture of extreme annoyance.

'They should never have caught all those smugglers so fast.'

Margaret wanted to laugh, but something in Lucy's face made her say instead:

'You're so pretty, Lucy, that I can't imagine that you won't be married before next year is out.'

'And what if I'm not?' she pouted.

'Why, then you must come to London to stay with us.'

Lucy flung her arms round Margaret's neck.

'Oh, Meg, do you mean it? Do you really mean it?'

'Of course I mean it.'

'I've always wanted to go to London so much.'

They lay for a moment in silence, side by side in the bed, each thinking of what London meant to her. For Margaret it meant Robert and her marriage—and her father and the book-shop and the endless talk about books that she heard in the shop. For Lucy it meant theatres and mantua-makers, and con-certs and tea gardens; but, most of all, it meant handsome, marriageable young men.

After one smiling look into the future, Lucy gave a final kick to the bed-clothes and jumped out of bed.

'I promised Mama that I'd help her with the syllabubs,' she exclaimed.

As she ran past the window, her eye caught sight of something outside and she stopped for a better look.

'There's such a funny snuff-coloured old man walking up the drive,' she laughed.

And then a second later:

'Do come and look at him,' she cried. 'He's picking his way round the puddles like a hen in the snow.'

Margaret leaped out of bed and stood at her side.

'Good gracious, Lucy,' she exclaimed. 'It's Mr. Stone!'

She hurried into her old, work-a-day dress, gave her hair a perfunctory pat with her brush, and ran down the stairs so quickly that she was in time to hear Mrs. Moore greeting the old man at the front door.

'Yes, this is Bush Farm,' she was saying, with a hint of suspicion in her voice.

'And you have Miss Pargeter staying with you here?'

'Indeed, we have.'

'Then I'll thank you Ma'am, for some breakfast and . . .'

'Mr. Stone,' burst out Margaret. 'How lovely that you've come!'

Her father's friend greeted her with his usual bite.

'Lovely is a word for a bride, Margaret,' he reproved her, 'not for a wrinkled old man like myself.'

He introduced himself to Mrs. Moore, who welcomed him by taking him into the kitchen and promising him breakfast in two minutes. In her absence, he cocked an eye at Margaret's untidy hair and shabby dress.

'I've mistaken it, now,' he grimaced. 'I should not have come!'

'Why, what have you mistaken?' she asked.

'I thought to see two young fools being wed here today.'

'So you will. So you will,' laughed Margaret. 'We're going to be married at half past ten. But how did you know? And did you really come all this way just for us?'

She was touched beyond measure by the thought.

'Nonsense, child,' said the old man brusquely. 'I was down with your father last night. There's a bookshop for sale near Charing Cross.'

'And Father told you?'

Mr. Stone nodded.

'Another twenty miles of your confounded mud didn't make much odds.'

'Mud?' asked Mrs. Moore, coming back with milk and eggs from the dairy.

'Mud, Ma'am. That's it. You country people should sweep it up as we do in the Strand.'

'Meg! Meg!' shouted Lucy from half-way down the stairs. 'Do come and see what they're doing!'

She was leaning half out of the stairs window and laughing so hard that it was difficult at first to understand what she was saying.

'Robert's . . . vaulting . . . over the gate. And now Dick. . . . And now . . . Robert's going to do it again! Come quickly. Do come.'

Margaret ran up the stairs and leant out of the window beside Lucy.

Robert's heels were flashing high through the air; and then down they came and up went his arms as he finished his ridiculous, graceful, joyous salute to his wedding day.

'How lovely! How lovely!' exclaimed Margaret. 'I wish I could go and do that, too.'

'Lucy!' thundered Mrs. Moore immediately behind them. 'Go and tell them to stop! Go at once! I've never seen such a thing! On his wedding day! And in his best coat! And Dick's in his best coat, too!'

She was still thundering on after Lucy as she sped laughing through the kitchen and out into the yard when the cabbage cart drew up at the front of the house with the party from the Tovells' farm. And Mr. Moore flung open the front door and shouted:

'We've come, Bet.'

Mr. Moore and Mrs. Neech and Elijah and Mrs. Dunnett and Emma Tovell crowded into the kitchen, their faces bright with the chill of the morning and with little pearls of mist glistening in their hair.

'Mr. Stone!' exclaimed Mrs. Neech.

Ten minutes later, when all the explanations and introductions had been made and Mr. Stone was settling happily to his second plate of eggs, Mrs. Neech looked across the room at Margaret and suddenly threw up her hands.

'Goodness, child, what a sight you look! It's your wedding day! You must go and dress.'

Everything about that bridal dressing conspired to make Margaret and Mrs. Neech gentle and quiet with each other, for both knew that it was the end of the road—a very long road—that they had travelled together. There was a sense of awe and a ceremony and a love in all that they said and did and a depth of feeling in their looks which brought a stillness to the little bedroom, setting it apart from the rest of the noisy household, preparing in such high spirits for the wedding in the drawing-room below.

'Brush my hair as you used to brush it,' Margaret smiled.

And Mrs. Neech made her sit down by the window and brushed and brushed and brushed, back from her forehead, up from the nape of her neck, sideways across her ears, fifty, sixty, seventy times, and more, with long, firm strokes that sent shivers of childhood memories rippling down Margaret's spine and made her red-brown hair glow like a chestnut that has newly burst out of its prickly green husk. As she felt again the strong, unyielding firmness of the hand that wielded the brush, Margaret remembered the battles of her childhood, the storms of temper, the rebellious tears, the passionate rights and wrongs. And always at the end, as constant and immutable as the motion of the planets, Mrs. Neech's unbudging, love-given strength. The housekeeper had offered Elijah a large maternal lap; she had offered Margaret only the inflexibility of her principles. And she recognized now, at last, in this final hour of her reign, that the wise woman had given to each of them according to their need.

Mrs. Neech's thoughts went farther back in history, and an intolerable ache of the pain of things past weighed upon her heart. She had brushed another head of chestnut hair but twenty years ago, had dressed another girl for her wedding day.

'Now, fetch your dress, child,' she said quietly.

And Margaret in a solemn, unsmiling ecstasy slipped into the beautiful white muslin gown.

Mrs. Neech pursed up her lips and then nodded her head. 'He has taste,' she said.

But she was not really thinking of either Margaret or Robert; she spoke so because it was owed to them. It was their marriage day. Her heart was elsewhere, and her eyes were dimming with tears.

'And now, your necklace, Margaret,' she said gently.

And Margaret went to the drawer and took out her mother's amethyst necklace that her father had put into her hands in the cellar in Holly Lane.

'Let me fasten it for you,' smiled Mrs. Neech bravely. 'It was always difficult to fasten it right.'

Hardly was the dressing completed when Lucy burst into the room, and then stood in the doorway, suddenly speechless with confusion and delight. She did not know which was the most astonishing and beautiful thing to exclaim at first: Margaret dressed as a bride or the news that she had come to tell.

'Meg, you look wonderful! You look wonderfully wonderful. And your brother has just come.'

Released suddenly from the solemn, tender ritual of the dressing, Margaret burst out laughing. Lucy's sentence had come out so comically.

'He's so handsome, Meg!' Lucy exclaimed, her eyes bright and her face flushed with excitement. 'I'd no idea he'd be so handsome. And he's got leave to stay for the barn dance after you've left.'

A voice sounded below them on the stairs. It was Mrs. Moore's.

'Lucy, hurry now. You must tie that ribbon in your hair.'

And then came Dick's voice.

'Come along, everyone. The Vicar's riding up the drive.'

It was over. They were married. Robert and Margaret, up in the gig, were bowling towards the open gate and the white fencing, looking back over their shoulders and waving good-bye to John and the Moores and Mrs. Neech and Mrs. Dunnett and the Tovells and the Vicar of Ikenthorpe standing outside the front door of Bush Farm, waving after them and shouting their good-byes, while Dick and Elijah were running beside them, laughing and breathless and red in the face.

'Take care. Take care,' Margaret called down at them, for Elijah was running far too close to the iron rim of the wheel.

But she needed not to worry, for as the gig reached the gateway and Robert turned left into the road, Dick swooped the child up in his arms and balanced him high on his shoulders.

'Good-bye,' they both shouted. 'Good-bye. Good-bye.'

They were alone now—alone together.

Robert looked at Margaret sideways, and the longer he looked the wider and more triumphant grew his smile. Then, he turned forwards again to the road and whipped up the horse, and the gig spun along towards the turnpike at such speed that the bare trees and hedges raced past, their branches and twigs lost in one huge, dark blur.

'Robert,' she gasped. 'We're going much too fast. At least nine miles an hour—if not more.'

'More. Much more,' he laughed. 'We're flying, Meg. There's nothing can measure the speed that we're going.'

At Ikenthorpe ford he slowed down.

'It's all right,' he assured her. 'I'm not going to kill us both before we've rightly begun. Life's too good, Meg. Much too good.'

Driving sedately through Ikenthorpe village, like a couple of respectable married citizens, they came back in their minds to the wedding.

'I believe Lucy's fallen in love with John,' Margaret laughed. 'It would be wonderful if he returned her the compliment.'

Robert considered the matter a little.

'I shouldn't wonder if he doesn't,' he said at last. 'He kept looking at her in such surprise.'

They talked of the rightness of the match. They were both of a suitable age, they said, and they sought the same things from life.

'He needs love and a little happiness to put himself right with himself,' said Robert.

'And Lucy needs them, too.'

And then, they looked at each other and laughed, telling themselves that they were as bad as Mrs. Fisher, the chemist's wife in Holly Lane, who was always inventing romances and marrying people off in her mind.

By the time that they reached the turnpike, they had left the babble of the wedding far behind and were looking straight ahead at the new life opening up before them. It was a good life, exciting and strenuous and full of hope. Yet, a single deep sadness cast a shadow across the sunshine. It was Robert's quarrel with his parents. They did not speak of the sadness because they were not yet experienced enough in each other's griefs. It was too new a bitterness and one which involved them both too nearly and in two such different ways, Margaret being the cause of the quarrel and Robert its chief victim.

What could she do? What could either of them do to heal the breach, Margaret asked herself. She knew that Robert would have to settle things with his father in his own way, for he had to forgive his father for something worse than hating her; he had to forgive him for breaking his doctor's oath—for his heartless indifference to the calls of humanity. It was not really Dr. Kerridge that grieved her so much. It was Robert's mother. She could not forget either the kindness or the suffering in Mrs. Kerridge's eyes, and she longed to be loved by her and welcomed at last as Robert's wife.

They had come now to the little town of Wickham Market, and Robert, reining in the horse, let it trot quietly and slowly down the middle of the High Street.

Suddenly, he pulled the reins even tighter.

'Meg,' he breathed. 'She's there.'

Margaret looked up into his face, where hope and disbelief were struggling for mastery, and then straight ahead in the direction of his gaze.

Drawn up in the little town square, under the beautiful wrought-iron device of The White Hart inn, stood an open carriage, and in the carriage sat a gentlewoman, by herself—waiting—her hands folded in front of her on her lap in an attitude of infinite patience and simplicity.

'Meg, take the reins. I must go to her.'

And Robert leapt out of the gig and ran across the square to his mother.

Directly Margaret saw that his mother was forgiving him, she longed to run across the square and join them, but she had been left with the reins and being ignorant about horses she was afraid of them. She was afraid that if she threw down the reins the confounded horse would take to his heels and bolt away down the street with Mr. Moore's precious gig rattling behind it and dash it to pieces against a corner stone.

They were smiling; they were taking each other's hands. Mrs. Kerridge was kissing Robert on the forehead. Margaret longed to be by their side. It was intolerable that she had been saddled with the wretched horse.

Her impatience was at that moment goldenly rewarded, for Mrs. Kerridge rose from her seat, took Robert's arm, and stepped out of the carriage and walked across the square towards her.

'Margaret, my dear,' she said smiling, as she put her hand up on Margaret's.

Robert relieved his wife of the reins, and with an abandon that belonged to a child rather than to a Christian matron, she jumped out of the gig and into Mrs. Kerridge's arms.

Three hours later they were with old Mr. Pargeter in Ipswich Gaol.

'My children. My dear children,' he greeted them, rising and flinging wide his arms in a large embrace.

Then he took Margaret's hands in his own and held her a little from him, while his eyes travelled slowly down over her burnished hair to her flushed and happy face, then down to the jewels at her neck and to the folds of soft white muslin dress to her feet.

'You've given her beauty, my son,' he smiled proudly.

Then, he asked them about the wedding.

'Come, sit down, and tell me how it was.'

They told him eagerly of their surprise at Mr. Stone's arrival, of the kindness of the Moores, of John's handsome bearing, of Mrs. Neech's quiet pleasure, of Dick and Elijah running after the gig and shouting their good-byes.

Yet, in spite of their gaiety, they could not help remembering the names that were absent from their tale.

Robert's parents were in all their minds.

Mr. Pargeter turned to his son-in-law.

'Your father and mother were not present at the wedding, then?' he asked gently.

Robert shook his head. It was an anguished moment both for Robert and for Margaret, for they could not explain the true reason for the doctor's refusal to accept his own godfather's daughter as his son's wife. It was too hurting for the old man. It was a wretchedness that they had to keep to themselves.

Mr. Pargeter looked from one unhappy, bent head to the other.

'It's my imprisonment, I think,' he said quietly.

Then he stirred himself in his chair, sighing sadly as he spoke:

'It is one of the penalties that are forced upon the children of outspoken men.'

He reached out his hands then, one to his daughter and one to his new son.

'You must forgive me, Meg; you must forgive me, Robert,' he said with simplicity, 'that my conscience has brought you this grief.'

They assured him then of their love and their gratitude to him.

'You have taught us, sir,' said Robert, his eyes bright with the admiration that he felt for Margaret's father, 'you have taught us how one should live.'

'If I have taught you that, Robert,' he said with great seriousness, 'then I must also teach you how to love. You must go to your parents, my son, as soon as you well can, and beg them for their forgiveness. And you, Meg, must forget utterly the hurt that you have received.'

They told him, then, of their meeting with Robert's mother after the wedding and of her acceptance of what they had done. She had welcomed Margaret and given them both her blessing.

'I am glad—very glad,' said Mr. Pargeter, smiling his pleasure. 'It was she, after all, who was most hurt by your going—unblessed.'

The cell had been wonderfully tidied up since Margaret's and Robert's visits to the prison; the torn scraps of manuscript that had lain heaped in the corners had been taken away, the hearth had been brushed, and two new chairs had been carried in. The rough deal table was now covered with a coarse clean cloth on which stood a flagon of ale, a basket of bread, and a hard, round Suffolk cheese.

'It's a homely wedding breakfast, Meg, that your father is offering you,' smiled the bookseller. 'We'll find a better way to celebrate your marriage when I'm out of gaol.'

His eyes grew bright as he spoke of the future .

He told them that Mr. Stone had found him a new bookshop as close to some of the most poverty-stricken courts in London as his heart could wish.

214

'We'll build our New Jerusalem there in a new way,' he urged.

And then, as a look of apprehension passed across Margaret's face, he added hastily:

'No, Meg, not with pamphlets that the Philistines can falsely accuse of libel, but with children's slates and reading books—and, Robert, with your sick dispensary in the room at the back. You'll do that, won't you?'

'Yes,' said Robert, smiling. 'And those I'm too ignorant to help I'll send with a note to Mr. Barnaby Coke.'

It was all settled. Their future was assured.

John had found happiness in the army. And in four months' time Mrs. Neech and Elijah would move from the lodgings which Mr. Moore had taken for them in Ipswich, and go with the bookseller to Charing Cross, to be at home again in another, more successful, Holly Lane. And as for Robert and Margaret, why, in four months' time they would be that much more confirmed in the joy of their marriage.

'Meg,' said her father as he surveyed the brightness of the dawning world, 'I feel like my old friend, Tom Paine, when he found that budding twig in the bitter cold of a February afternoon.'

The old bookseller laughed quietly to himself.

' "The spring is begun," Tom said. "The spring is begun." '

TITLES IN THIS SERIES